A QUESTION
OF MURDER

LOUISE FOSTER

OWL CAFE PRES LLC

A Question of Murder; A Crossword Puzzle Cozy Mystery

Copyright 2020 by Louise Foster

ISBN: 978-1-955458-07-8

*This book is dedicated to the men and women who are serving
and have served in the military.
Your sacrifices and those of your families are appreciated.
Thank you*

I'M TRACY BELDEN AND I'M HUNTING GHOSTS.

That is, until a tour through a haunted mansion turns up a murder victim.

The police are quick to connect the crime to a friend's mysterious past. Soon I find myself on the case and drawn into the world of fine art and million-dollar forgeries.

Though I know nothing about million-dollar forgeries,
I've never left a crossword puzzle unfinished.

Now it's time to solve this puzzle and prove my friend's innocence.

1

— ◦ —

23 Down; 7 Letters;
Clue: Frequented by a ghost
Answer: Haunted

So far, my first foray with Ghost Hunters 101 was not only lacking in ethereal spirits, I'd lost a son. While the rest of my group was in the second-floor music room of Rycliffe Castle listening for spirits, I was playing a worried mom and trying to find Marcus, my eleven-year-old Korean foster son.

I'm Tracy Belden, full-time cynic, part-owner of a handyman business, part-time PI, and a lifelong lover and creator of crossword puzzles. At the moment, I lurked in the semi-darkness at the top of the polished staircase.

Evidently, electricity interferes with manifestations, so the hall was lit only by the white light of January's full moon. The soft light shining through the intricate stained-glass windows painted dancing colors on the wall, lending an appropriately eerie feel to the evening. The ornate chandelier seemed to glow with an unearthly light.

The molding along the ceiling and the delicate wood carving spoke to the mining money that had built the four-story house at the height of the silver rush in Langsdale, Nevada.

I was contemplating my next move when a white form glided out of the rear sitting room. The shadowy figure came straight at me. Arms outstretched. White hair shining through the dimness.

My breath caught in my throat. My pulse spiked. Then the figure solidified into Mrs. Colchester, my widowed friend and apartment manager. My relieved smile froze a second later.

The woman looked as white as the ghosts we were hunting. She sped along as if her pink slippers had jet-pack power. Her eyes were glassy and unseeing. Her face was etched with horror.

My heart stuttered as my long legs closed the distance between us. When I reached her, her red, taloned fingernails dug into my arm.

"Is it Marcus?" Fear spread through me at the panic filling her pale green eyes. "Did something happen?"

"Not Marcus. Daniel." Her voice broke on the name. "I killed him decades ago. Why can't the dead stay buried?"

Any thought that she might be putting me on vanished. She was as frightened as I've ever seen her in our seven-year acquaintance. I sputtered for possibly the first time in my life.

Had I heard right? She'd killed a man?

"I killed him once," she repeated in a low, fast whisper. "Now he's come back. He's found me."

Her English accent, which had appeared out of nowhere several months ago, deepened as her agitation grew.

An almost over-powering urge to ask about her mysterious past rose up. Regretfully, I swallowed the impulse. "Are you sure you saw a real person? The organizers might be playing a trick."

Before Mrs. C answered, Marcus sprang out of the shadows.

I swallowed a gasp and scowled at the boy. "Where have you been?"

My former street urchin son ignored my question. He had always had a taste for trouble. He'd come hoping to see or hear a real ghost, but given his rabid interest in murder, a corpse would be an acceptable substitute.

"You saw the ghost of a dead guy?" Marcus crowded close. "Who? Where?"

I cringed at the way his excited voice reverberated through the hushed corridors.

While I'm an actual P.I., albeit part-time, I have no desire to solve crimes. I especially didn't want to mess with a murder. My interest is the money it adds to my bottom line. Marcus and Mrs. C, however, take a morbid and enthusiastic interest in my cases.

Mrs. C put a hand on her thin chest and drew a deep breath.

"Daniel Weatherington. In there." She pointed over her shoulder. She started to turn. "I must face him, clear the air."

"No way." Marcus shifted to block her. "Never go toward trouble."

"Especially dead bodies," I seconded the need for circumspection. With my arm around her thin shoulders, I helped Mrs. C to a padded bench against the wall. In the dim light, her ashen face made her look every day of her seventy-plus years.

The brick walls and brushed fabric wallpaper of the old mansion seemed to have been designed as a backdrop for drama.

"He found me. He wants vengeance." Mrs. C clutched my arm. She shook so much the wrinkled skin on her cheeks and neck quivered. She took a deep breath and appeared to regain control. "I evaded justice once. I won't run again."

She started to rise, as if planning to drift offstage like an aged screen star intent on one, final, dramatic scene.

I stood transfixed. Who was this woman? I'd seen her face down a gunman in a cemetery. Now she was giving up without a fight?

She placed one red-tipped hand over her heart. The parchment-like skin looked transparent in the light shining through the windows.

"No need for you to get involved." The hushed air seemed to gather around Mrs. C. "I'll speak with the bobbies. I'll tell them everything."

"Seriously?" On my best day, I couldn't get a straight answer from her. Now she was ready to confess to someone else? No way. I had more time invested in her mysterious past than the bobbies, er the police. If anyone deserved answers, it was me.

Marcus, my little force of constant motion, planted himself in front of the older woman. "Smart money says keep your mouth shut. Don't volunteer nothing."

Though I cringed at the syntax, I seconded his attitude.

She touched his straight, black hair. His golden skin appeared dusky next to her almost translucent hand. "You've always been such a good boy."

Talk about a final scene.

Marcus's black eyes pleaded with me. "We have to save her."

"Mostly from herself," I muttered.

Mrs. C's gaze remained riveted on the door of the sitting room.

I put my hand on her cheek and gently turned her face toward me. Though I hadn't forgotten the "I killed him decades ago" confession, I had to deal with the matter at hand.

"Take a deep breath," I urged in a soft, calm tone. "You've had a shock, but it's dark. They may have rigged an effect to make the image of a body appear."

Langsdale, a resort town of twenty-five thousand residents, lies three hours north of Las Vegas. The town pulls in upper-crust tourists with attractions that include golf-courses, art galleries, and pricey boutiques to gourmet restaurants and numerous concerts. Rycliffe Castle often hosts appealing activities, such as Ghosthunters, 101.

The mansion had been built by the Rycliffe patriarch who'd made his fortune mining silver in the late eighteen-hundreds. Located on the edge of town, the turreted, castle-like structure had been home to several generations of Rycliffes. The family history of intrigue, arguments, and violence was the basis of the hauntings credited to the building.

"There's money to be made from the dead." I cringed at my words. "I mean from the ghost trade. They'd pull out all the stops to get a good story going."

"It's him." From her blank expression and distant gaze, she didn't appear connected to the here and now. "I thought I was safe. I let down me guard, didn't I?"

"You're sure he's dead?" Marcus didn't hide the ghoulish interest in his voice.

"Blood on his temple." A shudder shook the older woman's thin frame. "A blow to the head. Just like the last time I killed him."

"Shhh!" I checked the empty hall for witnesses lurking in dark corners.

"Don't say that," Marcus whispered at the same time. "Never confess."

My son balanced on his toes, obviously eager to see for himself. He eyed me with a hopeful yet guarded expression. "I could go check."

I hesitated, but I had to know what we were facing. Though I was unsure what the older woman had seen, she was too overwrought to be left alone.

"Don't touch anything," I warned the boy in a hard, low tone. "Look and come right back."

I watched his undersized form dart down the corridor. Soon, his black hair blended with the darkness. He disappeared into the sitting room.

Before I could breathe or blink, he was dashing toward me.

My alarm meter shot to high. This couldn't be good.

Tension radiated from the tight set of his shoulders. He put a hand on my arm. "There's a dead guy. He's got blood on his head. It's dripping down his neck."

I filed away the image of gore. Containment. That was my priority. I couldn't let the older woman talk to anyone. Whatever she had done now or in the past, she was too frightened to make sense. Her confusion might land her in prison.

Luckily, only we three rebels had strayed from the main group, but it was only a matter of time before we were missed.

I grasped Mrs. C by the shoulders and bent from my five-foot-nine-inch height to meet her gaze. "Did this man hurt you?"

She nodded. Her shaking hands touched the loose skin on her throat. "He threw me against the table. The Tiffany lamp shattered on the floor. His hands were crushing my throat. I couldn't breathe."

Though the hall was cool, Marcus pulled his shirt away where it clung to his skin. "That's self-defense."

"Wait a minute." A full-blown attack and I hadn't heard a sound? That made no sense. "He just now attacked you? Who is this guy?"

"He's followed me across the ocean, across time." Mrs. C looked frantically around. "I have to confess."

Marcus put a restraining hand on her arm. "No."

The street ethics Marcus had grown up with before hooking up with me gave no thought to guilt or innocence. Protect your own was the first rule.

"We need the whole story before you do anything." I put a hand around her shoulders. "First, let's get out of here."

Marcus and I helped Mrs. C to her feet.

"T.R." A note of urgency rang in my son's tone. "Is that tape recorder still running?"

My breath caught in my throat. One person in each group carried a handheld tape recorder to catch any happenings. Lucky me, I had the one for my group. I'd hung it on my purse and forgotten it. My first impulse was to destroy the offending instrument, but I didn't dare. Instead, I thrust it at Marcus. "Erase it. We'll wait here."

He took the recorder while he handed me some electromagnetic thingamabob detector he'd been given. "Keep quiet."

He walked several feet away. His expression intent. After a moment, he wiped the recorder with his shirt, then set it on a nearby table.

I pointed him toward a room on the far side of the stairs. If there was a dead body, I wanted the three of us to be elsewhere when it was found.

I put my arm around Mrs. C's shoulders. "Not another word about the past, bodies, or vengeance. Marcus can't be involved. He might be taken away from me. We might never see him again."

Gut-wrenching fear shot through me at hearing my own personal nightmare aloud. Though the current caseworker was a good sort, I lived in terror of losing the boy I loved. Besides, I had to cut through the older woman's confusion.

Mrs. C's shoulders stiffened. The blank look in her eyes dissipated. "Quite right, dear. I can't drag you or the boy into my troubles. Not a word."

I put my hand on her shoulder while Marcus waved us forward. Once in the child's room, deserted but for us, I aimed our trio toward a door that connected to the music room. With luck, no one in the main group would notice we'd gone missing.

"Not a word," I repeated. "We stay together from now on."

Marcus nodded.

Mrs. C stared straight ahead.

I squeezed her shoulders. "Remember, think of Marcus."

She took a deep breath. "Right."

Slipping into the main group was amazingly easy. Between the darkness and the attempts to communicate with spirits, no one so much as glanced our way or seemed to realize we'd been missing.

I breathed a sigh of relief until I realized the real murderer would have been able to leave and return just as easily. I glanced at the shadowy ring of figures and wondered which of them was the killer.

A new worry sprang up, full blown. What if the murderer had seen Mrs. C head for the library? Even worse, what if they overheard her confession?

2

— : —

11 Across; 6 Letters;
Clue: The opening of a play, story, or drama
Answer: Act One

'Mrs. C found a corpse. Tell Rabi. Come for breakfast.'

That had been my text to my boyfriend, Kevin Tanner, last night. Though it wasn't my oddest message to him, it was in the top three.

None of us had been in any shape for a discussion last night. Now, semi-refreshed by sleep, I sat at my kitchen table. The morning sun streamed in through the window, and the aroma of frying sausages filled my loft apartment.

Ignoring the banquet of breakfast foods on my dining room table, I ran a hand through my short, spiky brown hair and shoved aside thoughts of last night's murder. My gaze lingered on Kevin, sitting in the next chair. I brushed a kiss on his cheek, thrilled as always at having him in my life.

Though his cobalt blue eyes, black hair, and Adonis-like looks drew the attention of every female on the planet, he was my guy. My boyfriend. For the first ten years I'd known him, he'd been my best friend. At thirty-five, I was seven years his senior. So, I'd thought it best to avoid romance. It was only a few months ago that I'd admitted it was more than friendship, and I let myself fall in love. I still felt giddy at the thought. "Thanks for being here."

"Where else would I be, Belden?" Kevin winked at me. Then he rose and pulled out a chair. "Mrs. Colchester, take a seat. We need some background."

Mrs. C set a plate of pancakes on the table next to bacon, sausage, French toast, and scrambled eggs. The woman cooks when she gets nervous. The spread on the table was our breakfast allotment for the next week and a half.

For a moment, she simply hovered. Faced with Kevin's steady, reassuring gaze, she dropped into the proffered chair. "I don't understand how he found me, but you lot need to distance yourself."

I planted my crossed arms on the table, elbows and all. Last night she'd worn the same look of defeat, like a condemned prisoner facing the gallows. I'd wanted to shake some life into her, but I hadn't dared say a word. Now I was under no such constraints.

"We can't walk away." I added a desperate note to my voice. Gazing directly into her eyes, I paused for effect. "I got Rabi out of bed on a Saturday. A murder investigation is the only justifiable excuse I can offer."

Jack Rabi, the man in question, sat at the end of the table. His black eyes showed over the rim of his coffee mug. Able to disappear in plain sight, he was skeleton thin with an ashen hue to his brown skin. His perfectly waved black hair hit his shoulders. He was a former US Army Ranger, a veteran with over two decades of service, and in the past five years he'd gone from delivery man to friend to adopted member of our ragtag family. A tsunami couldn't shake his calm.

As I'd hoped, a smile lit Mrs. C's face, multiplying the wrinkles around her eyes and mouth. The tension in the room eased.

Kevin's long arm snaked out. He touched the older woman's hand. "Belden and Company cleared me of murder in Vegas. We can clear you. You didn't kill the guy."

"Aye." The single word was expelled on seemingly the last breath in her body.

The sound was barely audible, though I sat straight across from her. Every muscle in my body clenched. I didn't want to miss a syllable.

"I did kill him."

The defeat in her gaze was far too incriminating. Good thing we'd made our exit last night before the police accused her. With her attitude, she'd be headed to the state pen in Carson City by now.

I could only hope that memories of the past were once again clouding her judgment. I had to admit last night's murder, with all the earmarks of a proverbial locked door mystery, was enough to throw anyone off their stride.

Did I mention there were eleven of us on the second floor where the body was found? Another group of eleven had been on the third floor. The organizers of the Ghost Hunters 101 event had locked all outside exits to avoid interference, or so they'd said. With a member from their team posted in the main lobby, there was supposedly little room for anyone to get lost or wander away.

Of course, we three knew that to be a fallacy.

Too bad we couldn't tell anyone.

Another problem with counting suspects was that the victim hadn't been on the list of attendees. He shouldn't have been in the house at all.

So much for locked doors.

"You didn't kill last night's dead guy." Marcus's straight black hair framed eyes clouded with worry. "His name was Daniel Neville

Weatherington, II. Everyone called him Neville. You probably killed his father, Daniel the first."

Mrs. C flipped her hand over to grab the young boy's fingers in hers. Her brow cleared a bit. "I did."

I leaned forward, marshaling my sincerity. "You said the father attacked you. You defended yourself. That's not murder."

She clicked her tongue. Rousing, she stabbed at her Tabasco covered scrambled eggs. "It is if you were raised on the wrong side of the tracks by a gin-swilling mother. Especially if you kill a member of the founding family of the Jerrone Auction House."

Kevin snorted. "No one is saying you wouldn't have been railroaded. We've all been on the wrong side of the law. This time, we've got your back."

Rabi shifted forward like a shadow in broad daylight, adding weight to Kevin's comments.

I stabbed the table with my index finger. "You have to keep the two men straight. If you talk about killing Daniel Weatherington, the police will take you seriously. The guilty party will get away with murder. We can't let that happen. *You* can't let that happen."

"Listen to her." Rabi's low, solemn tone reinforced my words.

Mrs. C put a hand to her throat. "The two men look so alike. The same coloring. The same build. The same..."

"Bash in the skull." Marcus finished her thought in his usual forthright manner.

I gave him the fish-eye. "You could be more delicate."

"Too bad he's never seen that style." Kevin pulled me against him. "It's odd both men died by a single blow to the head."

"And the note found by the body." Marcus stabbed the air. "That's lame. The murderer wanted to draw attention away from other suspects. Now the police will focus on Gracie Linden."

For that bit of misdirection, I had to give the killer full marks. "If that was the intention, it definitely worked."

When the corpse was found - for the second time - a note was discovered by the body. 'Meet me tonight to learn Gracie Linden's whereabouts.' The time and location had been listed, placing the victim in the middle of our ghost hunt.

Thanks to the crowd of spectators, everyone in the building knew of the message before the police arrived. A quick Internet search supplied the facts of Gracie Linden's brush with fame and death.

A British woman, she'd supposedly killed her married lover fifty years ago then disappeared. She had been in her twenties at the time.

That would make her a woman in her early seventies with an English accent who was intent on hiding her past.

Each fact tightened the vise around my lungs until I could barely breathe. Last night, I had to stop myself from looking at Mrs. C as each detail emerged. Fortunately, she'd chosen that moment to adopt a Southern drawl.

Murder. Not MI-6. No wonder my landlady had kept mum about her past. I'd missed the mark by quite a bit. Whoever had killed last night's victim had struck true.

Killing the victim with a blow to the temple.

When the dead man was identified as Daniel Neville Weatherington the second, I remembered Mrs. C's dazed comments about killing a man of that same name.

Marcus swirled his orange juice in his cup. "The article on the Internet said the documentary on the first murder is going to start filming soon. The dead guy, Neville, was working with the producers. Maybe he was looking for Gracie Linden for the show."

Kevin waited a beat before speaking. "Did you know about the plan to re-enact the first murder, Mrs. Colchester? The articles say it's been in the planning stages for several months. Neville was deeply involved. In his online interview, he said he hoped it would provide answers to Gracie Linden's fate."

Mrs. C was busy adding two pancakes to Marcus's plate, despite his protests. Then she took a pancake herself. Kevin waited with no outward sign of impatience. Finally, she met his gaze. "Aye, I read about the show; "Cold Cases; Hot Passion". Silly thing. Raking up the past, and for what?"

"Attention. Ratings. Money." I listed the possibilities as I cut a bite of pancake. As I raised the fork to my mouth and looked around the table, I found all eyes upon me. Too late, I noted her bitter tone. "Was that a rhetorical question?"

Mrs. C chuckled. "You're right, luv. People are always ready to watch other people's troubles on the telly."

The telly? Who says that anymore? She must be truly rattled. I settled in to give the other woman room. I wanted to hear her version of the past. "Tell us about Gracie Linden."

Marcus slanted a look at Mrs. C. "Are you her? Have you been hiding your identity all these years?"

Mrs. C freshened her tea with hot water and a new tea bag, evidently busying her hands while collecting her thoughts. "Gracie's dead. She died seven years ago during heart surgery. Three of her arteries were blocked."

"Too bad." Marcus's soft voice filled the moment of silence with sympathy. "That means they'll never find her. We'll have to clear you."

His oh so practical comment ended on an ah-well note that brought the moment of compassion to a screeching halt.

Kevin intercepted the glare I aimed at my son. My boyfriend stifled a laugh. "He's an eleven-year-old boy. He didn't know the woman."

Quietly acknowledging the truth of his statement, I motioned her to go on. "Who contacted you about Gracie's death?"

Mrs. C gave a sad smile. "We always e-mailed each other as soon as we recovered from a procedure. I never heard from her. A week later, I found her obituary."

"How did you meet her?" Kevin asked.

"Gracie was a friend. A dear friend. When hard times hit, we banded together."

"Like us." Marcus looked around the table, drawing us together as he had a knack for doing.

"What about Gracie?" What circumstances had caused my friend to kill a man, even in self-defense?

"She had a gift for painting." The older woman's expression took on a glow, quickly replaced by a cynical look. "She also had a knack for copying other artists. Weatherington mentored her. He encouraged her to copy the work of famous painters, supposedly to hone her technique. They became lovers. She trusted him. Until we traveled to Edinburgh and saw one of her paintings hanging in a private collection under the name of Ignacio Infantino."

Marcus typed hurriedly on his tablet. After five seconds, he held it up. "This is an Infantino. Abstract art."

It was a geometric assembly of bright shapes and ragged slashes. "Didn't you paint something like that when you were seven?"

Rabi's frown matched my reaction.

Kevin squeezed my hand. "You're a true connoisseur."

Marcus shook the tablet at me. "This sold for eleven million dollars five years ago. The artist died in the nineteen-fifties."

Mrs. C held up a hand to forestall our questions. "A fire enveloped Mr. Infantino's studio two decades before his death. A number of sketches and paintings were lost. Due to his secrecy, no one knew whether pieces had been sold or destroyed."

"Good game." Admiration warmed Kevin's tone. Raised by con artists, he appreciated the art of a fine scam.

Mrs. C nodded. "The Jerrone Auction House had fallen on hard times. Discovering lost Infantinos put them on a solid foundation once more."

"How did she become a skilled forger so young?" I pointed an accusing finger at my son. "You said you were going to research her background."

"I found stuff about Gracie's family." His voice held a smug note. "They were middle class. Two siblings. One of each. The family owns a business restoring old paintings. They clean them up. They're experts."

"That explains how Gracie knew the tricks to make an impeccable forgery." Kevin had been brought up in his own family's trade; fraud. "If you grow up learning a skill, it becomes second nature."

"That's good stuff," I told Marcus.

Marcus spun the tablet around on the table using his finger. "Jerrone has an art auction scheduled in town this weekend. Coincidence? I think not."

I allowed myself a smile at his dramatic tone. On the practical side, I had to agree. Suspicious soul that I am, I had to wonder if the Weatherington family might have held back one forged Infantino as a hedge for their future. Could Neville's death be tied to his father's indiscretion?

"Go back to you and Gracie." Keeping our group on task was no mean feat. "She was upset to learn the truth. Did she confront him? Was there an argument? How did he end up attacking you?"

"Gracie wouldn't say a word against him. She hoped to marry him." Mrs. C spooned salsa onto her scrambled eggs, then stabbed at the food aimlessly. "I was furious. I knew he was using her. I went to his office late one night and got in an argument with him. He attacked me and I struck him down."

Silence barely had time to settle when Marcus tapped his spoon on his plate. "What did you do then? Why did Gracie leave with you if you killed her guy?"

"I feared she'd turn me in," Mrs. C admitted. "I was dazed. By the time I returned to the flat, over an hour had passed. When I explained what happened, she all but collapsed. She kept saying: 'You killed him. You killed him.' We both knew she'd be suspected."

Marcus frowned. "Not you?"

Mrs. C dismissed the idea with a wave of her fork. "I had no ties to the man and no motive. She and I looked alike. The guard who saw me in the hall that night called me Gracie. If I'd ran off alone, she'd have been arrested. I decided to confess, but she insisted we both take off before the body was found."

Admittedly, Gracie was saving herself as well as Mrs. C, but I gave the missing woman full marks for loyalty.

Mrs. C stabbed at her eggs before tossing aside her fork. "I knew she hated to leave her family, but if she stayed, she'd have been convicted. I'd traveled all through Europe with me mum and dad. When he died, Mum moved us to England. I knew the tricks to crossing borders. Despite her picture being posted at every harbor and airport, I got us to the continent. It was actually quite fun."

I was relieved to see the twinkle in her eyes had returned.

She dabbed her mouth with her napkin. "It took a day for the press to paint Gracie guilty of murder. I offered again to confess, but she'd have none of it. We came to America a month later. Though we went our separate ways, we stayed in touch. She died several years ago."

My pulse quickened. "The note by the body implicates Gracie. If you prove you're not her, you're in the clear."

Kevin gestured toward Mrs. C. "Have you forgotten his father's murder?"

I shrugged the worry away, my practical side coming to the fore. "Everyone thinks Gracie Linden killed him. Mrs. C doesn't have a motive to kill Neville. Once Mrs. C proves she's not Gracie, she's home free."

"Yes and no." Mrs. C pressed her lips into a thin line. "I was born in a small village by a local woman. My birth wasn't registered. Gracie and I were both slim blondes with pale eyes. We could only afford one fake passport. I entered the States, then mailed the passport to her."

My shoulders drooped. "I should have known clearing you wouldn't be that easy."

Rabi pointed a scarred hand at Mrs. C. "Cops will connect you and Gracie. Sooner not later."

"I covered me trail, didn't I?" The fire in the older woman's eyes matched her belligerent tone. "Five decades. Multiple continents."

Kevin snorted. "The cops will investigate every woman of the appropriate age who was there last night. They'll tear their lives apart."

"They're right." I'd hoped for more time. I raked my hands through my hair. "I make it four or five attendees, including you. Maybe a few older women who are part of the Rycliffe staff."

Rabi sipped his coffee. "A day. Two at most."

I considered my options. "I called Crawford. He'll keep tabs on the official progress. I'd like some warning before the police arrive at the door."

Crawford was a retired police detective. After twenty-five years on the force, he'd opened a private detective agency. I work for him part-time. Despite my son's wishful thinking, I do not have my own agency.

I grabbed my phone, chuckling as I dialed. "Let's see if he still has enough contacts to have some answers by now."

"Hey, trouble." Crawford's gravelly voice filled my kitchen. With a volume that had cleared bars with little effort, putting him on speaker was pointless. I held the phone a foot away from my ear to protect my hearing. "Your calls are always bad news, especially this early on a Saturday morning."

I heard springs creaking in that old leather chair he refuses to give up. He was a big man, built like a brick outhouse as my grandmother was fond of saying. His sandy blond hair, streaked with white, was always combed straight back from his square-jawed face.

"I warned you it was going to get worse." I spoke without a hint of remorse, amused at his irritation. "Do you have any news about last night's murder victim?"

"Belden." His bellow made me wince. "You're in debt to me big time and the hole you're digging gets deeper with every call."

"You owe me." I brought the phone up to eye level. "Look at the free publicity my cases brought you."

Kevin raised a brow at my exaggerated claim.

So what if there'd been a few issues? Any publicity is good publicity, right?

"I owe *you*?" The crack of Crawford slapping the desk came over the line loud and clear. "Do you know how many favors I've called in to save you in the past? What am I getting out of this?"

"A warm, happy glow for helping a friend and for clearing an innocent woman." I gestured to Mrs. C as if he could see me. "Besides, we're buds. Friend. Pals. You love me."

Silence.

"You love Marcus."

My boy child nodded. "I'm easy to love."

Though I rolled my eyes, I had to admit it was true. Then, I focused on the call. "When I solve this case, I'll mention your name. That'll bring you even more publicity."

Crawford snorted. "You're nothing if not confident."

False bravado is all I have to go on most of the time. That and the mental crossword puzzles I build for my cases. This one was shaping up to be a doozy. "What did you find out?"

"Not much beyond the basics." The rustle of paper sounded over the phone. My boss is a dinosaur who prefers manila folders to the digital option. He cleared his throat. "Victim's name, Daniel Neville Weatherington, Jr, known as Neville. Age, sixty-five."

Marcus put both elbows on the table and hitched himself forward, listening intently.

I made a hurry-up motion, waiting with ill-concealed impatience for Crawford to get to the heart of the matter. "What do they have for cause and time of death?"

My bossman didn't answer directly. He simply continued reading. "Preliminary cause of death is blunt force trauma. The murder weapon was a paperweight. Time of death is not definite."

Though Rabi's expression was somber, he looked far less worried than I felt.

Marcus straightened in his chair. "The room was hot when I walked in it. Way warmer than the hall."

"Too bad the police don't know that," Crawford's flat tone held a note of accusation. "Thelen, the lead detective, can only speculate whether the gas fireplace was turned on to disguise the time of death. The victim could have been killed anytime from thirty minutes to four hours before he was found."

That was far worse than I'd hoped. Mrs. C, Marcus, and I had been in the building for over an hour when she found the body. She'd been out of my sight for several minutes when she ran out of the library. Not that I doubted her innocence, but the cards were already stacked against her. "This is not good for our side."

3

7 Across; 7 Letters;
Clue: Brought together as a unified whole
Answer: Reunion

After badgering Crawford into a promise to keep abreast of the police investigation, I ended the call. Despite his gruff manner, I knew he wouldn't fail me. The man is known for his loyalty. I met Mrs. C's gaze. "If someone is trying to frame you, we need facts to fight them."

Kevin pointed at Mrs. C. "Did last night's victim, Neville, contact you?"

"Not a word." Her British accent rang with conviction. "I knew the Jerrone company has been holding auctions in Langsdale for the last several years, but I don't run in that society, do I? The younger son, oversees the auctions, but he and Neville were boys when I left. They never saw me or Gracie."

Marcus was already searching, his fingers flying over the keys. "Jerrone is in town for a three-day art auction starting tonight."

Langsdale always has something going. Along with attracting visitors to tournaments at an internationally renowned golf-course, they had festivals, concerts, gourmet eateries promotions and more going on weekly. Well-heeled tourists with money to spend are a fact of life.

High-brow auctions were common affairs. Tourists, homegrown and international, bought art, antiques, and collectibles of all kinds.

"What's on the auction block?" Kevin asked.

"Paintings. Sketches. A different bunch of pieces every day for three days." Marcus read from the screen. "The lowest expected price is thirty thousand dollars. The highest value is eight figures. The highlight is an Infantino sketch valued at up to fifteen million dollars."

The amount was staggering. "People have definitely been killed for less."

"An Infantino, eh?" Mrs. C, pale in the morning light, twisted the silver necklace she wore. "It's come full circle. Come back to haunt me."

It was a rather ironic statement considering Neville had been murdered during a ghost hunt. I stared into space while the facts stacked up in my mind's eye. A horrible feeling gnawed its way into my gut and took up residence. "This can't be a coincidence."

Marcus slapped the table with such force that I jumped. "I told you it was a set-up, all of it."

With a hand over my heart, I glared at the boy. "Do you want to give me a heart attack?"

"The killer knew you'd be at Rycliffe Castle last night." Kevin's unflinching gaze zeroed in on Mrs. C. "You said you won the ticket in a radio contest."

"That was untrue, of course." The woman's admission came in a breezy tone. "When Marcus saw the ticket, it was the first thing that popped into my head. What with him always entering contests. Then, when he wanted to come, I couldn't think of what to say. I never thought either of you would be in danger."

Once he learned of the event, the boy had begged me to take him. I figured it would be interesting. Like Mrs. C, I hadn't expected trouble, but I hadn't known the whole story.

"How did you end up in the library at Rycliffe Friday?" I sounded like a live game of Clue talking to Colonel Mustard. "You finding Neville's body was obviously part of the killer's plan."

"I see that now." She took off the horn-rimmed glasses, rubbing the bridge of her nose. "It was foolish, but... "

Her voice trailed off.

"You received a note about Gracie." My intuitive leap was a statement, not a question. So far, all roads in this labyrinth led back to that woman and the first murder. "That's the only thing that would have drawn you out."

Mrs. C agreed with a sheepish nod. "I found a letter and a ticket in me mailbox two weeks ago. Addressed to Delia Alton, me real name. Gutted me, it did. Typed. Unsigned. No postage. The instructions were to arrive as early as possible. Then, immediately take the servant staircase to the library, but the stairs were closed for repair. I had to wait until we got to the second floor and the lights were out. I didn't know how to explain the note or even where to start. I... part of me didn't believe it could be true."

I have to admit that hearing about the first Weatherington murder would have been quite a bit to swallow coming out of the blue. But she could have tried.

Marcus shook his head. "Why did you go? You knew the meeting was trouble."

The survival instinct he'd learned on the streets still had a hold on him.

For one of the few times in our acquaintance, Mrs. C seemed at a loss.

"I didn't think anyone left alive knew the truth." Her voice shook. Her breath came in quick bursts. "Going was an admission of everything I've hidden for fifty years, but I couldn't help myself. I had to find out who knew my birth name, didn't I?"

"You have no idea who connected you with Gracie?" I couldn't help my dejected tone. I'd been hoping for a few breadcrumbs. "It's been decades since the first murder. In all that time did you ever confide in anyone? A close friend? Your husband?"

Mrs. C straightened her shoulders. "That life belonged to a different person. I'd been settled for over fifteen years when I met my Alfred. By then, my old life belonged to someone else. I never told him, or anyone."

If she hadn't told her beloved Alfred, the older woman had told no one her secret. Gracie had to be the source of the leak.

"Gracie must have talked." Kevin's gaze narrowed as he repeated my thought aloud. "Someone knows about your past. Who?"

"I can't believe Gracie would ever tell." Though her denial rang out clearly, uncertainty darkened her eyes. Mrs. C's pale blue orbs flashed a bit of fire. "That's what I went into the library to discover. Instead, I found that man. Dead. Looking exactly like I'd last seen his father."

Marcus scooted closer to the table, inching to the edge of his chair. "The dead guy had a note, too. Someone set you both up."

I nodded absently. The other woman's comment about the closed staircase circled in my mind. What if Mrs. C had entered the library earlier? "The notes. The timing. The instructions. All very detailed. I wonder when those stairs were closed. If they'd been open, how would the result have been different?"

Something told me it might have been worse.

"A split second can be the difference between disaster or success." Kevin's fingers tapped a staccato rhythm on the table. His family's intricate scams were timed to the second. "We have to analyze the victim. Find out if anyone else had a motive for his murder. What did you find on him, Marcus?"

"Tons." Marcus, whose gaze had flickered to his phone time and again, sat up straighter. "Jerrone was founded by Neville's great-great-grandfather. Family owned and run ever since. One of the top five international auction houses in the world."

"Along with Christie's and Sotheby's." I drummed my fingers on my coffee cup. "What about the family history?"

My son glared at me over the top of his phone. He didn't like to be interrupted during his reports. After a few seconds, he took up the story. "Neville was fifteen when his father was murdered. Liam, his only brother, was eleven. Their mother found the body. She was all torn up. Like Mrs. Colchester said, Gracie was the only suspect. She was identified as leaving the scene at the time of the murder."

"That was me, wasn't it?" Mrs. C clicked her tongue and shook her head with an air of regret. "No one ever knew."

Marcus made a half of a sandwich with a slice of toast and several pieces of bacon, seemingly unmoved by the woman's regret. He munched as he recited the facts. "Gracie's affair with the old guy was in the papers the next day. The cops figured he wanted to dump her, and she blew up. They called the killing a murderous passion."

The opposing views of the same story seemed to face each other from across the room. Mrs. C, young and scared, had struck out to protect herself, then fled the country. While Daniel Weatherington's death had left a widow and two sons without a father. A tragedy from every angle.

I took a long drink of my coffee, letting its heat dispel the gray mood. "How long was the investigation active?"

"A bloody long time, ducks." Mrs. C doused her eggs with a few shots of hot sauce. Her mouth tilted up in a rueful smile. "It was quite the lively chase for several years."

Marcus pointed at me with his phone. "The family kept the investigation alive. When Neville got older, he talked to the papers, called out the police for an arrest, hired private detectives."

I nodded. "Liam has lost his father and now his brother to murder."

"If the dead guy had stayed home like usual, he'd still be alive." Marcus set his phone on the table with a decisive thud.

Rabi, absorbing every detail but saying little, cocked his head in a silent question.

My son leaned in. "Neville never traveled to international shows. Liam, who's in town, or one of their cousins oversaw the auctions outside of Britain. Neville always stayed home."

"Timing." Rabi's low, deep drawl seemed to add a different twist to the word. "When did the man sign on to come?"

"Good question." Something had pulled the latest victim out of his comfort zone. Why? Had he been searching for a woman accused of a decades-old murder? Or had he wanted an art forger?

More important, had the knowledge of Mrs. C's past and her connection with his family died with him?

While the questions surrounding the victim multiplied faster than rabbits in springtime, a sudden realization smacked me between the eyes. "Oh, no, not this weekend. I can't believe I forgot. I can't have a murder investigation this weekend."

Kevin crossed his arms over his chest. His restrained amusement radiated through the air. "I'm sure Neville Weatherington and his family had other plans, too."

I gritted my teeth. "Mom and Pop are arriving this morning to spend the weekend."

"I can't believe I forgot." Marcus slapped his forehead. "It's my big contest win, the free stay at Silver Mountain Resort."

My son, the perennial contestant, enters every contest he hears about. For the last year, he's targeted anything that involved trips or travel as a prize. He'd been determined to give my parents something special for their forty-fifth anniversary. He hit the jackpot a few months ago with a free trip to Langsdale.

Kevin groaned like he'd been hit in the gut. "We've been on a countdown to this visit for months."

"It completely skipped my mind." I fortified myself with a long sip of raspberry chocolate coffee. "Murder has a way of overshadowing everything else."

"How many balls can you keep in the air?" The strain in Kevin's tone betrayed his tension. Since his relatives had disowned him and we were now a couple, he was stuck with my relatives by default. Now his drive to aid a friend warred with his loyalty to my family, pulling him in opposite directions.

"There's more." I gripped my warm mug. "Pop asked if we; you, I, and Marcus, were free to join them at the resort this weekend."

Surprise blanketed Kevin's face. "What did you tell him?"

"We don't have any handyman jobs scheduled for the weekend, either of us." I've tried to clean up my act for Marcus, but looking back, I maybe should have fudged the truth. "He said he and Mom weren't coming this far simply to stay at an over-priced motel. I haven't seen them in years."

The contracting business Kevin and I opened a few months ago was off to a steady start. There was always some errand to run or supplies to pick up, until now. The calendar was clear for their four-day visit.

Marcus's face lit up, a typical twelve-year-old boy sensing a treat. "We're staying at the resort?"

His response lightened my mood. So much for my mini-sleuth's sole-minded concern for murder. I nodded. "Pop traded in their king room for a double suite so we could stay together."

"This is for the best, ducks." Mrs. C pointed her fork in my direction, flinging drops of tabasco sauce across the table.

My quick reflexes helped me dodge the onslaught.

Kevin caught the splatter across his cheek.

Oblivious, Mrs. C dug into her scrambled eggs. "Spend the weekend with your family. Let the bobbies handle the case."

"I'm not having this discussion *again*." I added a touch of steel to my tone.

Anticipation lit Marcus's expression. "A weekend at a five-star spa, plus we scope out the dead guy's homies at the same time. Win-win."

My mind did a one-eighty. One minute I was locked out of a case that might put Mrs. C away for murder. The next, I'm at the front door with the suspects. "What are you saying?"

"People. Google is your friend." Marcus's straight, black hair reflected the light as he pointed at his tablet. "Where do you think the Jerrone auction is being held? Where are they housing their representatives? How about the most expensive digs in Langsdale?"

Among the trio of upscale resorts in town, the Silver Mountain held the edge in size, money, and amenities. With internationally trained chefs and high-dollar boutiques on-site, only tourists with deep pockets stayed there.

"That can't be." Mrs. C gasped. "The art auction… "

"Was scheduled for the Rycliffe Castle tonight, opening night. The other two auctions were always planned for Silver Mountain," Marcus declared, dancing in his chair. "The Rycliffe is now a crime scene. They changed the opening location to the resort."

Kevin gave the boy a pointed look. "I see your mind working. I suggest you pause before making plans."

My son's eyes narrowed. "In this family, you have to stay ahead of the game."

Mrs. C pointed her fork at me. "You can't involve your parents in a murder investigation."

I was torn. I couldn't -- wouldn't -- abandon Mrs. C's fate to the police. She had motive and opportunity. If her past came to light, she'd be halfway to the penitentiary by Monday. Besides, it seemed the universe had deposited this opportunity in my lap. "I don't plan to involve them. My parents don't know the first thing about the hazards of an investigation."

Marcus spread his hands out. "Why tell them anything?"

My streetwise son sometimes blinded himself to the obvious. I had to protect my parents from possible fallout from this investigation. "I'm not going to keep the facts from them. We were at the scene of the murder. This is a high-profile case. It'll be the topic of every conversation."

Marcus swirled a sausage link in his ketchup. "Which will be good for us."

I refused to admit that I'd had the same thought. "I wish I could send them home to Kentucky."

Kevin eyed me as if I'd sprouted a second head. "I can hear your dad selling that to his cronies at the café. He'd never live it down."

Marcus balanced his chin on his fist. "Gram's not going to pass on four days at a resort. Besides, she misses me."

After choking back a laugh at the boy's serious expression, I eyed Rabi. Perhaps wisdom could be found from a man who resembled a starving Buddha.

Rabi raised his cup in a semblance of a toast. "If you can't pick your fight, fight the hill you're facing."

It seemed I had little choice. Not that I was blind to the possibilities of being down the hall from the murder suspects. Yet, I couldn't ignore the danger. I shot a glance at Kevin. He returned the look with a knowing expression. The man can read my mind.

"This is a terrible idea." Mrs. C's vehement tone drew everyone's attention. She clasped her hands together. Her skin stretched tight and wrinkle-free across her knuckles. "Neville Weatherington couldn't have followed my trail to Langsdale. Someone told him."

"We covered that." But only in passing. "It must have been Gracie. You kept this identity a long time. Gracie could have tracked your e-mail somehow and discovered your name and location. If she stayed in contact with her family, she might have let something slip."

Mrs. C's pale eyes burned with intensity as she considered my scenario. After a moment, her whole body seemed to collapse. "Aye, Gracie was close to her family. If she reached out to them over the years, she'd never have told me."

I'd never seen the other woman so defeated. I patted her arm. There was worse to come. "Someone she told pointed Neville Weatherington to Langsdale. Even though the note didn't mention your name, someone else must know your alias."

Kevin's eyes hardened to sapphires. "If *anyone* contacts you... "

"Oh, ducks, you lot will know in the next breath." She held up her hand. "I've learned me lesson."

Part of me doubted that fact even now, but I had another nut to chew on. "Would anyone in the Weatherington family know that you aren't Gracie?"

The older woman waved a thin hand in a dismissive gesture. "Fifty years ago, Daniel Weatherington, Sr, his mother, and his wife met me in person. Those three people are dead. His wife died several months ago."

Exactly when Mrs. C's American accent had given way to the British version. At least, I had an answer to a question that had plagued me since that day. Despite the current complications, I happily filled in that part of my mental crossword puzzle.

"No one alive has ever seen Gracie or you in person, and according to the records, there's only one of you." Kevin's eyes shifted as if looking for a solution. "The murderer believes they tracked Gracie to Langsdale. No one will know you aren't her."

My head was beginning to hurt. "At least my mom can't be mistaken for Gracie or you. You're five-foot-six with your hair fluffed up. Mom is six-foot in her stocking feet."

She looks exactly like the horse breeder she is. Like my father and three siblings, my mother had been born in the right place, to the right life. I always felt like the stork carrying me got tired and dropped me at a Kentucky horse ranch at random.

Kevin took a long sip of coffee. "Your mother has the paperwork to prove her identity."

"So do I." Mrs. C sniffed at the perceived insult. She drew herself up as much as she could while sitting at the table.

Kevin's fingers resumed their tapping. "So, your history looks solid."

I felt the walls closing in around me. I'd been outmaneuvered by a fifty-year-old case. "The best-case scenario would be if I can talk my parents into going home. But, I'm here for you, Mrs. C. We all are. You're family. We'll do everything in our power to help you out of this mess."

"Odd you should say that, ducks." Mrs. C dug at the table with a red, taloned finger. "That's exactly what I told Gracie when I decided to confront Daniel Weatherington. Look how that ended."

4

3 Down; 6 Letters;
Clue: Extravagant living
Answer: Luxury

"Your father and I are staying at this resort, Tracy. Not another word." With that decisive statement, my mother, Sylvia Belden, marched into our suite at the Silver Mountain Resort. "Marcus won this trip for your father's and my forty-fifth anniversary. He was so proud when he called and told us. I am not about to disappoint my grandson."

I'd spent the last hour trying to dissuade Mom and Pop from remaining in town. My suggestion that they return to Kentucky was shot down. Then, I'd offered them my place. A cozy, though somewhat crowded, family visit far from any murder investigation.

No go.

Our discussion had lasted from our greeting, all the way through the car ride. Checking in at the hotel interrupted me briefly, but I'd quickly picked up the boxing gloves again.

Now stark lines of chrome tables topped with glass surrounded us on all sides. Plush furniture offered a welcome contrast, softening the severe lines. Sheer, flowing panels covered the French doors that led onto a spacious patio adorned with potted ferns. Enough of the bright, noonday sun sifted into the large room to make the stiff, modern lines of the room seem almost homey.

Mom surveyed the stack of matching set of luggage with an eagle eye. Satisfied each piece was accounted for, she faced me. "I listened to your reasoning, and I appreciate your concern. Your father and I are staying. This present means too much to Marcus."

I gritted my teeth against a comeback born of frustration. I'd known from word one I wasn't going to win. Once she set her course, a hurricane would have been hard-pressed to shift my mother. Still, no one could say I hadn't fought the good fight.

Kevin, Marcus, and my dad entered behind us.

Marcus, who loved nothing more than staying at expensive hotels, was already on the move. His wiry body bolted down the hall to the right. "I'll check out the place."

I watched him go, envying his ability to slough off worries so easily.

Kevin moved to stand beside me. His expression remained neutral, but I could tell from familiarity born of our long association that he shared my frustration. Though he'd reinforced my arguments early on, he'd fallen silent halfway through the discussion.

Perhaps, as an outsider, he wanted to stay on my parents' good side. Or perhaps he knew when to quit on a losing hand. This is only one reason why I don't play poker.

I fisted my hands on my hips. "A man has been murdered. Mrs. Colchester may become a person of interest in his death. I have to investigate. I don't want you and Pop caught in any issues that may arise. This is for your own safety."

Mom met my gaze with the same steady look that had waylaid my attempts as a teen to extend my curfew. My arguments had failed then, and they'd failed today. "So, you've said. Repeatedly."

She smiled at me with the advantage of three inches. My dad, at six-five and a solid two-fifty, overshadowed most people. My two brothers and one sister had all inherited the height gene as well. I was the runt at five-nine and, yes, the baby.

Maybe that was why I always felt I had to prove myself. That and the fact that, unlike me, they were all horse lovers who constantly beat the sun out of bed.

Not that horses aren't fun to ride. I love that part. It was the early rising and the endless chores that I never appreciated.

Pop came up from behind and pulled me close with one bear-like arm. His dark brown hair and hazel eyes matched mine. "You're circling, little girl. The horses are at the stables. The race is over."

What else could I do? Acknowledging defeat, I gave him a quick hug. After we unpacked, we took a tour of the grounds. Three pools, two spas, tennis courts, garden paths, and seemingly endless shops were laid out in shining crystal, polished wood, and gleaming metal. The best of everything.

Too bad murder, both past and present, had cast a pall over the weekend.

We put a hold on a full tour of the elaborate gardens to get ready for the dinner and art auction planned for the evening. The opening salvo of the Jerrone Auction.

In the privacy of my bedroom, I called Mrs. C. "Did Gracie have any children? They might be working to clear her name by laying both murders at your doorstep. Do you know what alias she used?"

I could try to get my hands on the guest list and cross-check the names. It was a long shot at best, but I was desperate.

Mrs. C drew in a slow breath. "Gracie was not maternal by any means. She never spoke of having children."

Too interested in Gracie, perhaps? "Okay, what about her sister and brother's names?"

"Hmm, Piers Linden and Audrey O'Keefe."

The names meant nothing to me, but information is never wasted. "I'll have Marcus do a quick check. See if anything shows up."

After hanging up, I walked into the main room of our suite. I smoothed my teal dress. My evening gown had long, slit sleeves, caught with rhinestones at the wrists. The sheath dress was form-fitting enough to flatter, but not skintight. Picturing walking into dinner with Kevin, I almost felt like prom had come around again. I couldn't stop a smile at the image.

Marcus's high-pitched whistle echoed in the spacious suite. "T.R., you clean up nice."

"You look very dapper yourself." I'd managed to wrangle the boy into the only suit he had by pointing out that Pops and Kevin would both be dressed up.

Kevin entered as Marcus was doing a preening strut.

"Looking good, sport." Then, Kevin's sapphire eyes roamed from my silver, open-toed sandals to the intricately knotted silver pendant.

I have to admit his appreciative gaze set my heart thumping double time. Kevin, with his wavy black hair and sapphire eyes, looked handsome in torn jeans and a dirty tee. In a suit and tie, he was dazzling enough to make me catch my breath.

"Belden, you always look good." He rested his hands on my waist and gave me a slow kiss. "Tonight, you're spectacular."

Marcus snorted. "You've seen the dress before. It's the only fancy one she owns."

So much for prom. "Thanks, kiddo."

I told him and Kevin about my latest call to Mrs. C.

Marcus noted the names and started to pull out his phone. I stopped him when my parents walked into the room.

Mom and Pop looked elegant in their best outfits as we headed to the ballroom. In the confines of the corridor, I put my arm around Marcus's shoulders.

"Remember, we're playing it low-key." I glanced up and down the hallway. A few other small groups were chatting among themselves. No one else was close to us. "We're not on the case officially. We don't want to draw attention to ourselves."

My mom patted my arm. "I think that's best, dear."

I held in a grimace at her slightly patronizing tone. She obviously thought I was blowing the danger out of proportion.

Marcus glanced up at her. "Keep your ears open for any comments about the dead guy, just in case. 'Kay?"

My dad gave him a thumbs up and a wink.

I groaned at the boy enlisting my parents when I'd done my best to distance them from the case.

Private conversation ceased as the other attendees closed in around us. We drifted through the double doors into the ballroom. The large room glowed with the subtle light of sparkling chandeliers. Oversized vases, brimming with wildflowers, scented the air with a sweet, subtle fragrance.

The dining tables were festooned with elaborately tied napkins, candles, and gleaming silverware. Silver vases filled with orchids served as centerpieces. Food stations and bars lined the side walls. The wait-staff, in crisp white shirts with black ties, threatened to outnumber the guests. They roamed through the crowd carrying trays filled with finger-foods.

French doors opened onto a patio that ran the length of the far wall. At least a dozen people strolled around, taking in the intoxicating view of the desert in the dimming light of the evening sky. The mountains, blending into the dusk, formed a dark purple chain on the horizon.

If only I could forget Neville Weatherington and whatever had motivated him to pursue Gracie Linden to Langsdale, Nevada.

I tapped Marcus as he started to wander toward a display. "Remember, low-key."

He gave me a thumbs up. "Subtle is my middle name."

Kevin's chuckle reached my ears. His warm hand against my waist urged me toward one of the food stations set up along the perimeter.

"Tracy Belden!" The high-pitched squeal brought our entire group to a stop. That and the blond bouffant who planted herself in my path. One hand reached out to me, hesitating as if I were a mirage that would disappear at a touch. "It *is* you, isn't it?"

Stunned didn't begin to describe my reaction. After an initial spike, my pulse settled into a normal rhythm. My brain busily searched for a clue to the woman's identity. She wore a lanyard with a stylized logo of SMR for Silver Mountain Resort. Maybe I wasn't supposed to know her. Finally, I simply blurted out. "I'm Tracy Belden."

She clasped her hands together. Her smile widened. "I saw Marcus, Sylvia, and Frank Belden listed as our contest winners. I didn't dare to hope they were your family."

Marcus had entered Mom and Pop as his co-winners. The three of them had been directed to the office shortly after we arrived while I'd called Crawford about the case. If I'd gone to that meeting, perhaps this scene could have been avoided.

Blondie sighed. Her gaze never left my face. "I've been crazy busy rescheduling the location of the auction today. I didn't have a chance to speak with them, or I might have learned they were your family. I can't believe my luck."

Nor I mine. When my brain still refused to update, I kept smiling.

"It *is* her." The blonde evidently had one volume. High. Though the comment was addressed to one young woman, everyone in a twenty-foot circle stared at us.

"There goes subtle." Kevin's murmur barely reached my ears.

A waif-like brunette with a Silver Mountain ID showing the name Jamie, walked up to the first woman. The young girl's gaze was like a deer caught in the headlights, unsure how to handle this unexpected blip in the flow.

"This is my assistant, Jamie." Blondie put a hand on the girl's shoulder, then pointed at me. "This is the famous private investigator I told you about."

I cringed at the description, and at the pained look on Jamie's face. "I'm not really famous."

Blondie couldn't hear me over her own voice. "Her picture was in the local papers when she solved that murder in Tahoe."

Shows what a slow week it had been for news in this region of Nevada.

"When Mr. Prushark was murdered in his mansion." Blondie's arm shook as she pointed at me. "She was there. She has a whole team of associates."

Marcus planted himself directly in front of me. He pointed at his chest, then included Kevin with a wave of his hand. "That's us."

I put a hand on his shoulder. With my other hand, I clasped Blondie's fingers and brought her arm down. The move forced her another step nearer. I had hopes that proximity would lower her volume.

She leaned in close enough to surround me with a cloud of expensive smelling perfume. "Are you investigating the Weatherington murder?"

Her stage whisper would have carried to the balcony.

Fortunately, most people seemed to have moved on from our encounter. However, one woman, thirtyish, with long, auburn hair froze in her tracks. She gave me a not-so-subtle sideways glance. Making a show of admiring the flower vases along the wall, her head remained cocked in our direction.

Another man stopped a dozen feet to the right. Pale red hair, shot with gray. Late fifties. Age had added girth to what looked to have been an athletic frame. His direct gaze studied me with undisguised interest.

I made a mental note to ferret out his name, then, I turned to Blondie. My assessment had taken only seconds. I kept a smile pasted on my face while seeking a diversion for this woman's enthusiasm.

"Holly reads mysteries all the time." Jamie, the Silver Mountain Resort assistant broke in with a shy smile. She looked like an escapee from high school with her ponytail and slight form. "Perhaps you two should talk after we finish taking pictures."

Blondie, aka Holly, smiled even wider at the gentle reminder. "You and your son being our contest winners means we'll have hours to spend together this weekend."

"Wow. I..." The polite smile froze on my face. "I don't know what to say."

"This is great." Marcus strained against my hand, edging closer to Holly. "You can give us the inside scoop on the people involved. Act casual."

Unlike Holly, my son's words barely reached me and Kevin.

In response, Holly clasped her hands then, another squeal. "This is so exciting to have you all here. You can tell me about all your cases."

I'd only had a dozen. Some were cheesy divorces.

Don't judge. That and the handyman business has boosted me into the lower middle class.

"Marcus sent us clippings of the McKiernan and Prushark murders." Pop stepped closer. Excitement gave his bellow more force than usual.

Anyone who'd turned away before, now checked us out one more time.

Mom was by Dad's side. She raised a brow in my direction.

Proper Southern ladies didn't get their picture in the paper. Of course, I had already done a number of things proper Southern ladies don't do.

"I had no idea Tracy was famous," was all my mother said.

Neither did I.

Jamie gestured to a huge poster with a photographer standing close by. The practiced smile on her face gave the young girl an air of added confidence. "Why don't we get your photo taken as the prize winners? Then we'll show you to your table. You have a front-row seat for the auction."

Marcus lingered behind as my parents moved on. "Having an 'in' with the organizers is great for our case. We can wrangle an intro to the Jerrone group."

The fact that no one else overheard his whispered comment seemed pointless now.

Holly had fallen into her professional mode, but she hadn't forgotten me. She matched steps with my mom and dad. "Do you remember the books about the Trixie Belden mysteries? I loved those when I was young."

Pop glanced over his shoulder. "Tracy had the whole collection. She got one for every birthday and Christmas present."

The Belden series of young adult mystery books had come out decades before Holly's childhood. Or mine for that matter, but my matching name gave me an excuse for having read them.

Marcus caught up with them. Determined to be involved, he pointed to my parents. "My family is related to the girl who inspired those books."

Mom and Pop, of course, looked totally confused by this announcement. For good reason, Marcus was working from false information.

Holly went into new spasms of delight. "I had no idea the stories were based on a real person."

I made the relationship up. I wanted to scream. I'd made up the relationship to win the trust of a street urchin. In those days, Marcus had haunted the local library. He'd read everything else when I fed him that line. I showed him the books to keep him talking. It was the only way he'd let me buy him lunch or give him food.

Mom's gaze held a suspicious glint. "I had no idea either."

"Tracy must have dug up the connection." Pop's offhand comment added weight to the story. "Once she gets her teeth in something, she won't let go until she has all the answers."

I smiled and slowed my pace, letting the others get farther ahead.

My boyfriend, being contrary, gave me a self-righteous look. "Oh, what a tangled web we weave… "

"I can't believe Marcus thinks that story is true." I cast a pleading look at Kevin as if hoping he'd unravel the complications of my white lie. "My parents surely know their own relatives. Not even Holly could believe this fabrication."

Kevin's jaw tightened to keep his laughter contained. "Haven't you learned by now that people believe what they want? That's the basis of every scam in existence."

The people who'd gathered for the auction were now whispering and pointing at me. I smiled politely then kept my gaze focused firmly ahead.

Kevin gestured at my parents, talking with Holly, gushing about our heritage. "You might as well go with the flow. Swimming against the current is how people drown."

The wisdom of his words seeped through my frustration. With a sigh of surrender, I slipped my arm through his and leaned in close. The woodsy scent of his cologne teased my nostrils. His nearness set my heart fluttering, but I kept my focus on business. "If the universe is going to stack the deck against me, I'm going to take advantage of the situation."

Kevin's chuckle sounded in my ear. "Now, I'm worried."

I shifted my body just enough to nudge him. "Since ignoring the murder is pointless, and Blondie – "

"Holly," he corrected.

"- has broadcast my profession to everyone within a hundred yards, perhaps I can use tonight to investigate the murder victim. Find out who he came here with. Who had a grudge against him." I flashed a bright smile. "This way, no one will think our interest is odd or out of place."

"Isn't that what Marcus said earlier?"

I ignored the comment. "The more information we have on Neville, the quicker we can find the killer. Was the old murder the real motive or a cover for a personal grudge? For all I know, Neville could have been done in by a jealous husband."

Holly had finished positioning Marcus and my parents in front of a poster and next to a life-size vase of hearts and flowers. She'd sent Jamie off on some assignment after an intense exchange.

Marcus had the undivided attention of the photographer and his assistant. He shot them both an innocent smile and nodded toward the stage where the first paintings waited to be auctioned off. He'd either developed a sudden interest in modern art, or he was scrounging for information on Jerrone.

You be the judge. It wouldn't be the first time he'd used his impish manner and talkative nature to charm answers out of someone.

Holly turned a searching glance our way, giving Kevin and me a hurry-up gesture.

Kevin cast her a dazzling smile but didn't change his pace. "Smart money says this murder isn't due to adultery."

"I know. Too easy." I chewed on my lip. There were too many threads, too many coincidences. "Did Neville know Mrs. C's identity? The killer must know, right? Those notes drew them together. I wonder... could they have been meant to die together?"

5

—◆—

12 Across; 7 Letters;
Clue: A public sale of goods
Answer: Auction

The photographer's flashbulbs all but blinded me. It brought to mind mug shots, except people rarely smiled in those pictures.

Another flash added fresh dots to the green ones dazzling my eyes. All the while, my brain wondered whether to worry about Mrs. C's safety or that my family's faces would be splattered all over the Silver Mountain website. They shouldn't be in danger. Marcus had won the contest months before, but the killer had to be close. Which meant, I couldn't help but worry.

"That's enough pictures." Holly ordered a halt in a business-like but perky tone. She started herding us to the front of the room. "You've been great sports. Are you sure you don't want bidding paddles?"

I confined our collective refusal to a smile and a shake of my head. My cash flow wouldn't have survived an initial bid on any of the artwork available this weekend.

My father waved away the offer as well. "I came to see the auction. I love the competition once the bidding starts."

Mom smiled in agreement. "I'm interested to see what prices the artwork brings, but I'm not buying."

"Then let me show you to your seats."

With Holly leading the way, our little group walked toward the front row of tables. Marcus rubbernecked, seemingly taking in everything.

I resisted the urge to follow his gaze. I'd hear all about his theories and suspicions later. I always did.

"There will be introductory remarks about the artists whose works will be auctioned off tonight." Holly's smile never dimmed as her smooth patter continued. "The Jerrone auctioneer who replaced Neville Weatherington will explain how the auction will be conducted. Then, there will be a short break for attendees to take a last look at the art."

According to the catalog, the auction was a three-night event, Saturday thru Monday. Tonight, prints and lesser-known originals were on the block.

"Only a dozen pieces will be sold tonight." The wattage on Holly's perkiness dimmed a bit. "The highest number will be auctioned tomorrow afternoon. Monday evening is reserved for our special items."

"What artists are featured this weekend?" My mother's interest came naturally. She'd minored in art in college. One more reason she'd refused to miss this weekend. "Any names we might recognize?"

Our PR person turned up the perkiness dial at the show of interest. "Tonight's feature is a small Picasso sketch. Tomorrow, a minor Kandinsky. The early Infantino sketch discovered by Archibald Smythe is scheduled for Monday. The sale has been especially anticipated since the sketch was thought to have been destroyed in the artist's studio fire."

Her words reinforced Kevin's earlier comment. What better item to copy than one believed destroyed? Fortunately, my ability to mask my thoughts had been well-honed. My time as a P.I. had reinforced a life of... shall I say shading the truth? There were many times in my teenage years when I practiced looking innocent in the face of damning evidence.

Kevin responded with a show of polite interest. His first eighteen years had been spent in the school of grifting taught by his family of internationally known con artists. The wrong reaction in that world meant a loss of big bucks, jail time, or even death.

"Those are big names?" Dad scoffed. "I've heard of Picasso, but his stuff is lousy. The other two... I never heard of them."

Holly responded with undiminished enthusiasm.

I listened to her explanation while I scanned the room. The elegantly clad women and men mingled with a nonchalant air honed over hundreds of weekends and evenings like this one. They nibbled on tasty hors d'oeuvres and sparkling drinks while they drifted through their lives.

Me? I watched faces. My brain had been nagging me for attention, which usually occurred when my subconscious was trying to tell me I'd overlooked a detail. I wondered if I might recognize someone from last night's ghost hunting gone bad.

A few people stared at our group as we walked by. Too bad I had no idea what prompted their interest. Was it the contest win or knowledge of my profession? I noted the faces of the interested parties for later.

Keeping a carefree expression firmly in place, I slipped my arm through Kevin's. "There will be no rest this weekend."

Nodding agreement, my boyfriend's gaze never paused. Another of the many abilities drummed into him was a skill at profiling that surpassed any FBI agent.

After all, when it came to money, the fate of the family depended on choosing a rich sucker over an undercover cop. Kevin's list of people in the suspicious range would be invaluable.

Same for Marcus. Survival on the streets had been *his* motivator in reading people. The boy had a more discerning eye than most adults.

Speaking of noteworthy gawkers, the redheaded guy who'd been eyeing me since Holly broadcast my profession was standing front and center next to the table by the main stage. A shaggy mustache framed his wide mouth.

I rubbed Kevin's arm in an affectionate gesture to conceal my whisper. "Check out the aged athlete. Faded red hair. Eleven o'clock. He's got to be one of the Jerrone crowd."

As if the man felt the heat of my gaze, he turned a pair of piercing green eyes on me. His gaze locked on mine with no pretense of subtlety. He gave a short, clipped nod as if to seal an agreement.

Kevin raised a brow. "He's been studying you since Holly ID'd you."

"I don't know him."

Kevin's attention flicked around the room. "You will before the night is over."

The redhead in question jabbed the young man next to him. The second guy frowned but stopped his conversation to respond. My unknown buddy spoke in a rapid-fire delivery.

Intense. Determined. From the bunched muscles beneath his suit coat to the tense lines etched in his face, everything about him screamed he would have his way.

The reserved sign on the main table seemed to underline his authority.

Marcus slipped away from my parents' side. He smiled as if the sights had dazzled him. "That old guy's talking about you. Bet he's one of the Jerrone hotshots."

Which could be very good or very bad. I gave my son a wink. "You took the words right out of my mouth."

Our party neared the stage. Holly, with the practiced moves of a model on a runway, pivoted and gestured toward a front-row table in one sweep. "This is where I leave you for the evening. Have a wonderful time. I'll see you first thing in the morning for the tour of the gardens."

She cast our party a wide, toothy smile.

I was impatient to nail down some facts in this case or, at least, scope out the Jerrone party for possible suspects. Spending a portion of my morning looking at flowers didn't fit the bill, but I gutted up and grinned back.

Holly turned toward the guys. "Another possibility is a trip to the Rowdy Reptile Ranch. There's a Rattlesnake Wrangling show tomorrow morning for our more adventurous guests."

Marcus caught his breath. His eyes lit with interest.

Pop smacked the table. "That sounds more like it."

"Sounds perfect." For them, I added silently. If Mom accompanied my dad and my son, Kevin and I would have our morning clear.

Holly gave a few last-minute, cheery instructions. "I reserved tickets just in case, so let me know. Again, if you need anything, call my cell or pick up a house phone and have me paged."

My mother responded with a cordial expression. "Thank you for your help."

"I'll see you tomorrow." Holly's thousand-watt smile managed to look sincere without being strained.

I envied her that skill. Though I can paste on a grin, sincerity usually escapes me.

She met my gaze. "I'd love to discuss your cases or maybe your ideas on poor Mr. Weatherington's murder."

"Of course," I assured her. I watched her walk away with a sense of relief. Her perkiness was draining.

My mother studied the array of desserts and finger food laid out in the middle of the table. "What a lovely girl."

Pop grabbed his napkin. "I thought the filly was never going to run out of air."

Kevin glanced around the room. "Looks like we have the table to ourselves."

"I hope so." I selected a tasty looking concoction of cake, nuts, and whipped topping. "I don't feel like putting on a polite face all evening."

Mom tut-tutted my comment. "A woman as pretty as you is always on stage when she's in public, honey."

"We sure were the center of attention." Pop nudged my arm. His chuckle brought a smile to my lips. "I had no idea you were so famous in these parts. My little girl a celebrity. Wait until I tell everybody at home."

"I wouldn't take Holly too seriously, Pop." I didn't want to give my parents the wrong idea. "She's probably the only person in the room who knew me."

"Not anymore," Marcus crowed. "Everybody knows who you are now, and your team."

"That fella at the main table sure enough does." My dad jerked his chin toward the same group who'd drawn my attention. "He's been staring a hole through you."

"I noticed that." My mother took a plate of bacon-wrapped shrimp Marcus passed to her. "I wonder what that man wants with you, Tracy."

So, did I.

"You have such nice manners, Marcus." My mother congratulated my son. "Your mother was more of a hoyden at your age. Thankfully, she grew out of that stage."

I swallowed a sigh. Time to focus. I turned my attention to the room. The people. The layout. Though I couldn't see any possible way of wrangling a paycheck out of this investigation, Mrs. C deserved my best effort.

The lights dimmed. The introductory remarks began. I zeroed in on the speaker. If the art world lay at the heart of the murder, I needed to learn all I could.

The murder victim's replacement, Stanley Peyton, an auctioneer from Jerrone, took the stage. He was slim, with a blond buzz cut and an oversized nose. He asked for a moment of silence for his fallen associate, a member of the Jerrone founding family.

As the seconds of silence ticked by, it struck me that Neville's death had left an opening in the upper echelon. Perhaps it boiled down to the prestige of standing on the main stage. In that case, the Gracie Linden angle could be a red herring. Anyone who knew about Gracie could have lured Neville to his death.

Note to self - find out how Barnes got picked for this gig. Was he next in line or had he simply been the man on-site?

Second note to self - find a way to get in with the Jerrone group. Holly could, no doubt, arrange an introduction.

Then again, the way the man at the main table had been eyeing me, I might not have to rely on the PR woman on steroids. A glance at his table showed the remaining seats occupied.

That's when my nagging voice went on high alert. The moment of silence ended, but I paid little attention.

One of the people at the Jerrone table was the auburn-haired beauty I'd noticed at the front of the room. She'd kept her back to me then, but something about her sparked a memory of last night. The tilt of the chin maybe or the way she tossed her hair over her shoulder.

The lights were dimmed for the speeches, so I couldn't see her face. Still, the nagging feeling persisted.

I'd have to check with my son. He'd snapped pictures of everyone in attendance at the ghost hunting foray, especially after the murder when we'd been sequestered together while waiting for the police. If she'd been in attendance, he'd caught her on camera.

I glanced around, wishing Holly or Jamie were present to identify the people at the main table. I'd have Marcus take pictures of the Jerrone players when the crowd started moving again. I tapped him on the arm and whispered the plan. Then, I turned my attention to the auction.

A short time later, I swallowed hard, stunned by the bid on the current piece. I squinted at the eight-by-ten painting being offered. Last bid, sixty-four-thousand dollars.

I leaned over Kevin for a better view. "These are the lower end items?"

His chin brushed my hair as he nodded. "We're talking serious money."

Marcus leaned toward me from Kevin's other side. "I wonder if the Infantino they're selling is Gracie's work."

"So do I." If so, the Weatherington clan could lose something more precious than money. They risked losing their sterling reputation. "Dig deeper into Jerrone's history of finding or selling Infantino pieces."

My son's eyes lit up. "Got it."

For the next several minutes, I watched the auction. The mostly silent, yet intense bidding rose to several times my yearly income. This was a world I had never belonged to and had rarely seen. I tried to picture myself living in this cut-glass, seemingly perfect level of society.

The image refused to form. Even in my imagination, I didn't belong. I let the daydream slip away without regret. Reaching across the satiny tablecloth, I twined my fingers with Kevin's.

He returned the pressure and cast me a warm look.

"Got it." My son's excited whisper pulled me closer. "First up, Gracie's forgeries. In the past four years, Jerrone bought back three of the pieces. The fourth is hanging in a museum on the east coast."

His eyebrows rose until his bangs covered them.

My boyfriend gave a silent whistle. "Someone in the family knows they sold fakes."

"How long have they known?" I clicked my tongue. "From the beginning?"

"No way to know," Kevin said. "They're covering their tracks."

That gave me something to think about. How did the information play into motive?

Selling the rest of the pieces of art took most of the evening. It was an amazingly short time to garner several million dollars.

Mom and Pop joined in the applause with evident enthusiasm.

My mother shifted her chair to face the table. "I love a good auction. Gets the blood pumping."

Kevin's look of surprise vanished as quickly as it formed. "I forgot. You two are practiced at this scene. You sell yearlings and two-year-olds at auction."

My dad gestured toward the stage. "Those pictures aren't young saddlebreds, but they brought in a tidy sum."

Marcus snatched the last piece of cake. Rather than shove it in his mouth, he shot me a knowing look. He sedately set the morsel on his plate and picked up a fork.

I smiled approval at him. "The high-dollar items will be on Monday."

"That's a lot of cash exchanging hands." Kevin spoke in a meditative tone.

Amidst the general bustle of movement, my peripheral vision caught the Jerrone table enmeshed in an intense discussion. Though none of them, including the redheaded man, glanced my way, a sudden feeling of being trapped shot me to my feet.

"Why don't we take a walk?" I suggested. "The view from the terrace is one of the selling points of this resort."

Marcus popped up. After sitting through the entire presentation without a complaint, the boy was ready to be on the move.

Mom put a hand on Pop's arm as they walked away. "Coming, you two?"

Kevin held out his arm. "Right behind you."

Several minutes later we reached the far end of the terrace. The sun was slipping behind the chain of purple mountains. Ribbons of bright orange and soft lavenders painted the sky above the desert. A cooling breeze wafted across the sand and sagebrush landscape.

Mom's gaze lingered on the mountains. "This view would be a painting worth buying."

"This is more like it." Pop threw out his arms as if to embrace the outdoors. "Fresh air and open spaces. I prefer green hills, but I can see why you like it out here, Tracy. Rugged. Colorful. Hard country."

A sudden stir of people to my left stopped the answer on my lips. I swallowed a smile.

The guy from the Jerrone table strode through the loitering crowd like a heat-seeking missile, aimed directly at me.

I felt more than saw Marcus's interest.

Kevin pressed his hand against the small of my back, then let his arm drop. He remained at my side in a show of support.

Appreciating his confidence, I squared off to meet the older man. Thankfully, we were outdoors. The man's intensity would have been hard to take inside, even in the oversized ballroom.

He put on the brakes a foot in front of me. "You're Tracy Belden."

The second time tonight I'd been confronted.

Thanks to Holly, everyone in the room knew my name. "Yes, I am."

"Liam Weatherington." His hand shot out.

We shook without breaking eye contact. Neville's younger brother. How much did he know about Gracie, his father's alleged killer? Was he as eager to see the documentary made as Neville had been?

The man let go of my hand. He continued to stare, his gaze sharp and assessing. "You were at the scene of my brother's murder."

I masked my surprise. Most families of crime victims aren't allowed knowledge of witnesses, but, for the past several years, the Jerrone Auction House had brought both prestige and publicity to Langsdale. That fact would likely ensure cooperation from the police.

I nodded coolly. "I was present."

"Official business?" Mr. Weatherington delivered the question with the speed of a bullet.

It took me a heartbeat to decipher his meaning. He thought I was on a job? "It was a family outing. I'm not on a case right now."

At least, not one Crawford was paying me for. Unfortunately.

A small circle of Jerrone associates watched and listened from a few feet away. Peyton, the auctioneer, was one.

Finally, the man facing me gave a sharp nod. "I want to hire you to find out who murdered my brother."

I squelched the urge to kick my heels. I remembered a football coach talking to his players about dancing in the end-zone. *Act like you've been there before.* "I'd be happy to discuss the job. However, I work for Crawford Investigations. Any official contract would have to be finalized with my boss."

Liam's jaw clenched at even this slight roadblock.

The man was a bulldozer used to mowing down all in his path.

"I can call him and apprise him of the facts." Getting my boss this case should even up my tab. "I'm sure he'll be agreeable."

Who was I kidding? Crawford would jump through the phone at the chance to charge top dollar and garner the publicity on such a high-profile case. And I was never going to let him forget that he owed it all to me.

While being paid to investigate this murder sounded like a bonus, a chill passed over my skin. I'd chased murderers before, but this time I'd be in the spotlight with a bullseye on my back.

6

31 Down; 8 Letters;
Clue: Study to establish facts
Answer: Research

Sunday morning found me on the patio outside the suite. I sat under an awning with Marcus, while Mom sipped tea from a delicate china cup.

Rocks in the Japanese-inspired landscaping gleamed golden in the morning light. The chain of purple mountains beyond the pale dunes served as a perfect backdrop for the scene. The view was almost enough to make me forget the case. Almost.

I ate the last piece of blueberry Danish, letting the sweet glaze and airy pastry melt in my mouth. The resort's coffee was hot and strong, just the way I liked it. The variety of flavors available in the suite added to my enjoyment.

Marcus shoved the last bite of a donut in his mouth, then licked his fingers. He swallowed before aiming a smile at my mother. "Now you and Gramps can see us work a murder case."

My mom set her cup on the matching saucer. "Does this mean you're on a job?"

"*I'm* on the job," I emphasized. I wished Pop were here. My parents both needed to understand the danger. Unfortunately, he and Kevin had gone off at oh-dark-thirty to watch the sunrise and possibly catch sight of desert wildlife.

I chalked Kevin's participation up to true love. Because not even for my own father had I agreed to the early morning venture. Of course, my mother hadn't gone either. She'd used me as an excuse.

Mom eyed Marcus, then shot me a concerned look. "Should you be involved in this? Think of your son."

"I know how to handle myself." I would have liked to say there was no danger. But with a killer on the loose, I needed her and my father to be alert to the risks. "Danger is always a possibility when dealing with a murderer. That's why the rest of you need to remain on the sidelines. Holly has a number of activities planned for you and Pop and Marcus."

Mom put her tanned, manicured hand over Marcus's golden-brown fingers and eyed me with a furrowed brow. From her pursed lips to her worried gaze, anyone watching would think this was our final farewell before I faced a firing squad.

I fortified myself with another long drink of coffee. "You three keep a low profile. Go on the resort outings. Sightsee. Most of all, don't discuss the murder."

Marcus scoffed openly. "Everyone in the city is talking about the Weatherington murder. We'll look too obvious if we ignore it."

The boy was unstoppable.

"There is real danger." I was treading a thin line between urging my parents and son to be cautious while reinforcing a "don't worry, I've got this" attitude.

"I'm not sure what you can do." My mother half-filled her cup with steaming coffee. She liked to drink her coffee hot. "The police are investigating the murder. They have more resources."

"I've thought that very thing in more than one case," I admitted.

"The family needs closure," she continued. "That man and his family deserve the best."

I masked the disappointment that stabbed at me. Clearly, she didn't think I fit the bill.

"T.R.'s great at this stuff." Marcus's confidence salved my pride. "Wait 'til you see her in action."

"I'm sure she is. She's always been stubborn once she got her teeth into a project." Mom patted his hand. "But I don't like any of you being involved. I don't know what I'd do if I lost you."

Her words served to confirm that her maternal instinct would make her as difficult to dislodge as Marcus. I couldn't bear putting them in danger. I had a plan. It started with laying all my cards, and the facts, on the table.

"Mrs. C knew people connected to the murder fifty years ago in England. If her past comes out, Mrs. C being on the scene of the second murder would make her a possible suspect." I splayed my fingers on the smooth surface of the glass patio table, painting the picture in sweeping strokes. "The police don't know about the connection. I have to find out who really killed the victim before they discover that fact."

Mom leaned in. "Why don't you explain the situation? Once the authorities have the facts, they can clear your friend."

"I wish it were that easy." If Mrs. C's motive for killing the recent victim wouldn't implicate her in the earlier death, it might have been. "I can't trust that an overeager DA won't jump at the chance to close a high-profile murder by pinning it on her."

My mother shifted in her chair, drawing away from the table. A familiar frown traced a line around her lips. "You've always led such a complicated life."

Disappointment lodged in my throat. A weekend without a murder would be easier. Too bad this was how my luck had always run.

Not that I was the one having the worst week. Neville Weatherington won that contest hands down. I just wish my options hadn't come down to choosing between my parents and my friend.

As much as I may have wished to accommodate Mom and Pop, I couldn't risk the police overlooking a crucial piece of this puzzle. After all, puzzles were my specialty. I already had the black and white grid in my mind for this case. Clues and questions were in place.

Besides, I couldn't shake the feeling that the danger to Mrs. C came not only from the present, but from the past. The vague misgiving lurked in a corner of my brain like a web being woven out of sight. The victim walked on unaware until the strands entrapped them.

I tried to find words to explain in a way my mother would understand. "I planned to investigate this case before Weatherington hired me. I can't risk the police settling on Mrs. C as the killer. She's my friend."

Though my mother still looked worried, her expression changed to one of resignation. Loyalty to a friend was something she understood. Good thing, since there was little more I could add.

"Speaking of being on the job." I caught Marcus's gaze. "I need to compare the pictures you took Friday to the ones from last night."

"On it." His intense expression ratcheted up several notches. He bounded out of his chair, returning seconds later with his tablet. He positioned his chair so all three of us could view the screen.

My mom smiled and inched closer. I hadn't thought she'd be interested, but I realized her hobby of people watching made comparing attendees at the two events right up her alley.

I watched my mother and son with amusement. Private investigating, a family affair.

Marcus tapped the screen. Two folders appeared. "I grouped the pictures by sex, race, and age."

Good thing the boy is too young to work on his own. He'd be more competition than I could handle. I patted him on the shoulder. "Good thinking."

"I'm impressed with all you've done." Mom echoed the sentiment. "When did you find the time?"

Marcus's cheeks flushed at the double praise. "I did some on my phone during the boring parts of the auction, then downloaded it to my tablet."

His latest, greatest phone was beyond my means. A fairy godfather in the form of Jack Rabi gave it to him as a Christmas present. The boy was a whiz, constantly discovering new features on the device.

"To work," he announced, pointing at the tablet.

Mom aimed a smile my way at his business-like tone.

Two folders, side-by-side, filled the screen. One was titled Ghost Hunters 101, the other said Auction Saturday.

I pointed at the screen. "Pull up the auburn-haired woman I pointed out to you. Mid to late thirties. Square face. Hazel eyes. See if you find her at the murder scene in the Friday pictures."

In less than a minute, Marcus had flipped through the photos of the women. He had two pictures displayed side-by-side.

The Friday night picture showed a mousy brown wig, colored contacts, bulky clothes, and bright eyeglasses. She'd pulled out all the tricks to hide her identity the night of the murder. The only thing lacking was a hat, which was good for concealing the face.

People focus on obvious, colorful details rather than a person's features. I've used the techniques myself, though not to kill anyone. However, the camera lens can't be deceived. I scanned her features.

"The rounded cheekbones, the nose." Mom waved a hand at the images. "It's obviously the same woman."

Marcus nudged my mom's elbow. "We caught her."

Not yet. "Why was she there? Why in disguise?"

"She must have known the dead guy would be there." Marcus's eyes narrowed. His straight, black hair seemed to shine with its own light. "They both work for Jerrone. He'd know her on sight."

That was the most obvious answer.

Mom's eyes widened. "Do you think she killed him?"

"Too early to tell." And far too easy judging by my other cases. "She may have learned about his meeting regarding Gracie Linden and wanted to be in on the score. If she's an up and coming professional, knowledge of either a possible forgery or Daniel Sr's killer would give her a huge advantage."

Mom sipped her coffee with a thoughtful air. "I hadn't thought of that."

Marcus swiveled in his seat. "She could still be the killer."

I bit back a smile at his encouraging tone, so at odds with his words.

Mom set her cup in the saucer with a careful touch. "This is so delicate compared to the mugs we use at home. I keep thinking I might break it."

A flash of camaraderie filled me. Her words of feeling out of place echoed mine on more than one occasion. Though I wasn't into horse breeding, I was still a country girl.

She studied the matching photos with an intense gaze. "What do you do now? Tell the police? No one else knows she was at the murder scene in disguise."

"Once the cops know, they'll shut us out." Marcus looked at me over his shoulder, a question in his eyes. "We should question her right away."

I nodded, thinking through my options. "*I* want to talk to her before I go to the police. I also want to find out her role at Jerrone's."

"Holly is due in a few minutes." Interest laced through my mom's voice. She reached for the pot. "She could identify the young woman. As a liaison for the auction, Holly can fill you in on the background of the people."

Marcus aimed one of his dazzling smiles at my mother. "You're a natural at this detective stuff."

Mom shared a smile with him, before she turned to eye me intently. "How will you know if she's the murderer?"

How to explain other than saying dumb luck? "A lot of answers have to be filled in to get the whole picture. I question everyone, see whose story doesn't stack up. With luck, I catch someone in a lie."

Marcus pointed to the screen. "Once a body hits the pavement, the lies begin."

All too true. "Most lies are meant to protect secrets unrelated to the murder. But there's no way to know without digging."

"I can see why you're worried." Mom sipped her coffee. "The closer you get, the more the murderer will feel trapped. That's when animals are most dangerous."

I wish I could say I had a better strategy, but the police method was no different. After all, I'd learned most of what I knew from Crawford, a twenty-five-year veteran of the force.

Marcus pulled the tablet close. "We should flip through the rest of the pictures. I didn't see anyone else from both places."

"We might as well cover all our bases." I reached for my coffee mug. "Even though we don't recognize them now, we may run into them later."

As it turned out, we found no one else who had been at the murder and the auction.

Mom sat back. "Watching you on the job is worth the trip. What's your next step?"

I tapped my chin. "I'll update Crawford. Perhaps he can work his police sources to get the names of the people who attended Ghost Hunters 101. I'd be interested to see if our mystery woman used her own name."

There was a narrow gap between questioning the woman on my own and obstructing justice. Of course, in the opinion of the legal authorities, I'd probably already crossed that line. So, the least I could do was drag my boss down with me.

A moment later his room-clearing bellow of outrage brought a triumphant smile to my lips.

"She's the missing woman." Crawford growled. "One name on the list of attendees was an alias and the person was gone by the time the police arrived and locked down the place. Why do you always mess up the simplest cases?"

"This case was complicated before I got involved." I yelled at my phone, held at arm's length to save my hearing. I loved a good argument with the old bear. "I've told you what I... we discovered. If you're scared, I'll call Wilson. I'm also going to talk to that woman soon as I can. She has to know something to be at Rycliffe Castle on Friday."

A loud growl came over the line. "I'll call Wilson. Keep me informed. No going off half-cocked."

"I would never do that." I ignored my mother's raised eyebrow and Crawford's snort. I'd worked with Detective Wilson in the past and I thought I'd be able to get around him, but having Crawford take care of it was easier. "I'll keep you up to the minute on my progress. You know how I love to file reports."

Marcus put both hands over his mouth to smother a laugh.

Before Crawford could respond, I ended the call. "I love hanging up on that man."

A tapping on the door heralded Holly's entrance. A moment later, she joined us on the outside patio. She reviewed the plans for the day, then segued into the main, or possibly the only, topic of the weekend.

"This is so exciting. You and your team working on a murder case here at the resort. Almost like a murder mystery weekend."

If the upbeat PR rep saw the tightening of my mother's jaw, she gave no sign.

"Death is far different when the victim is a real person rather than a two-dimensional character in a book." Sorrow for the tragedy threaded through my mother's tone.

Duly chastised, Holly sobered for the first time since I'd seen her. "I never meant to make light of the murder. We're all shocked and saddened."

Though she'd been standing, seemingly ready to deliver the schedule then leave, the woman joined us at the table. "Mr. Weatherington informed us he's hired you to solve Neville's murder."

I held up my hand to dampen her enthusiasm, but it was like trying to stop a runaway train.

"Not solve," I enunciated clearly. "Investigate."

The desire to dig into the identities of the players was my first instinct, then I took a drink of coffee and the business part of my brain went on holiday.

"This is delicious," I said in absolute sincerity. "Do you have any additional flavors not in the coffee bar?"

"We have caramel macchiato, black cherry, cinnamon hazelnut, among others." Holly slid a finger across her phone screen. "I can have any or all of them delivered to your suite."

My new best friend.

Marcus, frowning at me across the table, gave me a hurry-up gesture.

Ironing out the details about my favorite drink put me in a much better frame of mind. "I got the impression some of the other Jerrone representatives don't agree with Liam Weatherington's decision to hire a private detective."

"They don't see the point," Holly said in a forthright manner. "With the Jerrone's high profile and the publicity, the police have assigned multiple detectives to the case."

"That's what I told Tracy." My mom smiled at me. "Not that I want to do you out of a paycheck."

I returned the smile. My mother's practical nature had rubbed off on me. Fortunately, the handyman business I ran with Kevin brought me breathing room in paying the bills.

Holly inched closer. "The city would prefer a quick arrest. The police are getting a good deal of pressure."

I murmured agreement while fighting to hide my distress. If they made the Mrs. C connection, the push for a quick arrest was the worst news I could have heard.

"I've taken us off on a tangent," my mother apologized. "Would you like some tea or coffee? Then you can tell us about the history of Jerrone. I studied art in college and my husband and I sell thoroughbreds at auction. I'm interested in how the art world arrangements differ."

I shot her a grateful look. What a perfect segue and one Holly could hardly refuse.

Holly folded her hands in her lap. "Might as well start at the top. Last night, you met Liam Weatherington. He's the younger son of Daniel, the first murder victim. Neville, last night's victim, was the older brother by several years. His brother's murder has been devastating. Especially since the planned documentary was already raking up old memories."

The documentary again. Perhaps the re-enactment was a bigger threat to someone than I had first thought. "Was new evidence to be unveiled in the recreation? Any new suspects?"

Holly tapped a pink tipped fingernail against her matching lips. "Not that I've heard. I know Gracie was seen running from the scene of the crime."

"From the back." Marcus was quick to point out. "The security guard who saw her was ten yards away."

"Correct." Holly managed to sound like a game show host.

Marcus glanced my way. "I've been reading the stories."

"I knew you'd stay on top of the background research." I assured him with a touch of pride.

He nodded, intent on continuing his report. "Gracie and Mr. Weatherington's affair was discovered within hours of the murder. She was the only suspect. Then and now. The guards heard the yelling and the breaking of the glass lamps."

Holly's blond tresses danced in the sunlight as she nodded. "It was assumed he told her he wasn't leaving his wife. That's what the authorities believe started the fight."

In perfect tandem, Marcus took up the torch again. "It took the guards over ten minutes to open the connecting gate between the vaults where they were watching over the artwork and get to the office where Mr. Weatherington was working that night."

Which meant no one had actually seen Gracie, er... Mrs. C commit the crime. Gracie's assumed guilt had been based on circumstantial evidence. If her family knew she was innocent, how badly did they want to clear her name ahead of the condemning documentary? Especially since she wasn't alive to defend herself.

I slotted the information in as clues for my crossword puzzle then put the issue aside for now. "Who else traveled with the Jerrone group?"

Holly speared a small piece of pineapple before she answered. "You saw Mr. Barnes, last night's auctioneer. He's a junior partner and a third cousin of Liam and Neville. At forty-one, he's a dozen years younger than Liam. He was up for a senior partnership three years ago, but at the last minute, Neville eliminated the position. So, Mr. Barnes remained a junior in the hierarchy."

"Bad blood." I liked it, as a motive. With Neville's death, a senior position was open again.

Holly put a hand over her chest. "The remaining member of the Jerrone party is Payton Eberly, Neville and Liam's administrative assistant. I'm sure you saw her last night. Thirty-eight, a slim brunette with red tones in her hair."

Score. I had a name for my woman in disguise, Payton Eberly. To calm my racing pulse, I watched the white flowers nodding in the breeze behind Holly.

"Payton is crushed," Holly assured us. Her gaze scanned the area around the patio. Several seconds passed while a furrow marred her brow. "I'm not one to gossip."

If there is any better indicator of gossip than that statement, I don't know it.

"It's not gossip when murder is involved." Marcus jumped in before I could open my mouth. "This is official police business. It's your duty to give us the facts."

I concentrated on keeping a sincere expression on my face. Inside I was wondering when I or my investigation had become part of police business. I couldn't wait to see Crawford's reaction when I told him about this turn of events.

Holly's brow cleared instantly. "You're right. As a good citizen I should do everything I can to help you."

Mom added a confirming nod to the debate. "So true."

Oh, good, we all agreed.

"This is based on hearsay evidence." Safely buffered against any remaining guilt, Holly leaned forward. "In addition to working as Neville's assistant for the past few years, Neville and Payton were seeing each other. He was a widower, so no issues in that area. However, he had created a senior position again. She assumed for her, but Neville broke it off three weeks ago. Days before their arrival here, Mr. Barnes received the promotion."

My brain clicked off bullet points like a telegraph tapping Morse code. Any investigator knows that most murders result from the violent emotion of someone close to the victim.

Cancel Peyton's motive, add one to Payton's scorecard. She'd been at the scene of the murder. She'd given no sign of grief last night, but, then, neither had Neville's brother, Liam.

A quick sip of coffee fired a few of my synapses. "Has Payton been in town with any of their previous exhibits?"

Holly stopped with her cup of tea halfway to her lips. "Several times. The latest was two months ago. She was in Anaheim for an auction. She came to Langsdale at that time to review the arrangements for this weekend."

"Did she go to Rycliffe?" Marcus asked.

Holly nodded in wide-eyed innocence. "Of course. She worked extensively to organize the plans for the opening night, which, of course, had to be changed."

Which meant Payton would have known the layout of the murder scene.

Mom clicked her tongue. "How awful for the poor girl to have to be on the job at a time like this."

Holly's expression became appropriately mournful. "Horrible."

Though I'd already moved on from sympathy to suspicion, I murmured agreement.

After a moment, Holly's perkiness returned. "I've been instructed by Mr. Weatherington to assist you any way I can. If you need anything, please let me know."

I offered my appreciation with a nod.

A small, hopeful smile trembled on her lips. "It would be an honor to help with one of your cases."

An honor? Seriously? This woman needed to get out more.

Besides, how much assistance could I stand? With Mom and Pop on the scene, Custer's Seventh Calvary had ridden into Little Big Horn with less help.

Holly scooted her chair closer to mine, lowering her voice. "I won't tell anyone what we discuss."

Again, as soon as someone says that, you know they're going to blab. Unfortunately for my saner half, that's when inspiration struck. "Can you arrange for me and my mother to see the Infantino sketch? With her degree in art, she's interested in a closer look."

Holly's mouth bowed into a mew of disappointment. "Only registered bidders are allowed to view the Infantino sketch in person. The opening bid is seven million dollars."

"Wow!" Marcus's exclamation summed it up for all of us.

No way I could even pretend to be serious at that price.

Disappointed, but not defeated, I mustered an expression of concern, hiding a healthy dose of determination. While Holly's comment put me out of the running as a bidder, it did nothing to lessen my resolve. "Seeing the sketch could be integral to discovering a motive for Neville's murder."

Holly bit her lip. Then, her eyes lit up. "The picture is on the front of the catalog. It's our premiere piece."

The picture in the catalog was too indistinct to make out the finer details. When we enlarged it, the lines blurred. I needed a close up, especially of the signature block to send to Mrs. C. She swore she'd know where to look if Gracie had hidden a telltale clue in her forgery.

I gave a heavy sigh. "I suppose I'll have to approach Mr. Weatherington about obtaining permission."

Conflict warred in a silent struggle on Holly's face. Once again, deep lines marred her perfect brow.

Where was the unstinting support? I bit my tongue against the jab and settled on silence to weaken her resistance.

"You would be mentioned as an official consultant in T.R.'s report." Marcus's tone brought to mind the sea sirens that lured sailors to their death. "Crawford Investigations might even add you as a consultant in future cases. I can give you a card listing you as an official contact."

Laminated, no less. I have an official detective card he created in my billfold. He doesn't hand those out to just anyone, but I couldn't believe he'd try that with Holly. I was resisting the urge to roll my eyes when the blonde sucked in a breath and clasped her hands together.

"I'd be an official consultant with a real detective agency? And I'd be working with a relative of Trixie Belden?" The perky blonde heaved a sigh. After a moment of silent rapture, a touch of steel glimmered in her gaze. "I'll contact you when I've arranged the viewing."

I gritted my teeth at being face-to-face with the results of my deception. Seriously, would I never be free of that? Who knew this many people even remembered those old Trixie Belden mysteries? I forced a smile in the face of Holly's effervescent enthusiasm. As she walked away, I observed a suspicious glimmer of pride in my mother's gaze.

The possibility of Holly's deeper involvement brought with it a rush of conflicting emotions. Find the murderer. Clear Mrs. C. Protect all around me, including perky blonds. I hadn't felt this unprepared since my first solo case when I staked out my ex-husband.

Tension built in my gut. What would I do if anyone was hurt? How could I make them understand that trying to uncover a murderer was like pulling on the tail of a tiger? Once you started, you didn't dare loosen your grip.

As crazy as it seemed, only in the eyes of my twelve-year-old son did I find a hint of reality. For once, Marcus's slim face was solemn. Behind his surface enthusiasm lurked a hard wisdom won from life on the streets. He gave me a look of reassurance.

We got this, he seemed to say.

I hoped he was right. If Neville's murderer was one of his colleagues from the Jerrone camp, the killer would be watching my every move, while I, along with my family and friends, would be operating in plain sight.

I wasn't going to let them be easy targets for a murderer if I could help it.

7

9 Across; 6 Letters;
Clue: A watching device hidden in a visible object
Answer: Spycam

After spending several minutes on the phone, Holly left the suite with a set to her jaw and a gleam in her eye. She'd spoken first to her superiors, then to Jerrone representatives. Her chin stiffened with each refusal, but she persevered. She got through to Liam Weatherington himself.

No go. Finally, she rushed out, leaving behind the scent of her perfume and a promise to contact us as soon as she had news.

Marcus and my parents were scheduled to leave for the tour of the Rowdy Reptile Ranch in ninety minutes. Between their packed schedule as contest winners and Holly's duties, this morning was the only possibility for our private viewing. Privately, I held out little hope the publicity representative would pull off the feat. I was already searching for a backup plan.

Don't ask me what that would entail, since the resort had security blanketing the place.

I didn't understand the resistance to letting us take a peek. Liam Weatherington's company was auctioning off the piece and he'd hired me. It wasn't like I planned to stick the sketch in my purse and walk off. What I'd seen of Infantino's work, I didn't like. I certainly wouldn't hang one next to Marcus's caricatures on my refrigerator.

Unable to sit still, Marcus, my mother, and I took a walk through the Japanese garden while we waited. Five minutes after we returned to the suite, Holly called . Our showing was scheduled in fifteen minutes.

I was impressed and I didn't try to hide it. "That woman's toothy smile must hide the heart of a shark with lockjaw."

Looking smug, Marcus waved away my doubt. "I had my money on Holly the whole way. She wants to be one of the team."

Before I could respond, Kevin and my father walked in, windblown but enthusiastic after their early morning excursion. I gave a quick update as they headed to get cleaned up.

While we waited, my son brought up Holly again. For some reason, he found the PR rep fascinating. "We could make Holly a junior member of our team."

I had no doubt my expression matched my shock. Yet the stubborn tilt to Marcus's chin warned me to tread carefully. "I think not."

"What about making her a consultant for future cases? She has contacts in Langsdale we don't have." His innocent expression didn't fool me. He'd planned this step from the beginning. "She'd like being a member of our team."

Mom approved his play with a nod. "The girl went out of her way to do you a favor, adding her as a consultant is the least you can do."

Actually, the least I could do would be nothing, but I decided to give in gracefully. "Never let it be said I didn't do the least I could do."

Marcus raised a fist in victory, then turned to Mom with a stage whisper. "I'll print off a business card for Holly. She'll like that. We have our own logo."

Created by guess who?

"Very impressive." Mom patted his shoulder. "Your mother didn't have a tenth of your drive when she was your age. She was too busy chasing boys."

Pop grinned as he took a seat.

"Sounds like Belden." Kevin slipped into the chair beside me, his hair still wet from the shower. Smelling clean and masculine, he jumped into the conversation with enthusiasm. "She chased me for years until I finally let her catch me. It was all part of my master plan."

"I was into sports when I was young," I said in a self-righteous tone, before aiming a mock glare at Kevin. "And me chasing *you* is not how I remember it."

He dismissed my protest with a shrug. "Revisionist history is a global problem. What's next on the agenda?"

Marcus jerked his head toward me. "T.R. wrangled permission to see the Infantino the dead guy brought to the auction."

"I plan to send Mrs. C a close up of the signature." Anticipation of a possible clue had me eager to see the artwork. "If she recognizes it as one of Gracie's forgeries, that would be a huge motive. Then I'd have to figure out who knew the truth and who profited from Neville's death."

"The Infantino is their most guarded piece," Kevin observed. "Not even your biggest fan will approve of photos days before the big auction."

"She's actually my only fan, and I don't intend to tell her." Better to beg forgiveness than ask permission has always been a favorite motto of mine. I aimed a puppy-dog look at my mother. "I need a few seconds of distraction to snap the shot."

"I don't know anything about distracting people," she demurred.

"You love art. It was your minor in college." Enthusiasm carries a lot of weight in these discussions. Truth is even handier. "Be yourself.

Chat up Holly. She loves answering your questions. You can both ignore me. I'll pick my moment."

My father cast me a puzzled look. "They told you no purses or cameras. How will you manage to take a picture?"

Marcus grinned. "T.R. has a mini camera built into her watch. Real P.I. stuff."

A birthday present from Marcus. He was so proud of his gadgets.

Less than twenty minutes later, my mother and I were in a locked display room that would have done Washington's National Art Gallery proud. Holly waved us on while Jamie, her young assistant, spoke with one of two male guards roaming inside the room.

A female security officer was stationed in the hall outside. All-seeing cameras blinked at us from the ceiling.

"These pieces will lead off tomorrow's auction." Holly motioned toward a row of artwork with a graceful gesture. Mounted track lighting illuminated the prints and paintings in all their glory.

My mother stepped closer to a large white canvas with black squiggles and a yellow circle. Her intense study appeared amazingly sincere. "The contrast of colors and shapes is eye catching."

For a second, I debated whether the yellow dot represented an egg yolk or a traffic light. Then, I gave up. I didn't care. I wanted to get to the prize, take the picture, and retreat.

Fighting the fidgets, I turned to Jamie. Her position in the public relations office should provide further insight into the personnel associated with Jerrone.

The girl loitered behind us, evidently content to remain in the background. When I stopped and smiled expectantly, she had little choice but to join me. Her guarded expression almost had me promising not to bite. Instead, I dug deep for an extra dose of charm. Hopefully, a few questions about her duties would cut through her shyness.

"Coordinating a show of this magnitude must involve an enormous amount of detail work behind the scenes."

"That's part of my job." Jamie's expression warmed by several degrees. "Over the past year, Holly's been giving me more responsibility. As soon as an event is confirmed, I contact media outlets, write announcements, and e-mail our patrons. That way guests can make their travel reservations."

I had to smile at her enthusiasm. "I imagine you have counterparts at the art galleries who regularly send artwork to the auctions."

"Oh, sure."

This all laid the groundwork for my real interest. "Was Payton Eberly, Neville's assistant, your contact with Jerrone?"

Her gaze darted to her supervisor. "Don't you want to listen to Holly explain the background on these pieces? She knows all their histories."

"I'm enjoying our discussion." Her hesitation was like kerosene on the open flame of my curiosity. "I'm interested in the arrangements needed to pull this event together. Tell me more."

She licked her lips. "Payton was wonderful. She's very professional, with years of experience."

"It must be difficult for her to continue. She worked with Neville for years." I fought to keep my tone casual as my interest spiked. This affair was getting curiouser and curiouser. "I heard she'd been promised a senior position."

Jamie cast a glance at Holly and my mother walking several steps in front of us.

Mom stopped to study one of the pieces. "If I remember correctly, this surrealist predated Picasso."

If possible, Holly brightened even more at the display of knowledge. When she launched into the answer, I turned to Jamie, determined to keep the information flowing. "It would be normal for Payton to be conflicted about Neville's death. Sad that he's gone, but angry about him giving the promotion to Mr. Barnes."

My twenty-something victim cast one last hopeful glance in Holly's direction. Then, with a fatalistic sigh, she inched closer to me. "She's been distant since she arrived."

"It's a difficult time."

"She was acting odd before the murder." Jamie bit her lip. "On Thursday, I came up behind her to ask her a question about the auction. She slammed her laptop shut. Then, she screamed at me about sneaking up on her. I totally didn't. She was just so absorbed she didn't hear me."

Overreact much? Sounded like Payton had something to hide. "Do you have any idea what was on her laptop?"

When Jamie shook her head, her wispy, brown hair flew around her slim face. "I wasn't looking at the screen. I told her that."

Drat. Mrs. C would have noticed. Marcus would have the website memorized. I needed a better busybody. "Did she mention losing out on the promotion?"

Jamie shook her head before glancing over her shoulder. Both guards were by the door, well out of earshot. "She mentioned being busier than usual with Neville here."

Good thing I do a convincing act of being surprised since I already knew Neville didn't usually travel outside the British Isles. "Wasn't Neville being here always the plan?"

Jamie's light brown hair flew around her long, thin face. Loose to her shoulders, the feathery strands framed her intense expression. "Neville Weatherington hadn't traveled to Langsdale before this week."

Did Neville tell his brother why he had inserted himself into this show? I tucked the thought away, eager to keep on track of this line of inquiry. "Did anyone say why Neville was attending?"

"I never heard a reason." The young woman's large brown eyes met mine. "We received word of his plan to attend maybe six to eight weeks ago."

The timing of the event sparked bells and whistles. That was when Mrs. C heard of the plan to re-enact the first murder. Had that announcement led to the second murder? I fought to hide the leap in my pulse. "When was the Infantino added to the show?"

A trace of eagerness colored the look Jamie gave Holly and my mother. The two were engrossed in a discussion of a small painting full of orange and blue squares. With no call for her services, Jamie edged closer to me. "The Infantino has been listed since spring when it was authenticated."

Nothing to do with the documentary. Still, it seemed an odd coincidence. "Who found the sketch? Liam or Neville?"

"Neither." A quick frown furrowed Jamie's brow. "Archibald Smythe, a British art dealer, discovered it in Arizona in a small antique store."

Another name to add to the list. Who would be next? Maids and busboys? Whatever it took to clear Mrs. C of suspicion. "Has Smythe been to auctions in Langsdale before?"

She shook her head. "I only know him by reputation. His office is in England. He's been successful throughout the British Isles."

"Has he found other valuable pieces?"

Jamie's brow furrowed in thought. "He's made a few discoveries over the course of his career. Nothing like the Infantino. This sketch is the strike of a lifetime."

Bummer. No suspicious pattern. Oh, well.

"Mr. Smythe arrives Monday," Jamie continued. "He's coming specifically to see the piece auctioned off. After the Jerrone commission is deducted from the hammer price, the consignor will receive the balance."

What had Marcus said was the expected price range? Eleven to fifteen million? A commission of at least one and a half million was worth killing for. Especially, if the piece was real... "Who authenticated the sketch?"

"Mr. Smythe originally." Jamie's eyes sparked with excitement. "Of course, Jerrone had their own experts confirm the piece was an original."

Mom and Holly were wrapping up an animated conversation in front of a canvas that was half orange and half red, split by a thin white line.

My brain tabulated what I'd learned. I opened my mouth to ask another question, when Jamie motioned me forward with a smile on her face. "Here is what you came to see."

"Our prize for the weekend. Infantino's Cosmic View. Number I-38 in the catalog." Holly's breathless voice was hushed. "It's such a shame Neville won't be here to witness the sale."

Mom gazed at the pencil sketch with a judicious eye. It was an intricate assembly of squares, triangles, and lightning bolts in varying shades of pencil gray.

The piece was eleven-by-fourteen. Framed and under glass, the thick paper resembled a page from a heavy sketch pad sold at any art supply store. A nearby color poster showed the matching painting, currently on display at Sterling Art Museum in Cape Cod.

Hard to believe a few squiggles on a piece of cheap paper might have cost a man his life. The thought started a rash of heat burning deep in my gut.

What a stupid waste.

"This must have been done prior to the studio fire in the nineteen-thirties," I said.

Mom nodded appreciatively at my observation.

"Absolutely correct." Holly clapped her hands together. Her enthusiasm seemed a bit over the top. "This is one of his early efforts."

I swallowed a comeback. It felt too much like swatting the tooth fairy. Still, they didn't have to be *that* impressed at my spoonful of knowledge.

"I had no idea of the time period of this sketch," Mom admitted, beaming with pride. "You've obviously studied the artist."

"Not really." My brain's contrary nature couldn't leave well enough along. "The paper looks cheap. The kind a starving student would buy."

My mother's eyes widened but her smile remained in place. "I hadn't noticed."

My comment only added to Holly's enthusiasm. "That kind of deduction is why you're such a great detective. You notice details then put them together to unravel the mystery."

Her comment seemed over the top, but what could I say? "Umm, thanks."

Fortunately, Mom remained focused. "How was it that this survived the fire?"

In the manner of tourist guides the world over, Holly half-turned to face us as she gestured toward the piece. "An unknown number of preliminary sketches and finished paintings were in Ignacio Infantino's studio over a rented garage when the fire broke out. Due to the heat and combustible material, none were saved."

She put a hand over her heart.

I expected her to continue, but the pause lengthened into a moment of silence for the fallen little moneymakers. Jamie, and even Mom looked appropriately stricken. While mentally urging Holly to start the script again, I snuck a look at the others under my lashes.

My mother met my gaze with a knowing look. She didn't appear at all surprised by my wayward attention.

With my heart picking up speed, I snapped a quick picture of the sketch.

"The flames destroyed untold numbers of his works, including his early notebooks full of ideas and inspiration." When Holly chose this moment to start up her spiel, my hand jerked, screwing the shot. "The world will never know the artwork that was destroyed on that tragic afternoon."

If the destroyed artwork resembled this intersection of lines and shapes, the world hadn't lost much. However, considering what his doodles sold for, a lot of potential profit had gone up in smoke. "Where was this doodle, er drawing, discovered?"

"There is a detailed provenance." Holly's eagerness to relay her knowledge covered my gaffe. "Infantino exchanged the sketch for room and food when he was starting out. The artist relayed the incident in an interview later in his career. His landlord ran a boarding house close to the art school and had a number of art works from famous students. However, the man sold this sketch shortly after receiving it. Mr. Archibald Smythe found it hanging in an Arizona antique store."

Jamie's jaw tightened. She pressed her lips together.

I kept the younger girl in my line of sight while speaking to Holly. "There's no doubt about the authenticity?"

Jamie's eyes shifted down and away.

My heart flip-flopped in excitement. I would definitely be talking to her again.

"Jerrone experts confirmed the find before they moved forward with the sale." Holly assured me in a bright tone. Her eyes widened as if an epiphany had struck. "If the sketch was a forgery, that would be a motive for the murder, wouldn't it?"

My gut tightened. I so didn't want this too-enthusiastic woman involved in this investigation. That path led to disaster. "Anything is possible. Before I come to any conclusions, I have to collect information and sift through the details. Sometimes people keep facts to themselves, thinking the secrets aren't related to the case, when those details might clear an innocent person."

Though I spoke to Holly, I mentally aimed the guilt at Jamie.

"That would be horrible if an innocent party was blamed." Holly's tone was half-an-octave lower than usual. Her shocked sympathy made her far more approachable. Then, her mouth crept up into a bow as if it couldn't help itself. "If there's anything I can do, please let me know. I have full access to the records involving the discussions for this show."

She didn't know it, but this bit of news cemented her standing as an official consultant.

Full cooperation in a case was new ground for me. My usual style consisted of skulking around and conniving information out of people. "I need to learn everything I can about Neville Weatherington, who he spoke with, where he went, his relationships. Details regarding the exhibit will also be an enormous help. Thank you."

"No need to thank *me*." The thousand-watt smile was blinding. "Working with you is more than I ever hoped for. I'll be thrilled if any fact I provide leads to finding the guilty party. We can't let the threat of violence keep people from enjoying our beautiful city."

Wouldn't be good for the tourist dollars either. Not in this rocky economy.

A sharp intake of breath sounded from Jamie. "Mr. Weatherington deserves justice."

My mother patted the young girl's arm. "Tracy would never forget the man who was killed. My daughter has always been interested in what people do. That's why she's so good at what she does."

Good thing I never claimed to be psychic, because for the second time in five minutes, I had to hide my surprise. First, Holly promises to open their files. Then, my mother thinks I'm a people person.

I burned up a few brain cells on that. What usually drives me in a case is finding the answers for my mental crossword puzzle. Of course, to accomplish that I had to ferret out people's motives. In this instance, the possibility of Mrs. C becoming a suspect was driving my investigation.

I shook free of the musings. "Why don't we forget the case for the moment and simply enjoy the sketch? Presenting this Infantino is something Neville Weatherington will be remembered for."

Jamie gave me a grateful look.

An intricate knot of figures in a small circle sat at the bottom center of the sketch.

"Is that his signature block?" I asked.

"Yes." Holly's hands came together in a loud clap. The woman was over the moon with correct answers. She'd have made a great teacher. "He used various combinations of numbers and letters pertinent to the individual piece. His signature is found in different places in each work."

I met my mother's gaze full on. "Did you know that?"

My mother moved toward Holly, who retreated in the direction of the colorful poster showing the matching painting. "I read in the catalog that there was something unique about this painting."

Jamie drifted closer to the two women.

Noting the location of the guards and the angle of the closest security camera, I aimed the camera viewer at the sketch and checked the picture on the watch face. I snapped a portion of the drawing where the strokes stood out. Fortunately, the process was completely silent. Under cover of fiddling with the watchband, I took several of the signature block. Behind me, Mom kept the conversation and the information flowing.

"I read that Infantino signed each piece differently," my mother said. "But the signatures in the sketches always match the one in the corresponding painting."

Holly opened her mouth to respond.

"Except this one doesn't match the painting." Jamie's tone was clipped.

"Jamie's right." Holly's smile remained undimmed by her subordinate stealing her thunder. "This pair is unique. The artist's signatures don't match."

"Are bidders aware of that detail? Is it a problem?" Mom asked. "With the amount of money set to exchange hands, the authenticity would have to be beyond question."

Score one for Mom. Maybe Marcus was right. Maybe detecting did run in the family.

"The different signatures are attributed to this being the artist's early work. It's absolutely unique, which makes the sketch that much more valuable." Holly's confidence was undiminished by the question. "Jerrone has built their reputation on tracing the provenances of the pieces they sell. Their word is unimpeachable."

A chill pervaded the air at her words. Or perhaps it was my imagination. The presence of spirits was said to lower the temperature by several degrees. Considering that Neville died in a supposedly haunted house, I had to wonder if his ghost was walking among us, listening to our attempts to unravel his secrets.

If Mrs. C identified this piece of art as one of her old friend's forgeries, I might be able to narrow down the motive for murder.

Had the dead man been ready to auction off a lost treasure? Or a forgery that would bring his family's livelihood tumbling down to its rocky foundations?

8

8 Across; 6 Letters;
Clue: A natural aptitude or skill
Answer: Talent

As my mother and I walked out of the gallery, I glanced over my shoulder for a last glimpse of Jamie. Holly was talking to her, but the younger woman's gaze remained on the sketch.

"That girl is scared." Despite the circumstances, my mother's soft Southern drawl brought back memories of the rolling hills of Kentucky. "You should talk with her."

"I intend to." The secrets of the living rarely die with the dead. I just hadn't expected Jamie to be the one with the answers.

My mother and I walked down a main corridor. As my feet sank into the plush carpeting, I noted the ornate mirrors and cool marble with little appreciation.

With my crossword puzzle mostly empty, curiosity gnawed at me like a hungry animal. I'd quelled my first impulse, which had been to corner the young assistant like a lioness would an antelope. Instead, I decided to bide my time and track her down as soon as the shuttle departed for the Rowdy Reptile Ranch. Tamping down my impatience, I followed my mother into an outside courtyard.

While everyone else in our party seemed to find their way around the resort with little problem, mastering the multiple halls of the complex eluded me. There were too many paths and too many turns. Then there were the trees and decorative sculptures that blocked any chance of getting an overall view of the layout.

"The landscaping is gorgeous. The different theme in each area is delightful." My mother's gaze floated from one flowering cactus to another. Taller bushes provided sparse shade from the sun. "These southwest desert plants are a nice contrast to the rock garden by our rooms."

"They're beautiful." I murmured, barely registering her words. "I have to get to Jamie when Holly's not around. I want her input before I breach the Jerrone citadel."

Mom gave a soft sigh. "You are as single-minded as your father when you latch onto a problem."

I smiled an apology and linked arms with her. "Consider the problem shelved for the moment. I'll focus on family when we're together."

Her light laughter floated on the hot, dry air. Though in her late sixties, no one seeing her would guess at the hard work she put in at Pop's side to make the ranch a success. "I won't hold you to that promise."

A smile tugged at my lips as we walked to a covered promenade bordering a tennis court. With a bit of imagination and a glass of sweet tea in my hand, I could picture myself and my mother strolling around the green hills of home on a hot summer day.

Feeling nostalgic and comfortable, I said. "Did you mean it when you said I was a people person?"

She bit her lip, looking amused. "Your outspokenness is a bit off putting to people, honey. I believe I said you were interested in people and curious."

"Nosey was what I heard, but I'll take it." Hope buoyed my spirits. The case was long on questions and short on answers, but promising leads had reared their little heads. "We had a good morning. You got your private viewing. I got pictures of the sketch."

Mom patted my arm. "Nice to know all your youthful sneaking around is paying off."

I shot her a sideways glance to check for sarcasm, but she sounded relieved. A conspiratorial air sprang up between us. "You knew about my midnight excursions?"

Her laughter was full blown this time. "You were my fourth teenager and, compared with your brothers and your sister, by far the most inventive."

I caught my breath, unable to stop a wide grin. "Those paragons of virtue? Tell me more."

An amused mask blanketed Mom's expression as she drew herself up. The thudding of tennis volleys sounded in the background. "I do not tell tales on my children."

"If it's any comfort." I slid my mom a sideways glance. "My practice at spinning yarns has come in handy more than once in my P.I. career."

Her features settled into a motherly expression, that neither condemned nor approved. "Nice to know it served some purpose."

"I'll contact Mrs. C as soon as we get to the suite." After my parents and Marcus left, Kevin and I could plan our next move. "I hope she recognizes the sketch or the signature."

Mom watched the tennis players while we circumvented the court. "Your friend's information should be of enormous help with your case."

The game ended on a stinging backhand.

"That's the plan." The promise of additional information danced like a carrot just out of reach. "Knowing Jamie is involved might prove more valuable than the photos."

We reached the end of our circle and turned onto a straight-away to our suite.

My mother's gaze turned inward. "I think you're on the right track. Passion is a powerful force. It drives people."

Her words dovetailed perfectly with the decades-long history of this case.

"Marcus is right," I said. "You're a natural."

As soon as we entered the suite, Mom hustled my father out the door to buy gifts for my nieces and nephews. With time of the essence, Kevin, Marcus, and I sat around the bleached oak coffee table. The sand and sage coloring of the room echoed the beautiful but harsh desert that surrounded the resort.

Marcus Face Timed with Mrs. C and Rabi then propped his tablet in its holder. Rabi had a laptop on their end. I'd e-mailed pictures of the sketch to Mrs. C.

On the screen, the older woman adjusted her reading glasses and leaned toward us. Her furrowed brow and narrowed eyes filled the screen.

I pulled away reflexively.

Kevin chuckled. "She's not going to land in your lap."

"Well?" Marcus demanded. "Do you recognize the sketch or the signature? Is it Gracie's?"

Mrs. C clicked her tongue. "The point of a forgery is to make the fake indistinguishable from the real thing."

I braced my hands on the buff colored love seat. "You said you'd know. I figured she had a code she shared with you."

"I can't say for sure." The older woman retreated. Her face returned to normal proportions, but her expression was puzzled. "A couple of the marks look like Gracie's. However, other symbols are ones Infantino used in his signatures, aren't they?"

Shock electrified my entire body. Stunned silence filled the room before I found my voice. "Are you saying this sketch is the real deal?"

She cocked her head to one side. "I can't swear it's Gracie's. Though it might be, don't you know."

I fought a wave of irritation. At the moment, I didn't know anything. Evidently, neither did Mrs. C. I sought to master my whirling thoughts. "Did she mention which works she forged? Did you see any in the flat you shared?"

Mrs. C's mouth flattened, erasing some of the wrinkles. "Gracie wouldn't tell me. She wanted me to have deniability and all that rot. Of course, I would have just lied."

Though I admit to being far from perfect at presenting a solid moral compass for my son, I could have done without the older woman's comment.

However, Marcus's silent nod echoed the code of the streets.

Kevin remained focused on the scam. "Did you see any of her forgeries? Sketches? Final paintings?"

"Nary a one," Mrs. C admitted in her British accent. "Weatherington provided a private studio for her. He needed to ensure there were no witnesses, didn't he?"

The explanation set a bee buzzing in my brain. Yet I failed to find anything beyond the obvious need for secrecy. I tucked the odd feeling away. In the past, my mental notebook tagged discrepancies that later proved instrumental in unknotting tangled threads.

Mrs. C's intake of air heralded another comment, but my quick-draw mouth beat her to the punch. "Were you ever with her and Weatherington when they were together?"

Marcus raised an eyebrow.

Kevin cast me a questioning glance.

The question had bypassed my brain. I had no idea how to explain what prompted the query. The itch lurking in the shadows of my mind refused to come into the open.

"I only saw Gracie and the cad together once." Mrs. C's ruminating accent dragged out the words. "She invited me to attend a gallery opening. A few of her actual works were on display. After a brief introduction, Weatherington kept his distance."

The older woman had never seen the couple interact in a personal setting. Did that matter? I wasn't sure. Evidently some part of my brain thought that fact was important.

Marcus inched closer to the tablet. "What kind of stuff did she paint?"

"Slices of fruits and veggies melting off kitchen counters and such. Dark backgrounds emblazoned by bright, bold colors. Very eye catching."

I jumped as if struck. "Like the piece hanging in your kitchen?"

Mrs. C's expression tightened at my accusing tone. She straightened, which took her face out of the camera's view. "Gracie sent me the orange slices flowing off the ebony cube after we settled in the States."

Astonishment struck me speechless. Five decades of hiding behind false names and a fake American accent. Moving constantly to avoid detection. Assuming numerous identities before settling on this one.

Yet Mrs. C had displayed the one item that could tie her to a past she was trying to outrun? A past that connected her to a murder?

Not to mention that Gracie had resumed painting in a style from her youth? Both women had been foolish beyond belief.

"Take it down." Kevin, who'd carried out countless flawless scams in his first eighteen years, gave no sign of disappointment at Mrs. C's lapse. However, his tone brooked no argument. "Give it to Rabi. Put up another picture, same size."

Mrs. C sniffed. "I'll fix it today."

Marcus thrust himself in front of the laptop. "Don't *buy* a replacement."

Too easily traced if the police focused on her as a suspect.

"I'll take care of it." Rabi's low rumble sounded off camera.

The conversation brought home that I was surrounded by people with a nefarious twist to their brains. Though their skills came in handy regarding cases, I always seemed to be swimming against the current when it came to the moral compass thing.

My heart rate slowed from worry fueled adrenaline. "Could Gracie have made a living selling her own work?"

"Absolutely." Mrs. C's voice rang like the tolling of a small bell, full of pride at her friend's skill. "Talent ran in her blood. Her father was a well-known art restorer. Gracie was a rare hand at imitating other artist's styles. It ran in her blood, you might say."

Kevin snorted. "Perfect training for a forger."

"That man took advantage of her." Mrs. C's voice shook in anger. "If she hadn't been hoodwinked into forgery, she'd have been able to concentrate on advancing her own promising career."

I chewed my lip in concentration. The possibility that the sketch was real still had my brain ablaze. "Do you have any idea how many forgeries she completed?"

"Not many." Mrs. C centered herself in front of the laptop's camera. "The forgery scam was only in place for a few months."

"The sketches couldn't have taken long, but research and practicing would take time. I have no idea the amount of time required for an oil painting." I barely mastered coloring inside the lines before I gave up art. Yet, I couldn't help but think a private studio seemed rather elaborate for a short-term scheme. "More to the point, if this is a real Infantino, is it a motive for murder? If it's a forgery, where has it been all these years?"

Kevin's fingers tapped a soft rhythm on the love seat. "Weatherington couldn't risk flooding the market with lost Infantino's."

He spoke with the certainty of having planned countless scams.

"Too suspicious." Rabi's gravelly voice confirmed.

Marcus spun around. "Jerrone sold two Infantinos the year before Weatherington died. One the next year. Then, ten years later, one more. No paintings since. Never any sketches."

The curiosity in his tone matched my own. I'd been so certain it was fake. "It's odd this would be the first forged sketch. If it is a fake."

Anger darkened Mrs. C's green eyes like trees shadowed by a thunderstorm. "Gracie believed he disposed of the works she'd completed. She quit the scheme after she and Weatherington argued."

I mused on the timing. "No wonder the old guy went ballistic when you told him his gravy train was disappearing. He had no time to prepare."

The conversation had given me a lot to think about. The photos of the sketch had opened a can of worms.

"My concern," Mrs. C's voice interrupted my thoughts, "is not whether this sketch is a forgery, but whether the painting it matches is the real thing."

I felt my eyes widen. Ton of bricks.

"Mrs. Colchester," Kevin's voice rang with admiration. "You have a knack for getting to the heart of a scam."

Marcus grabbed his phone. "I'll find out when the painting was first sold."

"Most of the early sketches were believed to have been destroyed in the fire." Kevin's gaze narrowed. "Gracie never had to worry how she signed her paintings because no one knew the artist gave this sketch away. When Neville saw this piece, he may have realized the painting was a possible forgery."

"Guess what?" Marcus held up his phone. "The painting that matches this sketch was the one Jerrone sold ten years after old man Weatherington died."

Dramatic music thundered in my mind.

"How does this play into a motive?" That was my concern. "Did Neville know the sketch could expose the fake painting? Is that why he decided to be on-site for the auction? Or was he focused on the documentary and finding Gracie Linden?"

Though I've never profited from a crime, the black and white of right and wrong isn't what motivates me. I'm not that noble. Curiosity drives me.

I shared a calculating glance with Kevin. He twined his fingers around mine. The corners of his mouth turned up at the tips. My tendency to focus on motives rather than morals always amuses him. Perhaps that's why I fit in so well with my acquired family.

Despite a few half-hearted guesses, no one had a satisfying answer for my question.

Gears whirled in my mind like a kaleidoscope spinning through different patterns. "I have to talk to Jamie. She knows more than she's telling."

"Rabi, did you find leaks in Mrs. C's trail?" Kevin asked.

"Nothing." The other man's deep voice sounded from off screen like the voice of God. Or of doom. "Good work."

Wow, high praise.

Kevin's brow furrowed in puzzlement. "Which confirms that no one tracked her here. Either Neville or the killer were given Mrs. Colchester's identity."

Again, no help.

"We'll keep digging." I surrendered with a shrug. "Mrs. C, Rabi, keep a low profile. Any developments, check in."

"The cops are pushing for answers." Kevin snapped his fingers in a rapid rhythm, a sure sign of agitation. "They're bound to question her. Time is not our friend."

"Time. Dates." I tossed what I'd learned up in the air to see what connected. Not much. "Gracie died seven years ago. The sketch came to light in the spring. Jerrone professionals authenticated it soon after. Yet Neville only made plans to come to Langsdale when the documentary was announced. Why?"

The others eyed me patiently. They knew better than to expect a stunning announcement. I was just thinking out loud.

Kevin flipped a coin over his knuckles. "Gracie's family might have led Neville here to expose Mrs. C and salvage Gracie's reputation before the documentary condemned her."

I had to agree. "The leak *has* to be with Gracie's family."

Marcus prompted his chin up with both fists, scrunching his cheeks up. "If they knew Mrs. C's current name, why not call the police years ago? That's what I'd do."

"Anyone would." Rabi's certainty added weight to the words.

I voiced the first thing that came to mind. "Perhaps they don't know her name, only the town."

A smile wreathed Mrs. C's face. "Oh, that would be lovely, wouldn't it?"

Improbable was more like it. "Perhaps that was all the information Gracie had. Did you use your aliases when you corresponded?"

The older woman shook her head. "We had code names. She never heard of Alice Colchester."

Kevin stilled the dancing coin, balancing it on his knuckle. "You think the upcoming documentary prompted one of Gracie's relatives to contact Neville and slip him the only piece of information they knew?"

"That doesn't work." Hearing the theory out loud made me realize the glaring flaw. "Someone sent that letter to your apartment. Someone knows your name."

Mrs. C's expression tightened as if she'd been shot.

I gritted my teeth one second too late. Though we all knew her identity had been compromised, I regretted causing her pain. My talk first, think last failing had claimed another victim. This time a friend. "Mrs. C, I'm-- "

"Nay, luv, don't apologize. There's no point denying it, eh?" Her jaw stiffened as her ancestors' stiff upper lip must have when the Brits carried on during the Blitz. "We must face facts if we're to win out. Lying to each other will bring ruin upon us."

She ended on a stirring note Winston Churchill would have envied. But I faced the same unanswered questions. Who knew Mrs. C's name and why hadn't they exposed her to the police or given Neville her name? Why toy with her, and him, like a cat with a mouse?

Gracie's family had to be the ones who knew the truth. One of them could be in Langsdale anonymously. Or they told Neville and *he* sent the note to Mrs. C. She met him and killed him rather than be exposed as a murderer.

I felt a twinge of guilt, but I kept my mouth shut. Was my scenario disloyal? Certainly, but it was far from impossible.

I rested my chin on my fist. The squares in my crossword puzzle remained empty. Taunting me. "Did Neville intend to expose Gracie or did he want to silence her so the forgeries would never come to light?"

Greed, justice, or revenge? Which one put the man into an early grave?

9

---◆---

10 Across; 9 Letters;
Clue: Freely offer to undertake a task
Answer: Volunteer

Marcus swaggered as he walked into the hotel lobby flanked by my parents. He spun on his heel, pointing at me and Kevin. "Last chance to see venomous reptiles eye-to-eye."

After what happened in Las Vegas, you'd think he'd know better. As it was, I repressed a shudder and pointed right back at him. "Still passing."

I was eager for him and my parents to be safely away from all things connected with murder. Then I could concentrate on finding answers to my mental crossword puzzle. Clues, witnesses, and leads beckoned to me.

Kevin gave an exaggerated sigh of regret. "Someone has to stay behind to watch Belden."

My father put a hand on Marcus' shoulder. "Looks like it's just the three of us getting up close and personal with the cold-blooded crawlers."

In the lobby, my parents and my son turned toward the front entrance where the shuttle waited. Mom lifted a hand in farewell, then gave her full attention to Marcus and Pop's discussion on who'd win a fight between a rattler and a scorpion.

When the shuttle drove off, I sighed in relief. "This gives us a good three hours. I can concentrate on the case knowing they're safe."

Furrows marred Kevin's forehead. "Maybe *they* are, but the snakes and scorpions have no idea Marcus is on the way."

"The critters are on their own." I hooked my arm through his and aimed us toward the wing where the business offices were located. "I've already mapped out our agenda for the morning. Top of the list is finding out what Jamie is hiding."

Fifteen minutes later I leaned over the receptionist's desk, hands fisted on my hips. If the guy hadn't scooted his chair back, we'd have butted heads. "You're telling me Jamie Mueller is an escort on the reptile excursion?"

The young man swallowed hard then nodded. "One of the scheduled guides called in sick. We planned to go with only two escorts. We do that a lot. Rowdy Reptiles has their own people, but Jamie insisted."

Ice cold shock cooled my anger. What game was the girl playing? She'd known before the Infantino showing that my parents and son were on the tour. Was she being solicitous or was she involved with the killer? Worry spread through my veins like slow poison.

Though Kevin's outward demeanor didn't change, I felt him tense. "Is Holly Reynolds available?"

I admired the way his tone remained calm and business-like.

The man's Adam's apple bobbed nervously. "She's with the Jerrone party, finalizing details for today's auction. I can text her."

He reached for his phone, giving me a wary look. He was evidently ready to throw anyone into my path to save himself.

I waved away the offer. With my emotions swinging from fear to fury, I was in no mood to deal with another dose of perky helpfulness. My new goal was to corner Jamie when she returned. "I have Holly's number. I'll contact her later. Thank you."

The cool air that made the corridors an oasis in the desert did nothing to lessen the irritation fermenting in my gut.

"I don't know whether to be annoyed or worried." I chewed my lip. "Either way, that girl and I are going to have a one-on-one the second the shuttle returns."

I followed Kevin, assuming we were aimed toward the lobby. In the maze of corridors, I couldn't be sure and I was too distracted to ask. "Liam Weatherington is probably with Holly. Even if he's free, I want more ammo before I speak with him. I need to know what Neville told him about coming to Langsdale. Did Liam know about the meeting with Gracie? The articles Marcus read only mention Neville being involved with the documentary."

I threw up my arms. "I need answers. Facts. A solid lead."

"It's cliché, but there's always the scene of the crime, if it's open on Sunday."

I hadn't been to the Rycliffe Castle since the murder. "That's a good idea."

"I'm full of them." Kevin winked. "It would help if we knew how Neville managed to stay out of sight Friday night."

"Let's find out."

A short time later, Kevin and I walked on the cobblestone path leading to Rycliffe Castle's stone edifice. One turret rose from the front corner of the building to bask in the morning sun. Another soared above the rooftop from somewhere in back. A long driveway on the right led to a covered carriage entrance from bygone days. With the wrought-iron gates behind us, the mansion had the feel of a grand manor.

I took the stone steps at a slow pace, mulling over Neville's motives. Had he believed he was meeting Gracie? Had he intended to kill her or confront her? Surely, he would have told Liam about a lead on their father's murderer. Unless he wanted to be certain it was the truth this time.

I stopped as a new possibility sprang to mind. "If Neville didn't know about the forgeries, he wouldn't know Gracie could expose the truth and destroy his family's business."

Kevin looked at me from the top stair. "From a PR angle, finding his father's killer would have drawn huge publicity."

The man views crimes through the lens of a con artist.

I took the hand Kevin held out and joined him under the stone arch. "If publicity was Neville's motive, that means... "

"Coming to Langsdale makes more sense." Kevin finished my sentence. "He was determined to find his father's killer. That was his only goal."

The sun warmed the skin on my arms and neck while I let the idea stew. "Someone led him here with the promise of finding Gracie."

Kevin's blue eyes narrowed. "And that someone has Mrs. Colchester's name and address."

Panic chilled my blood at his words.

"Why not expose her?" My frustration multiplied each time I confronted that unanswerable question. Not turning Mrs. C over to the police didn't make sense. "What if the sketch and the old murder are red herrings? If that's true, the motive for Neville's murder is personal or a power play for his position."

Kevin eyed me for a moment, his hand on the doorknob of the Rycliffe Castle. "Do you have anything resembling a plan for this interview?"

He had to be joking. "How long have you known me?"

"Hope springs eternal." He opened the thick wooden door and waved me on.

"I have my usual, foolproof plan." I stopped in the small entryway, tiled in a white and black design that reminded me of a crossword puzzle grid, and smiled at him over my shoulder. "Rattle cages until something gives."

My volley drew a smile. "Go with your strength."

What did I hope to accomplish? As usual, I was making it up as I went. At least, I'd called ahead. The administrative offices for Rycliffe were open. Though the library where Neville had died was off limits, the police had released the rest of the house. "I'll see who's here and find out what they know."

I preceded Kevin into the two-story foyer. I stood for a moment, soaking in the atmosphere.

From the polished hardwood floor to the gleaming bannister, the nineteenth-century mansion lived up to its landmark status. Stained glass in the windows painted rainbows on the walls and floor. However, the bright sun couldn't dispel the heavy atmosphere that drifted down the winding stairs.

"It feels anti-climactic to just walk-in."

Kevin's hand urged me forward. "I'm sure you'll have a chance at breaking and entering before we solve the case."

"Very funny."

Kevin gestured at a sign pointing toward the back of the building. "Administrative offices."

"I'd like a list of attendees from Friday night." I whispered, thinking aloud more than anything else. The ghost hunter company had refused to turn over the names to me. The police were dragging their heels. Neither Crawford nor I had made headway with our contacts on the force. "Two, maybe four, of the women looked to be in Gracie's age range. I want names."

Kevin frowned. "Gracie's dead."

"If Neville planned this weekend for publicity, he couldn't afford to come up empty handed. If whoever he expected didn't appear, a well-coached actress would have made as big a splash in the media."

Kevin stared at me for a moment. "Your devious mind rivals my grandmother's."

I raised a brow. "Is that a compliment?"

"Huge." Even though he was no longer in the business, he couldn't hide the admiration for his clan's matriarch.

The place seemed devoid of life. No hint of the ghosties that other attendees on Friday had sworn they felt or heard. No hint that anyone knew we'd arrived. Surely, they had cameras or dinging bells to alert them to guests.

As if the thought sent out a silent call, the clip of heels on the hardwood floor sounded from the hallway.

A matronly woman marched toward us. Gray threaded through her cap of black curls. A navy dress in a conservative cut matched her reserved smile. She gave us a quick once over, pausing a few extra seconds on Kevin. Then, she included us both in a nod. "I'm Brenda Bryant, may I help you?"

After making introductions, I held out my card. "I called a few minutes ago."

"You didn't mention you were an investigator." Brenda set her jaw at a determined angle. A wary look nestled in her brown eyes.

"If you've come for information regarding the murder, you should contact the authorities."

Kevin grimaced in sympathy. "I'm sure you've had to speak with the police several times."

The man is adept at empathizing with people. I remained silent and let him work.

The cautious look in Brenda's gaze thawed. "The crime scene technicians made a mess of the library. The press is constantly trying to invade the halls. We had to cancel two weddings. In all my fifteen years, I've never seen anything like this chaos."

"You've been volunteering here fifteen years?" Kevin's admiring gaze lingered on her before scanning the polished cherry wood. "The house and grounds are beautiful. The role of Rycliffe Castle in the community is a credit to everyone involved."

"We do our best to uphold the reputation of the estate." Brenda folded her hands across her middle. "I won't contribute to sensationalism."

"The murder isn't why I've come." Faced with a stonewall, I flipped my story. "I was one of the guests Friday night. I brought my son. He was very interested in the event."

A spark of interest glimmered in her eyes. Brenda's head tilted by a hair's breadth. "Was he your *only* reason for being here?"

A slight nuance shaded Brenda's tone. Not quite conspiratorial, her tone was more akin to Holly's interest. Brenda wanted the inside scoop.

Carefully glancing around the hall, I made a grand show of confirming we were alone. "My son was a cover for an assignment. The Ghosthunter group may be manufacturing the encounters they're reporting."

The woman caught her breath. "I don't believe in contacting the dead, but the members of the paranormal group seemed so sincere. I would hate to have them using the Rycliffe home for cheap exploitation."

"Nothing's confirmed." I jumped in before the spark exploded into a firestorm beyond my control. I wanted an "in", not to smear the Ghosthunters' reputation. "I was sent to get a feel for the event. I would *never* have brought my son if I expected violence."

"Of course not." Brenda's tone warmed at the image of a protective mother.

Kevin moved forward, closing our little circle. "Have you attended the paranormal events in the past?"

"I've been present on several occasions, but not to participate." The tightness in the woman's shoulders relaxed. Her folded hands dropped to her sides. "A staff member has to be here to open and close the premises."

"I didn't realize that." I couldn't remember anyone mentioning that fact on Friday, but with Marcus's nonstop chatter and my wandering mind, I'd barely heard how the electromagnetic equipment worked to detect spirits. "How many volunteers from the Rycliffe Foundation were here for the event?"

"Only one besides me." The woman's firm tone implied certainty until she frowned. "No, two. Edna's great-niece was here to help set up. She left early as well."

Kevin focused on the woman as if she were the only person in the world. "What do you remember from Friday night?"

Evidently not wanting to derail the focus of the conversations, Kevin didn't stop to ask for names.

She straightened her shoulders like a soldier ready for duty. "I arrived early to help set up the chairs and tables. I manned the sign-in table initially."

Again, news to me. "You weren't there when I signed in."

"I only stayed for the first half of the evening," Brenda explained. "I had to go home to sit with my mother."

"Could I get the names of the other volunteers and the attendees? Perhaps they saw something during these events that would help." I added the final bit to reinforce that I wasn't here about the murder. "Everyone I spoke to on Friday was very sincere. I doubt there's any basis to the allegations, but I should be thorough."

Brenda's shoulders relaxed. "Why don't you come to the office? I'll get the names for you."

A moment later we were in a small office. Sun poured in through windows topped with colored glass. Kevin and I sat in the chairs opposite a dark wooden desk.

Brenda fingered the list of attendees in her hand. She'd written the names of the volunteers on the bottom. "Let me know if there's anything I can do to help clear up this matter. We can't have fraud being perpetrated on the premises."

As opposed to murder. I took the folded slip of paper she held out and smiled my appreciation. It was so much easier to gather information when everyone was on the same side.

"How early does everyone arrive?" I had to remember not to mention Neville. I've learned the hard way to keep track of my stories. It's difficult to recover when you mess up your own plot line. "Do the paranormal investigators have free access to the house?"

She sat forward, her arms on the desk. "They've never been restricted, but they rarely wander off. They prefer not to disturb the spirits prior to the event."

"Were any restrictions placed on them Friday?" Kevin asked. "Considering the Jerrone auction was scheduled for Saturday."

He was so clever, sneaking in the auction.

"There were no special rules. None of the pieces were on-site." Brenda's demeanor had thawed all the way to tropical. "We had all Saturday to get ready for the next night's event."

I had a flashback from Friday night of a velvet covered chain set across a door in a back corner. I described the scene to Brenda, my new friend.

The other woman frowned. "That's the servant stairs. How did you get there? It's nowhere near the front room where the seminar was set up."

Okay, so I snuck away from the group before Marcus did. I'm not nosey. I'm an investigator. "I wanted to see if there were other means to access the upper floors out of sight of the attendees."

For my then non-existent case. I didn't so much as glance at Kevin. No need. I could feel his amusement.

Brenda nodded knowingly. "I understand."

I was glad someone did. "So, is the door locked?"

I realized in a late epiphany that the staircase in question was the one Mrs. C had been instructed to use. The one she'd found locked.

Brenda glanced at the security monitor on her desk. No activity. She focused on me. "It's usually left open to provide quick access to the upper office. Wedding parties also use it. The dressing rooms are on the third floor. We had to close it late Friday afternoon. One of the janitors nearly broke his ankle when a step gave way."

My busy brain latched onto the unexpected information. "Was Ghost Hunters 101 informed of this issue?"

"No one outside of our staff knew of it." Brenda brushed off the idea without hesitation. "I locked the staircase. The closure had no impact on the event. They never use it and it wasn't needed for the auction on Saturday."

"That makes sense." Kevin's tone rang with approval. "Why alert Silver Mountain Resort or Jerrone's if there was no need."

A staircase that was usually open had been suddenly inaccessible. No one from the outside knew. While Brenda basked under Kevin's almost flirty look, my mind noted the closure for my crossword clues. The answer, like most of the others, remained annoyingly empty. How had the unexpected closure affected the killer's plan? "Where does that staircase lead?"

Brenda pointed up and to the left. "The stairs come out to a hall on the second floor. A hidden door allows entry to the main hall outside the library."

The library. My brain silently supplied the answer at the same moment. Mrs. C would have walked into the library unseen. Had Neville been alive? Or had the killer been lying in wait?

I felt the blood leave my face. If Mrs. C had been found dead by Neville's body, the case would have been tied up in a neat, horrible little package. The police would have concluded that the two of them killed each other during a confrontation.

I starred the clue on my puzzle, then looked encouraging. I had to keep this woman talking. "Getting back to the Ghosthunters' event, have you had any complaints from participants?"

"Any complaints were due to do a lack of manifestations." Brenda shifted in the chair. "We a problem last year when someone walked in off the street after the electricity had been turned off."

"Is that when they started locking the doors and leaving someone in the lobby?" Kevin's direct gaze served to draw the woman in even more.

"Exactly." Brenda nodded. "After that incident, all the doors were locked and monitored before the event began. We've had no trouble since."

"I don't see any issues here." Kevin's voice held a hint of "I'm ready to be done". He tapped his fingers on the arm of the chair before focusing on Brenda. "No one arrived early in the day with some excuse?"

"None of the paranormal investigators." The woman shook her head. "One of the caterers for Sunday's wedding brought his staff in to look at the kitchen. Holly Reynolds from the resort and Payton Eberly from Jerrone reviewed the plans with our staff Friday morning. They were gone before noon."

Except Payton returned for the paranormal event.

Kevin twirled a pencil in his hand. "I'm guessing Neville Weatherington wasn't a member of the catering staff?"

Brenda laughed in answer to his amused tone. "Of course not. I know the caterer well. There were a group of three, two men, one woman. They've worked here many times."

I noted the information. Rycliffe Castle had multiple people coming and going most every day, including Friday. Anyone who'd been to an event on the grounds could have learned the layout of the building and the schedule of events. "Are there security cameras throughout the house?"

Brenda looked away quickly before meeting my eyes. "We don't have the money and it hasn't been an issue before now."

"One more thing," I was trying to cover all my bases while I had my chance. "Was the library unlocked all day?"

"The police asked that same question." The comment coupled with the tone of her voice indicated she didn't have a clear answer. "It's usually open. Edna did a walk-through that morning, but no one went upstairs that afternoon. There was no need."

I wasn't as disappointed as she evidently expected me to be. That meant Neville could have snuck up the back stairs, met the real killer, and been struck down hours before we arrived.

The other woman sighed softly. "That poor man."

"His death was a tragedy." Kevin sounded bored, and only vaguely interested. He gestured to a small fireplace wedged into the corner of the room. "That's an interesting piece of architecture. Does it work?"

"Yes, it does." Brenda brightened at his interest in the house. "All the fireplaces were converted to gas years ago. They're used periodically."

Including the one in the library, I added silently. Which, if turned on, would have muddied the time of Neville's death. I couldn't let the thread derail. "Was Neville here with the resort people that day?"

"Only the two woman I mentioned."

I bunched my legs to stand then relaxed. "Just a few more questions. Who locks the doors before the event? Their people or yours?"

"Only our staff have keys."

"Do you know who locked the doors on Friday?" I hadn't expected the trail to lead to the Rycliffe staff, but I was willing to harass anyone.

Brenda's gaze focused on the ceiling. "I left before they started the event. Edna locked the front and side doors. I didn't see who locked the back door and the delivery entrance."

I sat on the edge of my seat. "Could you try to remember? I should check with them before I close my case."

She clicked her tongue. "The police asked a lot of these same questions regarding the murder."

"I doubt they'd give me any information on this matter." Actually, even the ones I knew well had ignored my pleading or I wouldn't be here. "I don't want my investigation tied to the murder. I'd like to keep this just between us."

Especially since my entire story line was built on air.

"Of course," Brenda murmured. Her understanding expression marked us as conspirators. "No need to mar anyone's reputation."

I gave Kevin a self-righteous look.

His response was just short of a smirk.

So what if my caution was self-serving? It was true. I didn't want my story to leak beyond these walls.

Brenda tapped her chin. "I did see a figure at the door as I pulled out of the rear lot. It was too slim to be Edna."

I sat so far forward I was at risk of falling off my chair. The police would certainly have questioned the person, but that wouldn't stop me from doing so as well. "Who did you see?"

The Rycliffe volunteer smiled. "Edna's great-niece was in the carriage drive. Jamie must have locked up."

Shock rippled through me. It couldn't be. I unfolded the slip of paper the woman had given me. There were the names of the other volunteers, including one as big as life. "Jamie Mueller."

"That's her." The woman looked pleased that she'd remembered. "She knew the man who died. She arranged for Rycliffe to host the auction through her job at the Silver Mountain Resort."

"Did she?" That young woman had kept quite a few key details hidden. "I'll have to ask Jamie if she saw anything suspicious... regarding the Ghosthunters."

I kept my tone casual, not easy with my heart thudding in my chest and a firestorm racing through my veins.

Brenda's brow furrowed. "Do you think I should tell the police I remember seeing Jamie by the door?"

"Definitely." Kevin's tone left no wiggle room. "They need to know."

I barely heard him over the wheels racing in my mind. I would have liked to ask her not to mention my name, but being caught in a lie was the least of my problems.

I had questions galore for Jamie. First, I had to find her.

10

17 Across; 6 Letters;
Clue: A pressing or critical situation
Answer: Urgent

As I faced Holly in my parents' suite, I reminded myself that she was an ally. Jamie was the one who'd held back information. The younger woman's game playing had the fiery desert heat burning in my veins. When my fisted hands tried to settle on my hips, I forced my fingers to unclench and kept my arms at my sides.

"I had no idea you had questions for Jamie." Holly's crushed expression bordered on melodramatic. The blond woman's hair was pulled into a chignon. A high-necked blouse and a suit gave her a professional appearance. "She'll be so sorry she missed you."

I exchanged a skeptical glance with Kevin before turning to Holly. "Did you know Jamie was at the scene of the murder?"

Holly's chocolate brown eyes widened. "I know she works there part-time. Surely she would have told me if she was at Rycliffe on Friday."

"She was *seen* there." Frustration set the pressure cooker in my gut to boil. "If she kept this information from the police, she could be in trouble."

A bland expression of innocence gave way to suspicion as the implications worked through Holly's synapses. "Why would Jamie have kept such a secret?"

I fought to control my irritation. Was Holly being deliberately obtuse? Did she not realize Jamie's silence might implicate the young woman in the murder?

When I finally drew a breath through clenched teeth, Kevin touched my arm. "Tracy and I need to find out why Jamie didn't mention being at the scene of the murder."

Maybe because she was involved in this murder up to her skinny, little neck. I held in the words with an effort of will. Jamie had to know I'd find out.

"I'm sure she has a good reason." Though the tight lines around Holly's mouth eased, the woman didn't look convinced by her own reassurance.

Having regained a measure of control, I forced a calm expression. "I need to speak with her at the earliest opportunity."

About why she might have let the murder victim in the back door of a supposedly locked building.

"Jamie worked so hard to make this auction a reality." Holly's gaze became distant as if searching for a reason to explain her assistant's actions. "She was devastated when she learned Neville had been murdered."

First, Payton, Neville's assistant, turns up at the murder scene, now Jamie. Except neither woman had admitted being present. Had they been working together?

The connection flared in my brain. "Jamie was in close contact with Payton Eberly for several months, wasn't she?"

"Absolutely." A fresh spark lit Holly's expression. Discussion of business details put her on firmer ground. "Jamie and Payton communicated constantly to iron out the necessary details for the auction."

Did I smell a conspiracy? "Where is Payton?"

Holly pulled out her phone. After a few swipes, her brow cleared. "She's off-site. The mayor's office called a meeting with the police chief. Mr. Weatherington and Payton were among the attendees."

"That's a dead-end for now." I cringed at hearing my words, then hurried on hoping no one would notice. "I'll talk to Jamie when she returns."

"The excursion is due to return at two," Kevin said. "It's one-thirty-four now."

I checked my watch. I needn't have bothered. Kevin's skill in tracking time had been drilled into him since birth. Coordinating a high-level con-game requires split-second timing.

I angled my body toward him. I don't know what I intended to say. The *Sherlock* theme song, Marcus's ringtone, interrupted me. I grabbed my cell phone on the fifth note. Holly's phone rang as well.

"Hello." Since Holly had moved to the other side of the room to answer her call, I put my phone on speaker and held it between Kevin and me. My Spidey senses tingled with alarm at the unexpected call.

"Gram got stung by a bark scorpion. It's a bad one." Marcus's voice was strained. "We're on our way to the hospital."

My heart seized. "Which one?"

"Ah, Good Sam."

The next thing I knew, Kevin and I were flying down the corridor. Then, we were in the car weaving through traffic like the streets were a racetrack. The trip was like a slideshow with several scenes missing.

Finally, I found myself sitting in a plastic molded chair reminiscent of waiting rooms everywhere. A hospital spokesperson had greeted

Kevin and me at the door. The woman's platitudes echoed in my ears. A freak accident. Scorpion stings aren't as dangerous as believed. They rarely require hospitalization. Anti-venom was administered immediately. Never happened before.

According to Marcus, they'd been at a special demonstration. The bark scorpion wasn't even supposed to be there. No one had a satisfactory explanation for what happened or how.

The representatives from Rowdy Reptiles and the Silver Mountain Resort had withdrawn to play the blame game.

I didn't care about that. I wanted to see my mother, to speak with my father. I tightened my trembling fingers around Kevin's hand.

He caught my cold fingers between his two strong, calloused palms, encapsulating my hand in his warmth. "She'll be fine. They administered anti-venom on-site."

"Anti-venom for the most dangerous scorpion on their grounds."

Kevin's expression solidified to a glacial stillness. "Once the cops finish with Jamie, she's ours."

I nodded silently. I was done playing with kid gloves.

Jamie had been on the excursion.

Jamie had *insisted* on going.

Jamie had eluded me long enough.

My father's hard, thudding footsteps echoed from the hall.

Marcus, glued to his side, walked double time to keep up.

I rushed to embrace my dad. After a second, he pulled away. His large body aimed itself toward the door. Instinct told him that action solved problems. Get free, attack. Except that wasn't how this problem would be resolved.

Realizing where he was, he turned abruptly to face me.

"She'll be fine. Scorpion stings can't kill healthy adults." I put my hands on his shoulders and repeated Kevin's reassurance. I didn't mention that bark scorpions are the one lethal scorpion in the USA, though no fatal stings had been recorded in the past fifty years. Calming my father helped me rein in my own rioting emotions. "How is she feeling?"

Like me, focusing on something concrete calmed him.

Gazing out the window, he let out a slow breath. He always sought the blue sky for comfort. "Better. She's got color. She's ordering the nurses around."

That drew a smile from both of us. At home, mom had their room organized just so, from the temperature, to the bed's position, to the lighting.

The news loosened the knot tied around my heart. "Are they going to release her?"

Dad's face solidified into a mulish expression that had faced down countless Kentucky storms that dared to threaten his ranch and his horses. "They want to keep her overnight for observation."

His grudging tone conveyed his displeasure. I could tell he blamed himself for failing to protect the love of his life. How could he guard her if they were separated?

Kevin put a steadying hand on Dad's shoulder. "Keeping her here is best, at least for one night."

I quickly moved to reinforce that opinion. "She can recover her strength. It's only Sunday. You'll still have two days in town when she's released in the morning."

Marcus, who'd been hovering in the background, stepped forward. "The hospital said family members could sleep in the room. They can bring in recliners. Rowdy Reptiles is picking up the tab. I told the resort guy they had to ship in real food. I also had them order flowers. Women like flowers."

His take charge attitude helped ease the tension.

Kevin patted him on the shoulder. "You covered all the bases."

"Good job." I hugged Marcus. Holding my son close for an extra heartbeat, I faced my father. "Crawford is sending additional security."

Marcus perked up. "Have him send Rickson."

Kevin met Marcus's gaze. "We need to stay in contact."

The boy gave a sharp nod. "I'll be in charge here."

"Pop, you and Marcus should sleep here tonight." Between my son and my mother, the hospital staff would definitely be kept on their toes. Having the three of them in one place would give me more latitude in my hunt for answers. "She shouldn't be alone."

Dad frowned. "Why do we need a guard? The scorpion bite was an accident."

Was it? I squared my shoulders. I don't like coincidences. "I just don't want to take any chances."

The sting *could* have been an accident. After all, hurting my mother made no sense. No one had warned me to back off of the investigation. Those rationalizations didn't stop the guilt from crashing on my shoulders. Though I'd warned my parents of the possible danger, I should have insisted they leave town. I shouldn't have stayed at the resort with them. Regrets and what ifs choked me.

My father's worried eyes searched mine. "You think this is tied to that murder?"

"It's a possibility." If so, I was going to find out who and why. "How did the scorpion sting her?"

Pop exhaled a long, slow breath. "Marcus was letting a tarantula crawl on his shirt. Your mother was sitting next to him. There was a row of small, plexiglass cages. One of the workers saw the scorpion on your mother's arm. Just as he pointed it out it stung her."

My father's jaw, dark and weathered from the elements, tightened. The same guilt that ate at me darkened his usually open gaze. The tension from Pop was palpable. "You told us to leave."

"Someone told me once that guilt won't undo the past." I put my hand on his arm. The tightness around his mouth and eyes eased as I repeated the advice he'd given my younger self. "We have to move on from here and do our best."

Marcus edged closer. His determined expression was a good match to Dad's. "We'll protect Gram."

"You got that right." Pop squeezed Marcus's shoulder before focusing on me. "What will you do?"

Fire flashed in my gut, feeding a heat that swept through my veins. "I'm going to continue investigating the murder and find out whether Mom's scorpion sting was an accident or deliberate."

Conscious of Kevin's support, I met my father's gaze, including Marcus in a sweeping gesture. "We're going to stop them."

The two women in my life were now in someone's crosshairs. Whatever secrets remained hidden, I was going to dig up and post for public view.

Kevin and I stayed until Crawford's guard arrived. Rickson, a monolith of a man and a former Marine, gripped my shoulder in silent assurance. The *Semper Fi* tattoo on his bicep matched the one on his soul.

Promising to be careful, I took leave of my family. Knowing Rickson was on duty eased my worries as Kevin and I sat in the large, now empty, suite at the Silver Mountain Resort. The silence echoed eerily. I gripped a large mug of steaming coffee as though the cup were the murderer's throat.

I'd called Holly on the drive to the resort. She promised to deliver Jamie to our suite when we arrived. There'd been no word from her since Kevin and I hit the door seven and a half minutes ago.

But who was counting?

As I reached for my phone to call Holly, it dinged beneath my fingers. I frowned at the readout for the text message. "I don't know this number."

Kevin raised a brow. "What does it say?"

I swiped it open. "Scorpions are dangerous."

As my voice stiffened, then faded, he crossed to my side with cat-like grace. With the light glinting off his jet-black hair, he looked like an angry panther stalking prey.

With the thudding of my heart suddenly deafening me, I continued reading. "Humans are worse. Be careful."

Kevin slipped the phone from my slack hand. He checked the information record on the message to no avail. "No name attached. A burner."

The horror of my mother's attack returned. Fury swept through my veins like acid, leaving one thought behind. "My mother was attacked. The sting was a threat."

My voice shook with anger.

Kevin pulled me close, enveloping me in his arms. "She's okay."

I returned his embrace. His muscles trembled beneath my fingers. "Rickson is guarding the three of them. They're safe."

The beating of Kevin's heart steadied in his chest. We stepped away from each other. Our gazes met in a silent communication born of our long relationship.

"We'll get them." Our voices synced in perfect accord, easing some tension.

I squared my shoulders. "I'll forward the text to Crawford. Perhaps his computer genius can pull some useful information out of this message."

A moment later, Crawford's guttural tones filled the suite. "Odds are the phone is in the trash."

"I'll call Detective Wilson and report the message." With my blood still racing, I bit the words off.

"For all the good it'll do." Crawford's voice echoed off the walls, fueled by frustration. "Report a text on scorpion behavior and a warning to be careful? The police can't do anything."

"I know that." I yelled, relieved to blow off steam. "I also know it's a threat to warn us off."

"Knowing and proving." Crawford's well-worn wisdom came over the line along with a heavy sigh. "That's two different things in the legal world."

"Ain't that the truth." Kevin rubbed his hand over my shoulders, spreading a welcome warmth up my spine.

Despite the circumstances, a chuckle escaped my lips, echoed by Crawford's explosive bark of laughter. Kevin and his family had escaped trials and prison more than once because of the truth behind that maxim. Suspicion without solid proof counts for nothing under the law.

"There speaks a man who knows." My boss man's voice was heading to full volume.

I pulled the phone farther away from my ear. Some of my tension eased.

"*I'll* call Wilson," Crawford said. "You get people riled up."

"That is so not true." Well, maybe, a little. I glanced at Kevin, looking for support.

He smiled. "Agitating people is a good thing in investigations."

"Not the police. The police are our friends." Crawford spoke slowly as if I didn't understand the concept. Yet humor underscored his words. "I'll call Rickson, too."

Not that Rickson could be *more* vigilant. When he was on duty, the man operated at one level: full alert. "Thanks. For everything."

"I have to tell you... " Crawford's tone held ominous undertones. "The cost of the guard is coming out of your pay."

Outraged, I jumped to my feet. "Oh no it isn't. I got you this contract."

Kevin's laughter floated over our argument. "Way to go, Crawford. Poke the tiger."

My boss man's laughter sounded just before the line went dead.

"Crawford." I glared at the phone. "Smart-aleck."

"Who?" Kevin looked up at me from the plush sofa.

"Both of you." I plopped down next to him, putting my feet on the coffee table. I rubbed my thumb across my phone screen. With a flick of my wrist, I threw it onto the polished surface of the coffee table. "Let's get back to the murder."

Kevin snorted. "Yeah, we're doing much better solving that problem."

"I think Neville died hours before the seminar began on Friday." The certainty solidified in my mind. "After the introductory remarks, we were in total silence, listening for spirts. If he'd fought with his killer, everyone would have heard the commotion. Raised voices would have carried. When people started arriving, even an argument would have been overheard."

"That would put his death at mid-afternoon." Kevin paused, a thoughtful look on his face.

I lined up my bullet points to shoot down the problems. "Holly finished her walk-through. The Ghost Hunter people didn't arrive until later. No one went upstairs."

Kevin rose and paced to the window. "So, in this scenario, the killer turned on the fire to disguise the time of death. Then, they waited for Mrs. Colchester to arrive, but the step broke and the staircase was locked at the last minute."

His words opened my eyes to another realization. "The murderer wanted to make sure Mrs. C found the body. That's why she was directed to go to the library right away."

He raised a brow. "What if Mrs. Colchester had been on schedule? Would *she* have survived the night?"

"I thought of that very thing." So many unanswered questions. So many holes in my theory. "Two deaths would have closed the book on both murders."

Kevin stood in silhouette by the window, overlooking the courtyard and the resort's layout. His highly trained brain could have drawn a mental map of the exact proportions. The man also never got lost, another of his annoying talents. He flicked the blinds closed, then spun around and resumed his pacing.

He halted abruptly, facing me. "Remove Gracie Linden from the equation. What's the motive for murdering Neville?"

Interesting question. My mind sent feelers in all directions. "His position at Jerrone. Jealousy. Power. A thwarted ex-lover."

Gracie Linden's colorful past, coupled with worry for my mother and Mrs. C, had distracted me. I'd lost sight of the victim. Who were his associates? What were their jealousies? Passions?

Time to regain control of the investigation. "We need to attack this problem more efficiently."

A coin flipped in rapid sequence over Kevin's knuckles. "What are the odds that a woman would die from a scorpion sting with anti-venom steps away?"

"Very small." Had Jamie, a waif-like figure with a ponytail, been part of the plan? She'd stuck with my parents and Marcus when the larger group split into smaller ones.

Coincidence? I think not. I could almost hear Marcus delivering his favorite phrase. A bitter smile tugged at my lips. A surge of frustration quickly followed. "I'm tired of waiting. I want answers. If Holly and Jamie don't appear in one minute, I'm going to hunt them down."

The threat partially worked. Holly knocked on the door with seconds to spare.

She was alone.

I glanced into the empty hall behind her then shut the door harder than necessary. "Where's Jamie?"

"I don't know." The PR rep smoothed her worried expression into a business-like mask. "Jamie left the police station after giving her statement. She didn't come to work. She's not at home, and she's not answering her phone."

The news electrified my nerves, leaving a dazed, heavy silence with its passing.

Kevin's somber aura and flint-like gaze conveyed the same worry I felt.

The murderer was getting rid of co-conspirators.

Holly continued before either of us could respond. "The police offered to drive her here, but we sent a car for her. When the car arrived to pick her up, she was nowhere to be found."

Jamie had been taken or she'd run. As angry as I was, I hoped it was the latter.

I had no time to scour the city. Good thing I knew people who had resources for this kind of problem. Crawford and Rabi both had contacts. "You said you could hook me up with Jerrone employees?"

Holly nodded so fast her head looked ready to topple off her body.

"Find me Payton Eberly." I was determined to get answers out of someone. "Now."

"She's either in the Jerrone suites or with the artwork." Holly assured me.

"Is there a conference room where I can talk to her? I don't want her to know she's meeting me." I work best by ambush.

Holly gave me the room location. Relieved to have Jamie's disappearance off the table, she moved toward the door with the speed of a cheetah chasing a gazelle. "I'll have her there in ten minutes."

11

5 Down; 7 Letters;
Clue: To believe someone is guilty without proof
Answer: Suspect

Holly was as reliable as she was perky. Not fifteen minutes after leaving, she delivered an unsuspecting Payton Eberly to me in a small conference room by the business offices.

As soon as the victim's former assistant saw me, she spun on her heel and headed for the door. However, Kevin's muscular frame standing in front of the door stopped her cold. My stern reminder that her boss had hired me earned me a glare.

Holly struggled to hide her eagerness behind a professional mask. "I can stay."

"I don't think that's necessary." I had plenty of sidekicks. Besides, what would she do? Take notes for a press release?

Payton, with her back to the door, was less than an arm's length away from the PR rep.

"Are you sure?" At my second refusal, Holly quickly hid a flash of disappointment. The silver and aqua decorations of the small meeting room framed her blond coloring. "Tracy, Mr. Weatherington requested you meet with him. He'll be available in his suite until one o'clock."

That gave me over two hours. I perked up at the chance to confront the victim's brother, er update the client. With Liam Weatherington on my list of suspects, I had to remember he was the money man for this case. Either way, this was the perfect time to gain insight into how much he'd known of Neville's plans for this weekend.

"Kevin and I will head to Mr. Weatherington's suite as soon as we're done here." I shifted my attention to Payton until I realized Holly was making no move to leave.

Kevin turned his charisma on high and aimed it at Holly. "You've been a huge help with the investigation. Having you on the front lines gathering information is invaluable."

Holly brightened. "Don't hesitate to call on me for even the smallest request."

Sure. Fine. Great. Get out.

For an instant, I feared I'd spoken out loud. When I realized my clenched jaw had prevented that, I smiled in a silent apology.

Kevin twisted the knob, then leaned into Holly's personal space with a conspiratorial air. "Keep your eyes and ears open for information on our other contact. Call if you hear anything."

Holly's expression became solemn at the reminder that her assistant was still missing. "You can count on me."

I barely heard her whispered words before she left. Evidently being deputized was prize enough for missing this interview.

A frown puckered Payton's forehead. She studied Kevin as if her intense scrutiny could pierce the meaning behind his words.

Her curiosity reminded me that few others knew Jamie had taken a powder. I'd done what I could to set the hounds on her trail. Rabi had put the word out among his street contacts. Crawford's computer expert was searching online. My boss was keeping tabs through his police channels on any Jane Doe who might show up at hospitals or the morgue.

I could only hope the last two avenues turned up zilch.

Kevin closed the door then leaned against it, evidently so Holly couldn't sneak in.

Payton slanted a look at me. "What was that about?"

"I'll ask the questions." I added a dose of irritation, hoping to put her on edge. "If we have time later, I'll open the meeting up for audience participation."

My snarky tone drew a look of cool disdain. Her auburn hair framed her wide face and generous lips. "I can only spare five minutes. I have a number of things to see to for the auction."

"Can the attitude. Your employer hired me to investigate his brother's murder." I pulled out a chair and sat facing her. "I would think you'd be as eager as Mr. Weatherington to find Neville's killer."

Something flickered behind her eyes. "Of course, I want his murderer found."

"Then help me." I softened my attitude. "Tell me who might move into Neville's position at Jerrone."

Payton met my gaze head-on. A wrinkle between her brows conveyed puzzlement. "The work will be dispersed among several managers."

"Did he have enemies within the company?"

Her frown deepened, then the light dawned. "You think someone he knew killed him?"

I shrugged. "He was a powerful man. With him out of the way, the door is open for someone to step into his place. Family. Friends. Co-workers. Someone had to want that chance."

She shook her head. "Jerrone is an international company. There's plenty of work for everyone. As you said, Neville was family. Liam will take over the administrative duties. Neville's and Liam's children have grown up in the business. They, along with several managers, will assume additional responsibilities. Truly, none of them were vying for Neville's job."

She made my inside job theory sound less than promising. But she would, since she was one of my chief suspects.

"Not even you?" I asked in a sweet tone. "What about the recently created senior position you thought was yours?"

She sucked in a breath while a deer-in-the-headlights look froze her expression. Seconds later, her clenched fists and bright red cheeks betrayed her anger. "That is none of your business. You are a rude, pushy, annoying woman."

What else is new? "Answer the question."

It took a moment for her to loosen her clamped jaw. Finally, she took a deep breath. "I may have nursed daydreams of receiving the promotion. However, Barnes deserved it. He grew up in the business."

"But you were angry," I persisted.

"Disappointed," she corrected me in patronizing tone. "I certainly didn't murder Neville because of it."

Like I'd believe her. "Why were you in disguise at the paranormal event?"

She stiffened. A denial hovered in her guarded expression.

"I have pictures of you in the Goth get-up," I warned. "I also know you were there under a phony name. So do the police."

I didn't know what name, but Payton Eberly wasn't on the list of attendees. If she had been, the police would have been on her like flies on honey.

Payton's eyes searched mine. "Did you arrange to meet Neville at Rycliffe Friday night? Were you working for him?"

This was the second time someone had accused me of being on the job Friday. And hadn't I told her this was *not* twenty questions?

I debated, then gave a mental shrug. If trading answers loosened her lips, I'd play, for a while. I could always resort to the bad cop later. It came to me so naturally. "I went to Rycliffe with my son. You, however, followed Neville."

Her shoulders slumped. "He shouldn't have been here. He never travels to auctions. Why this one?"

A desperate tone underlined her question as she searched my gaze. I hope she wasn't expecting an answer. All I had was a slew of my own questions.

She ran her pink nails through her auburn hair. "That question puzzled me since Neville told me to make the travel arrangements."

Kevin crossed his arms over his chest. "What was his answer when you asked him?"

Payton's mouth flattened. Her disgusted expression robbed her face of its beauty. "He fobbed me off with talk of the increasing sales in this venue. He wanted to see the resort and meet the staff. As if I hadn't known him long enough to know he was lying."

I leaned across the table. "He never alluded to another motive? Did anything happen that would explain his change of plans?"

The tense set to her jaw relaxed. "I assume you've heard of Gracie Linden?"

Kevin's eyes narrowed.

The rules of give-and-take are that each player has to answer one question before asking another one. However, being a rule-breaker myself, curiosity overcame my scant regard for structure.

I crossed my arms over my chest. "The note found by his body mentioned her. According to the news stories, she killed Neville's father. It's ancient history."

Not so much actually, but no need to show all my cards.

Payton drew into herself like a coiled spring ready to explode. Her jaw tightened. Her narrowed gaze flicked to Kevin, who now stood like a sentinel at the curve of the table mid-way between us.

The woman remained silent for so long I began to wonder if she was waiting for me to fill in the details of the first murder.

"Neville was consumed with finding her." The words burst forth from her lips as if breaking through restraints. "He kept the investigation active long after leads on Gracie's whereabouts dried up. When I kept asking him why he was traveling to Langsdale, he finally admitted he had information that Gracie Linden was living here under an alias. He intends to expose her."

She stopped suddenly. The awareness that her boss was now in the past tense lanced through her eyes. "He *intended* to have her arrested and returned to London to be tried."

Though her confirmation that Neville had known Mrs. C's location wasn't a bombshell, an anvil settled in my gut. I felt Kevin tense, but I kept my attention on Payton. "Did he give you the name of her alias?"

"No." She clipped off the word with such ferocity I almost believed her.

Kevin snorted.

"You're saying Neville found a lead fifty years after the fact?" His skeptical tone painted the woman a liar. "What was his source for this *revelation*?"

Payton shot him a belligerent look. Violent emotions marred her pretty features, but Kevin's provocation failed to elicit a response.

I studied her reaction, then I realized the truth. "He never told you where he got his information. Do you have any ideas? Could it have been Gracie's family?"

"He refused to share any details." She slapped the bleached oak table at each word. The action seemed to fuel her roiling emotions. Her cheeks flushed red.

I shared her frustration. Sending Mrs. C that note made no sense. A quick phone call would have put her behind bars.

Unless, she hadn't received a note telling her to come to Rycliffe Castle. What if Neville contacted her directly? Offered to keep her secret if she created another forged painting? What if *she* asked him to meet her that afternoon to rid herself of the threat to the life she'd built?

That made sense.

Don't look at me like that. It's my job to suspect everyone.

Annoyed at myself, I turned my anger on Payton. "How did Neville find Linden? A private investigator? A tip?"

She glared at me. "I told you. I don't know."

"Did you look for a clue?" Kevin asked.

"In every paper, computer, and mobile device he has." In her agitation she reverted to the present tense. "I checked his finances for payments to an investigator."

"You couldn't get any details from him? Gracie's alias? His source of information?" A healthy dose of disbelief underscored my tone. I wanted to make sure the self-assured woman wasn't keeping anything back. "You couldn't have failed. You're better than that."

She recoiled as if I'd slapped her. Her hands clenched into fists.

"You think I didn't try? We had a huge argument over him wasting his life pursuing this wild goose chase." Her sigh echoed the regret in her voice. "After I called him a crazy fool, he barely talked to me except for business."

"Yeah, men don't like that." My observation earned a raised eyebrow from Kevin.

He responded without missing a beat. "While it's well-known that women adore being called crazy and foolish."

I met his gaze and hid a smile.

Rather than debate men versus women, Kevin set his hands on the chair. "Eight weeks ago, the documentary recreating the first murder was publicly announced. Could the producers have been the source of Neville's new information?"

I perked up at the possibility. How had I overlooked that avenue? Then, again, how would they have found the information?

Payton was shaking her head before I finished my thought.

"I took notes at all the meetings for the documentary." The woman rubbed her fingers across her glittery, manicured nails in a quick, nervous gesture. "Their script is straight out of the police report fifty years ago. Nothing new. Certainly not the alias and hiding place of the killer. If they knew, they'd have told the authorities."

"Anyone would." Except whoever sent the notes... unless it was Mrs. C.

My brain whispered that last part, not me.

"How does the sketch tie in?" I was surprised it hadn't been mentioned before. "When did Neville become involved with the Infantino piece?"

Payton had to stop to consider. "Archie Smythe found and confirmed the sketch over a year ago. He approached Jerrone last December."

"Why Jerrone?" Kevin's tone teetered between disbelieving and bored. "The sketch was discovered in Arizona. Why not go with Sotheby's or Christie's?"

Payton straightened her shoulders. "Jerrone's has a history of selling Infantino's. We know the clientele. We were the natural choice. The only choice."

So, she was a loyalist.

"Smythe is also a Brit," I noted. "He chose the home team."

Payton sent me a withering look. "Archie would work with his worst enemy to ensure the best sale."

"Then, why isn't he here?" I made a sweeping gesture to include the city at large. "Shouldn't he be on-site?"

"There's no need for him to attend." Payton's condescending tone coupled with her attitude was grating on my nerves. "He'll receive his fee when the hammer falls."

"Of course." When Payton arched a brow, I faced her with a stern mask. When interviewing involved parties, it's best to feign certainty in all matters. In this case, I actually *did* know the hammer fall marked the final sale in a fancy art auction. "Did Neville say or do anything out of character since arriving?"

Her narrowed eyes bored into mine. Intense. Suspicious. Unsure. "Neville and Liam were scheduled to attend a special dinner Friday night. Neville refused. He said since he wasn't supposed to be here, his absence wouldn't matter. He wouldn't budge and he wouldn't explain, not even to Liam. I was out of patience. So, Friday morning, I hacked into Neville's tablet and found an entry about the Ghost Hunters 101 event."

"Ghost hunting was out of character for him, I take it?" I asked in a flippant tone.

"It was ridiculous." She bit off the words, making no attempt to hide her disdain. "I asked him about it, but he brushed me off. He didn't trust me."

This from a woman who hacked into her boss's tablet?

She chewed on her lower lip. "He was a no-show for his afternoon meetings. I called him but he didn't answer."

Was he already dead?

Kevin's eyes narrowed. "How long was he out of touch?"

Payton paused in thought. "I hadn't spoken with him since one."

I hid surprise behind a neutral expression. Neville couldn't have been killed that early in the day. Where had he been? Meeting Jamie? Meeting Mrs. C? Already inside Rycliffe Castle?

"You had a ticket to the event." Kevin pointed out. "Neville didn't. How long had he been planning to attend?"

"I discovered his plans Friday morning. That's why I kept calling him. I made my excuses for the dinner in order to attend the Ghost Hunters event." Payton set her jaw in a hard line. "Are you going to ask me who he was meeting? Who sent him the note?"

Frustration stamped itself on her attractive features. The rapid-fire questions came to an abrupt halt.

"I don't know." She answered her own outburst. "If you find the answers, you tell me."

I waited a few heartbeats to let her irritation spend itself. "Did you speak with Neville while you were at Rycliffe?"

She dropped her gaze. "When I didn't see him among the attendees, I felt like a fool. Then, that man yelled that he'd found a body. I rushed in with the others and... I saw Neville. Dead."

Taking a shaky breath, she pressed her lips together. "I couldn't believe it was him."

Her display of sorrow was convincing. However, just because she mourned him didn't mean she hadn't killed him. "Did Neville know Jamie Mueller, the PR assistant?"

The strained muscles on her face relaxed. She took a deep breath. "He was introduced to her. She attended the planning meetings over the past few days."

"Did you tell her he had a lead on his father's murderer?" Kevin's stern voice sliced through the give-and-take.

Having witnessed Jamie's sympathy for Neville, I was willing to bet the young woman had been the recipient of the small scrap of knowledge. A man on the trail of his father's killer. What harm could it do to let him into Rycliffe by the back door?

Payton jerked as if he'd slapped her. She couldn't hold Kevin's gaze for a second. "We e-mail and text constantly while arranging these shows. On my first night in town, Jamie and I went out. Holly was busy. I may have mentioned my frustration with Neville's supposed lead."

"You may have been tired of the subject, but Jamie was sympathetic. After all, he had his first clue after fifty years of searching." I tried to fill in some of the blanks in my crossword puzzle. "Did he know she worked at Rycliffe Castle?"

Payton blinked in surprise. "All the senior staff knew. We've held opening nights there more than once. It's a beautiful setting. Liam always credits Jamie at the first meeting for acting as a liaison. What are you saying?"

The epiphany sparked in her eyes, then the realization flowed over her face.

Payton spread her hands on the table. "Neville spoke with Jamie several times in the days before his death. Did she let him into Rycliffe Castle? Is she in league with Gracie Linden?"

I thought Jamie was in league with you. I didn't have time to say that out loud.

Payton half-rose out of her chair. "Did Jamie set Neville up to be killed?"

"There's no evidence of that. She also has no reason to wish him dead." That I knew of... Though Jamie knew more than she was telling, she wasn't high on my suspect list and I had no reason to move her up. I waved Payton to her chair. "The most she might have done is let him in without anyone else knowing."

"Which got him killed." She ground the words out between her clenched teeth.

"Neville's pursuit of his father's killer cost him his life." Kevin reminded her in a no-nonsense tone. "That and the murderer."

Which brings us back to the case. "Who else knew the real reason Neville came to Langsdale? Liam?"

"Of course not." She bit off the words.

I could feel my eyebrows rising of their own volition. That didn't ring true. "He didn't tell his brother he had a lead on the woman who killed their father?"

Payton's hazel eyes met mine. "He wanted to be certain of his facts before telling Liam."

Kevin cast me an infinitesimal nod that Payton missed.

I'd mostly believed her excuse, but it was disappointing to have him confirm she was telling the truth. What else was she holding back? My job would be so much easier if people cooperated. Like children. Or feral cats. "How did you escape the dragnet at Rycliffe Friday night?"

She studied me for a moment, then shrugged. "As soon as I saw his body, I ran downstairs. No one was around. I slipped out the rear entrance. In the confusion, no one saw me."

"The door was open?" How many loopholes did this supposedly locked mansion have? "No one stopped you?"

She cocked her head to one side. "I forgot the doors were supposed to be locked. I walked out and drove off."

I threw up my hands. "So much for airtight security."

Kevin leaned on the table. "Were you with your designated group the entire time?"

"Of course." The words were out of her mouth while she was still blinking in surprise at his accusing tone.

Her outraged look left the impression that sneaking away from your designated group was more offensive than murder. Not to mention leaving the scene of a crime.

Since honesty was not one of Payton's strongest character traits, I decided to prompt her to do the right thing. "You have to tell the police you were at the scene when Neville was murdered."

"That would be pointless." She dismissed my suggestion with a toss of her head. "I didn't see anything helpful."

"They know someone is missing. They're detectives." Though I didn't crack a smile as I resorted to a patronizing tone, I was dancing a jig on the inside. My boss has used that line on me more than once. It's a heady feeling, being able to shoot down other people's excuses without blinking an eye.

Kevin met my gaze with a knowing look. He knew I loved being self-righteous. His expression remained neutral as he addressed Payton. "This is murder. The police won't stop until they account for every attendee on the list."

"Fine." The word exploded from her lips with ill-grace. "I'll talk to the authorities. Are we done? I have things to do. This is a very important night."

"We're done for now." I so did not like her attitude. "Don't run off again."

The door slammed with resounding force.

Kevin jerked his head toward the door. "Not a fan of yours."

"I still have Holly." Who was more than enough for me. "Payton made sure that we knew Liam had no idea of Neville's true motive for coming to town."

"No mention of the forgeries either."

"I thought they'd be the heart of the case." They still could be, but more digging was required. "Why would she protect Liam?"

"He's waiting in his suite." Kevin opened the door and waved me to go first. "Let's see what the man has to say."

12

2 Across; 13 Letters;
Clue: Hostile meeting between opposing parties
Answer: Confrontation

I walked through the corridors, focused on the meeting with Liam Weatherington. With clues and crossword puzzles demanding my attention, I barely heard my phone ring.

Until Kevin's cell buzzed with a text message at the same instant.

My feet dragged to a halt. Good news does not come in pairs, especially when it was my boss's ringtone. I barely drew a breath when he trampled my greeting.

"An arrest warrant has been issued for your landlady for the murder of Neville Weatherington."

Crawford's announcement drove the air from my lungs. Kevin and Rabi had warned me that Mrs. C's past identity would be uncovered sooner rather than later, but the suddenness stunned me. It was early afternoon, barely forty hours since Neville's murder. "Can they do that? They haven't questioned her since Friday."

"They're the *police*." My boss snarled. "If they have the evidence, they can skip a few steps."

Kevin grimaced at the readout, then turned the phone toward me. "Text from Rabi. 'Police here for Colchester.'"

Crawford's deep voice, thickened with years of smoking and liquor, continued. "The cops should be picking her up any minute."

"They just arrived." Resignation filled my tone.

Kevin glanced up. "Rabi's clear. He was checking the street when the cops pulled up."

"At least he wasn't caught in the middle." One point for our side. It was a tiny victory, but, at this point, I'd take what I could get. I started walking again. I had to make progress. I was also determined to glean all the details I could from my boss. "This morning the police only knew she was among the attendees. Now they've arrested her for murder?"

"Big leap." When I turned to the right, Kevin took my elbow and shifted me ninety degrees toward an archway leading outside. "The Weatherington suite is across the courtyard."

I stepped onto a mosaic pathway shaded by overgrown palm trees and leafy ferns. Focused on the next question, I stubbed my toe on a jutting rock. Between groaning and cursing, I decided I shouldn't try to walk and talk. I stopped on the deserted side of a cactus. "What evidence does the district attorney have?"

"Howell isn't talking." Crawford's voice dragged. He hated when the DA and the police locked him out.

I tapped the speaker button so Kevin could hear both sides of the conversation. Then, I lowered the volume so the entire resort didn't overhear the former detective's booming voice.

"They have something substantial," Crawford continued. "Howell moves fast on high-profile murders, but he won't risk an arrest on a weak case."

The last breath of air left my lungs. "They must know about Mrs. C's past."

"What about her past?"

I updated my boss. Keeping him in the dark while he was trying to help didn't seem wise. Besides, he detests secrets among allies. He's funny that way.

"Wait." Even on low volume, Crawford's commanding tone startled me. A thump of feet hitting the floor was followed by a rustle of papers.

My heart picked up speed at the thread of hope in his voice.

"What's up?" I demanded. Patience was never one of my virtues. "What do you know?"

"Wait." The pre-emptive command came again.

I gritted my teeth. Counted to ten. Scowled at Kevin's perfectly composed, endlessly patient gaze. The man's calm only fed my irritation.

"Tell me something," I demanded again, knowing Crawford wouldn't answer until he was ready.

No reply.

Two couples with tennis rackets sauntered up the hill. One pair nodded and waved at me and Kevin. I gave them a tight smile. A stream of air escaped through my clenched teeth after they were gone.

"Alice Colchester." The triumphant note in Crawford's voice was unmistakable. "The name on the arrest warrant. No aliases."

"Well, duh, that's her name." As soon as I said the words, the lightbulb went off. My mind flipped through my mental notebook of legal procedure. "They usually list a person's legal name on the warrant with her aliases. Right?"

"If they know the legal name." Crawford's confirmation held a note of triumph.

"That means… " I tried to think through the ramifications. "That's good news. Right?"

Kevin's narrowed gaze studied the tourists and resort staff moving in the background. He drew closer to the phone. "Mrs. Alice Colchester has no motive for murdering Neville Weatherington."

Not as Mrs. C.

"What does that tell us?" Actually, it told me very little, but I was hoping for more from my boss. He'd been on the force for twenty-five years. "They don't know about her past. What motive can they have?"

"The DA must have a witness or a murder weapon with prints." The squeaky springs of Crawford's office chair groaned as he shifted his weight. His voice deepened even more. "Something to prove beyond a doubt that Mrs. Colchester struck the fatal blow."

"That's impossible." My protest was a gut reaction. "She didn't kill him."

"I'll be in touch." Crawford disconnected without another word.

I stood under the desert sun. A cold rivulet of sweat snaked down my spine.

Kevin put a reassuring arm around my waist.

I shook my head, more in confusion than denial. "How could the police have physical evidence she committed the murder? The woman's innocent."

Well, innocent of this particular crime I told myself. She could hot-wire a car like a pro. She was a walking "how to" on avoiding detection. She knew more about the seamier side of life than most criminals, certainly more than me. All that was a given. But she wouldn't hurt anyone, certainly not murder.

Not even to protect the life she'd built? The family and friends she'd found?

The insidious questions bubbled up from the dark regions of my mind. Contrary thoughts that refused to remain silent.

What if Neville had taken her by surprise? Threatened to expose her past after she thought she was safe?

"The evidence is a plant." Kevin's tone held complete conviction.

"You're right." My brain refused to commit. Some detail nagged at me. After all, wouldn't the DA be absolutely sure of the facts before making an arrest?

"Someone discovered her identity." Kevin's steady tone sounded as a backdrop while my mind ran in circles. "They led Neville to Rycliffe and murdered him, now they're painting a target on Mrs. Colchester's back."

Once again Kevin's phone buzzed. He eyed the readout, then did a double take. "Mrs. Colchester's missing. The cops can't find her."

"How could she be gone?" Was nothing simple with this case? "Wasn't she in the apartment when Rabi went outside?"

Kevin called Rabi. Several minutes later he pocketed his phone and gave me the lowdown.

Mrs. C took a call. A moment later, she insisted Rabi check the perimeter. Her words. When he left, she locked herself in the apartment. The other entrances to the building had already been bolted and were still locked from the inside. Nobody went in the building until the police arrived.

"They went in. They came out." Kevin demonstrated the actions with his hands. "No Mrs. Colchester."

"She didn't answer the door?" That wouldn't work. The cops would have broken down the door, or would they? Was that legal? "Did they go inside? She could be hurt."

"Rabi heard them talking. Her apartment door was open," Kevin explained. "The place was empty. No sign of violence."

I listened with increasing disbelief as possibilities came and went. A mental picture formed of the older woman scuttling down the alley in pink slippers. Her top speed is a fast shuffle. Amusement bubbled up inside of me. "They're going to put out a BOLO on a seventy-plus woman wearing bedroom slippers?"

Kevin's mouth creased in a smile. "They already have."

I snorted. "I bet she has a friend at the police station who warned her."

Her list of contacts was a continual surprise - county clerks, taxi drivers, funeral directors.

"Where could she go?" Kevin asked. "The police are bound to find her. Rabi was outside for five minutes."

"Who knows?" Debating between ourselves would accomplish nothing. I started walking again. "Time to find out what Liam Weatherington knew about his brother's plans."

"Tracy Belden, please find a house phone and call the hotel operator." The outside speakers broadcast the announcement in a steady drone. "Tracy Belden... "

The message repeated twice while Kevin and I went inside and located the nearest phone.

"Who would page me?" I asked, not expecting an answer. Then a possibility popped up. "Someone who can't risk anyone tracing the call. Someone like Jamie."

I waited with eager anticipation while the call connected.

"This is Tracy Belden."

No answer.

"Who is this?" I barely breathed. I was ready to be comforting, stoic, or demanding. Whatever it took to get the girl to confide in me.

"Ms. Belden, this is the British Imports Company." A stiff, nasal, upper class British voice sounded over the line. "I've called to inform you that your overseas package has been temporarily misplaced."

Confusion blanked out my circuits. Several seconds passed until synapses flickered to life. Only one person, one woman, could be behind this call, but that was... not impossible, but totally unexpected. "Umm."

That's me. Rapier comebacks.

"Who is it?" Kevin mouthed. He waved his hands in front of my frozen expression. "Earth to Belden. Earth to Belden."

"Not to worry." The official sounding voice continued. "No doubt the package will return to safe harbor in no time. We have every confidence in your ability to bring the ship about."

"Sure. Absolutely." How had Mrs. C eluded the police? How could she sound so casual? By all rights she should be in handcuffs or in jail. For that matter, where was she calling from?

"We'll keep in touch. Ta-ta."

A click sounded in my ear. I stared at the phone. Were hallucinations usually this solid? Because this couldn't be real.

"What's wrong?" Kevin gripped my shoulders, concern etched on his face. "Was that Jamie?"

"British Imports. My package has been misplaced."

His confused frown barely had time to form. His eyebrows shot upward. "Mrs. Colchester? Where is she?"

I shrugged. "My place? A hidden room? The Ritz? With her, there's no telling."

I wasn't sure I wanted to know where the woman was hiding. Let the police search for her. I had enough troubles trying to clear her of murder.

13

1 Down; 7 Letters;
Clue: Continue obstinately in a course of action
Answer: Persist

By the time we reached the Jerrone suite, Kevin had updated Rabi. I still had no answers as to where Mrs. C might be.

However, one look at Liam Weatherington's digs diverted my attention. His suite was to ours what the Taj Mahal was to a cardboard box in an alley.

Kevin and I waited in the main hall while a representative fetched the lord of the manor.

Kevin looked completely at ease in the opulent suite. I stood out like a stray cat.

I glanced down a couple of halls but the endless reflections of chrome, glass, and shining Italian marble made me dizzy. I settled on the view of a small garden just beyond the French doors.

Water jetted out of the sprinklers. Tiny rainbows flared to life only to vanish in tiny bursts of sparkles and air. The dancing drops reminded me how quickly Neville's future had evaporated.

"Ms. Belden." Weatherington's voice sounded directly behind me. The plush carpeting had muffled his heavy stride. "I'd like an explanation."

Irked at the arrogant tone, I spun around and deflected his question. "And I want answers."

A fast blink and a tight jaw rewarded my demanding tone. I gestured toward the window. "How far would you go to ensure you don't lose all this? If Neville's actions threatened your family business, would you stoop to murder?"

Fury raged in his hard gaze. His heavy jowls shook with indignation. "I don't like what you're implying."

I held my silence.

"Have you forgotten I'm paying you to find the killer?" He bit off the words with a hard snap of his teeth.

"Even if you're the killer?"

"Don't be ridiculous. The police have a suspect, an older woman. They believe she may be Gracie Linden. If so, she obviously killed Neville to protect her identity." He thrust his head and shoulders forward, the better to look down on me from his greater height. "What have you accomplished?"

Not much, but I wasn't about to tell him that. I fought not to sigh at his obvious maneuver of trying to use his height to intimidate me. My siblings had tried that trick on me all my life. It didn't faze me then, or now.

"I'm aware the police have a suspect." I held his stare. "Do you have a theory as to why the authorities haven't released details to the press?"

The older man remained silent rather than rise to my bait, but uncertainty crowded into his gaze.

Kevin, standing to one side, exuded an air of certainty. He shifted closer in perfect tag-team timing. "The arrest is an attempt to cool the heat from the press, the public, and the mayor, all demanding results."

Weatherington leaned close enough that I could smell the mint on his breath. "They have evidence."

Since Crawford had told me as much, I had no trouble shrugging away the jab.

"The woman in question didn't know your brother," I said. "She has no motive."

None I was willing to reveal to the possible murderer. I searched the man's expression, looking for any hint that he knew Mrs. C had a tie to his family's past.

No overt reaction. His ire at my poking seemed focused solely on the present.

He stabbed a finger at me. "You know Neville's killer. You were with her the night of the murder."

Kevin watched but made no move.

I ignored the other man's attempt to dominate the conversation.

"I am acquainted with the woman the police suspect," I admitted, fisting my hands on my hips. "She didn't kill your brother."

I had to keep repeating the words because, really, the facts were aligning against her.

Weatherington shifted his bulk away from me, giving me room to breathe. "Is she Gracie Linden?"

Assuming Mrs. C had told me the truth, I could answer that question with total honesty. "No."

My treacherous brain couldn't help but consider the possibility that the reason none of the Weatheringtons knew of Gracie's friend was because she never existed. Perhaps only one slim blonde had been involved with the first victim and only one woman had escaped England to come to the States.

Perhaps Mrs. C *was* Gracie Linden. Nothing I'd discovered so far proved Gracie and Mrs. C weren't the same person. Fifty years after *their* disappearance, how could anyone confirm both women truly existed?

Don't blame me. I can't be held responsible for the way my mind works. "Do you want to find the real killer or simply pin charges on anyone?"

I focused on his eyes, debating whether fear or grief glimmered in their depths.

His expression remained masked. "My father was murdered when I was eleven. Mum was devastated. Neville was the one who got me and my sister through that dark time."

No one could remain unmoved by his litany. However, his response could also be a ploy to distract me.

"Now, my brother has been murdered on the eve of his greatest success." Weatherington walked away. His long fingers traced the gilded frame of a painting. His shoulders lost their rigidity, giving him an air of defeat. "I want to know why."

Call me heartless, but the opening was too good. "Perhaps because he was about to expose the Infantinos your father authenticated as forgeries."

For a big man, the guy could move. The accusation had barely left my lips when he was in my face again.

Rage darkened his skin to purple. "If you're going to make such a statement, you better have proof."

If the man was covering up, he was an excellent actor. "I've heard rumors the Infantinos your father sold in the months before his death were forgeries."

"My father would not have made such an error." His words blasted me with the chill of the north wind.

I wasn't implying his judgment was in error. The old man had perpetrated outright fraud. "What do you know about Gracie Linden?"

He followed the quick change of topic with a slight narrowing of his eyes. "She's the painter who murdered my father."

I didn't answer right away, noting the puzzled wrinkle on his forehead. "She and your father were together during the time he found the Infantinos."

"You believe she switched the real paintings with forgeries?" Weatherington asked. For the first time since Kevin and I stepped into the suite, a sense of common interest imbued the air. "I heard she had a hand in discovering the Infantinos. Perhaps that was her motive for the murder. Father found out the truth and planned to expose her part in the deception."

Weatherington could spin as good a theory as I could. However, I got the impression he believed his version.

Who knew? Perhaps he was correct. If her family had been involved back then, that would give them an added motive to kill Neville.

In the brief intermission between rounds, Kevin entered the fray. "You sound unimpressed with Gracie Linden's talent. Have you seen her paintings? Could she have made a successful career in the art world?"

Weatherington's snort of derision dismissed the idea. "I studied her works when I was young. No real talent. Her skill lay in her proficiency as a copyist. Her family had a business as art restorers. She could copy most any style."

More than Infantino? I filed away his words for later. "If the Infantinos weren't her motive for killing your father what was?"

He studied me with a keen intelligence. "They were lovers for a short time. He broke it off. She became irate. Refused to accept that he didn't want her."

Again, no mention of Gracie's close friend. "How long were they involved?"

He shrugged. "Her family worked for us for years. They were involved for three or four months. No more."

The same basic facts Mrs. C had supplied. However, Liam's version had Gracie as the aggressor in the forgery scheme. What if it *was* her idea? "There was no hint at the time that the paintings were forgeries?"

"None." Weatherington's denial struck me as a touch over-done, too fierce, too quick. His jaw shook with the force of his emotion. "Who gave you this scurrilous information?"

I took refuge in the P.I. manual. "I'm not at liberty to divulge the name of my informant."

The man balled his hands into fists. "I'm your client. I am paying you to investigate this matter."

I met his demanding visage with a cool stare. "I haven't confirmed anything regarding possible forgeries. If I do, I'll let you know."

Easy to say, hard to do. In fifty years, no one had spotted Gracie's counterfeits. Besides, I had a nagging suspicion this case wasn't about the Infantinos. At least, not directly.

Don't ask me what it *was* about, so far, my mental crossword puzzle remained woefully blank.

"We've heard Neville was almost obsessed with bringing your father's murderer to justice." Kevin rubbed a hand across his mouth. The gesture gave him a thoughtful air. His calm demeanor helped defuse the tension. "Did he mention he came to Langsdale to follow a lead on Gracie Linden?"

The older man's shoulders drooped. "I'm the last person he'd tell. Finding that woman consumed his youth. It's been years since Neville spoke of our father's murder or the woman who killed him. I thought he'd moved on until the documentary was announced. Then they found the note by his body."

Kevin met my gaze in a silent exchange.

Thanks to our long association, I knew what he was thinking as if we'd planned this interview in detail beforehand.

In the blink of an eye, Kevin turned on an aura of comradery that always drew people to him.

Weatherington was no exception. The other man's attention was drawn to Kevin as if they were alone. The older man stepped closer to Kevin. "What do you know?"

Kevin paused for a heartbeat. "We haven't been able to confirm how he came by this information or if it's true. It's likely that his murderer led him here in order to blame Gracie Linden for his death."

My guy delivered the news in that compelling tone that had once earned his family of grifters several fortunes.

The other man froze. Not a breath escaped his lips. Not a blink betrayed him. He held Kevin's gaze in total silence.

After a second, Kevin continued. "Gracie's name in that note has centered the entire investigation on her and the first murder. There's no proof the woman is even alive."

Weatherington's face seemed to tighten even more. His gaze shifted down and to the right.

Most likely thinking, not concocting a story.

The man spun to face me with such speed I was taken aback. "It's that friend of yours. Neville came here to confront her."

Even as I marshaled a defense, I couldn't help noticing that, though Kevin had been speaking, I had to face Weatherington's wrath.

Something about me tends to antagonize people.

It's a gift.

Deep lines etched themselves around the other man's taut mouth. "The woman the police suspect in Neville's murder is Gracie Linden. She murdered my father. Now she's killed my brother."

So much for Kevin's attempt to open a field of suspects closer to home.

"She is not Gracie Linden." I repeated, hoping to convince both of us. "The police have investigated her background and confirmed her identity."

I wasn't sure that failing to uncover Mrs. C's contrived history counted as confirming her past, but I wasn't about to punch holes in my own defense.

I pasted on a business-like mask. "I don't believe your brother's murder is about exposing Gracie Linden. Someone fed Neville that information and preyed on his well-known obsession in order to lead him to his death."

The man crossed his arms over his chest. "So, you have a theory after all."

I ignored his patronizing tone and proceeded to make my case. "The note mentioning Gracie Linden that was so conveniently left by Neville's body. It was manufactured to point to the first murder. How could Neville or anyone have uncovered her location after fifty years?"

That was the biggest argument in Mrs. C's favor. Regardless of whether I bought into her version of the past, I refused to believe Neville had been able to track her to Langsdale when the police, Crawford, and Rabi combined still hadn't found a loose thread in her story. Someone led him to her.

Finding out who was proving to be a problem.

Weatherington's stern posture didn't relax. He hovered over me like a vulture looking for a sign of weakness. "What's your theory?"

"Look at the end result." I spread out my hands. "Neville's dead. Who benefits? Who profits? Who replaces him?"

"No one can replace him." Sorrow echoed in his tone. His shoulders slumped as if this tragedy were too heavy to bear.

I refused to let his grief derail me. "Who will take over for him?"

With obvious effort, Weatherington straightened. "His work will be divided."

I froze like a dog on point. "Are any of his possible replacements in town?"

His jaw tightened.

"I'll need their names and their schedules. I have to talk to them." His jaw clamped shut, heightening my hunting instincts. "Would one of them happen to be Payton?"

Weatherington's expression could have been carved from stone.

"I'll take that as a yes."

He studied me silently for a moment. His jaw worked until finally words came out. "I will get you the information, but I expect regular reports of your investigation from this moment on."

Yeah. Right. Him and Crawford.

His hard gaze bored into mine. "I find it best to keep my friends close and my enemies closer."

Somehow, I doubted our little tête-à-tête had earned me a place on the man's Christmas list.

14

—— ◆ ——

4 Down; 9 Letters;
Clue: Release from a hospital; Fire a gun
Answer: Discharge

"Being called an enemy by your own client is a first even for you, Belden." Kevin's tone held undisguised amusement as he slapped the elevator button in the hospital lobby.

It was Sunday afternoon. I'd been on the case less than twenty-four hours and I'd alienated almost everyone except Holly, my number one fan. Visiting my mother in the hospital could only improve my day.

"At least Weatherington didn't fire me." I grimaced at having to face my boss if I lost him the biggest case to hit the city in years. "Even if we lose the contract, Crawford has gotten more publicity from this investigation than he could ever buy."

Kevin laughed out loud. "Your boss won't be satisfied with publicity if Weatherington cuts you loose."

After leaving my client's suite, we'd met Rabi at a local barbecue dive. Rehashing the case proved how little I knew, especially about Jamie's involvement with my mother's scorpion sting. On my earlier visit, I'd been the worried daughter. This time I'd stay in P.I. mode and dig for details.

Jamie, the PR assistant with a bobbing brown ponytail, had insisted on being present at Rowdy Reptiles. She'd been close when my mother was stung. She'd been on hand at Friday night's murder. Did the young woman have a hand in the violence? Or was she simply unlucky enough to be in the wrong place?

Repeatedly.

Though her waif-like build made her look underage, Neville could have reeled Jamie into a scheme under the guise of a publicity stunt or sympathy. Unfortunately, since she'd disappeared this morning, I hadn't been able to question her.

Neither Rabi, Crawford, nor the police had found any sign of the young woman. No Jane Does had turned up at a hospital or the morgue. That was the good news.

In order to get a feel for the woman's state of mind, I had to ask the last people to see her: my parents and my son. Hopefully they could provide insight into her actions.

I heaved a sigh and turned to my captive audience, Kevin. "Even if Jamie is a willing partner, I can't see her acting alone."

My boyfriend's only reaction was a slightly raised eyebrow. He was used to me arguing cases aloud.

His lack of comment didn't slow me down. "I still like Payton, as the culprit. She was in disguise Friday. She bought an advance ticket to the ghost tour. She toured Rycliffe Castle months ago. That gave her a chance to plan every detail of the murder."

The elevator's arrival saved Kevin from rehashing our luncheon discussion. He waved me in without comment. A buzzing from my cell phone distracted me from my one-sided debate.

"It's an e-mail from Holly showing Neville's itinerary." With my gaze glued to the screen, I skimmed through the appointments.

The calendar was crowded with meetings from last Tuesday morning through Monday. I studied Friday in detail. No revelations. As I scanned Saturday, then today, my gaze slowed.

Meetings he would never attend. People he would never see again. His hopes, future, and long-sought justice, gone in a single, irrevocable instant.

Sympathy welled up inside me. For some reason, the missed meetings brought the tragedy home. Now, in addition to proving Mrs. C innocent, I felt an obligation to find justice for the man who'd lost his life seeking his father's killer. "What a waste."

The elevator counted up to the fourth floor at a snail's speed.

With my arm around Kevin's waist, I flipped through the schedule. "Meetings with the other principles. His brother. His assistant. The resort's PR team. No mysterious, private time marked off saying 'Here I meet my killer, see attached notes.'"

Kevin gave me a sideways glance. "Guess you'll have to solve the case the old-fashioned way."

When the elevator doors opened, my gaze remained glued to my cell phone. I walked blindly, relying as ever on Kevin. I knew he'd wouldn't let me walk into a wall. When we turned the corner, he pulled up short.

I rocked on my heels, narrowly avoiding a collision with my father. Beside him, a nurse jerked my mother's wheelchair to a halt. Marcus reined in a cart crowded with bouquets of flowers and gave a jaunty wave.

Rickson, a bodyguard on my boss's payroll, brought up the rear. "Beldens never stay put. Never do what they're told."

"Where are you going?" The answer was obvious. My mother was leaving. "You can't walk out of the hospital."

Marcus, flashing a grin, pointed to the wheelchair. "She's rolling out."

"The doctor dismissed me." My mother's tone made it sound as if the news had come as a total surprise. "My stay was strictly a precaution. People are rarely admitted for a scorpion sting."

I folded my arms across my chest and gave her a stern look, feeling as if I was the parent, she the child. "There has to be more to the story."

Mom's eyes widened. "I may have spoken to him about being dismissed."

"A few times," Rickson interjected.

Dad shifted his feet. "The doctor assured us your mother is well enough to leave. He arranged for a visiting nurse to check on her."

"I feel fine. No more muscle spasms. My blood pressure is normal. So is my heart rate." She gestured to Pop. "The more I thought about your father missing tonight's auction, the more I realized how unfair that would be to him."

My dad made herding gestures. Standing in one place too long wore on his nerves.

Arguing was obviously pointless. "I'm surrounded by rule-breakers."

"I know my own mind," Mom clarified. "Your father, Mr. Rickson, and the rest of you will be watching me like hawks."

Marcus waved a paper in the air. "They gave us a sheet of instructions."

"Time to surrender." Kevin swung me around and we headed toward the elevator.

While we waited, Mom turned to me with a conspiratorial air. "I'd hate to miss this auction, too. I love watching people fight for the same piece and see who wants it the most."

Her eyes lit up with unconcealed glee.

When the elevator dinged and everyone got on board, I leaned into Kevin. "My mother, the adrenaline junkie."

He answered with a smile. Holding the elevator door open with an outstretched arm, he entered last.

I pulled Marcus close and planted a kiss on the top of his head. My reward was a look of disgust before he wiggled away and positioned the cart between us.

I glanced at Kevin to share the moment.

However, my boyfriend's gaze was fixed on the closing doors. He stiffened just as the doors snapped shut. "Jamie."

His yell fired the air with electricity. He hit the closed doors to no avail. By the time he found the "open door" button, the elevator was sliding downward.

Rickson tensed. "Jamie's the girl who went missing this morning?"

Kevin stabbed the button for the next floor. "She was peering around the corner."

Marcus balanced on the cart's wheels. He leaned closer. "You think she was spying on Gram?"

Kevin eyed the floor indicator, which changed with agonizing slowness. "Very likely."

That would explain why neither the cops nor Rabi's contacts had found her on the streets. I maneuvered around the cart and stood by the door with Kevin.

My heart revved up to full speed. I pointed at Rickson. "Stay with them."

His sharp nod and determined look reassured me.

The elevator stopped on the third floor. The doors separated.

Kevin pushed through the slim opening and took off at a run.

I was hot on his heels.

"Go get her." Marcus's cheer followed us as Kevin aimed toward a door tucked into the corner marked Stairs.

I followed Kevin into the stairwell.

He stood frozen on the lower step. Muscles tense. Head cocked.

Running footsteps sounded on the stairs above us.

He flew up the stairs and out of sight. Though I'm no slouch when it comes to running, his speed carried him out of sight before I cleared the door. He was long gone by the time I hit the first landing. His feet thudded infrequently on the stairs, barely touching the steps.

"Jamie! Stop!" His voice echoed off the walls. "Let us help you."

The woman's footsteps echoed somewhere above my head.

I hit the first landing and pivoted. Above me, the door to the stairwell was closing as I started up.

A figure in a dark, long-sleeved top stepped between me and Kevin. The form hurried up the stairs to the next level.

Adrenaline rushed through me as I groaned at the thought of an innocent bystander being caught in harm's way. I took the stairs two at a time. I had to warn the person to get out of the way.

By the time I hit the bottom step of the next set of stairs, the figure was almost to the top.

The hood of the oversized sweatshirt covered the face. Driving gloves hid the hands.

Still running at top speed, I saw a gun swing up at the runner's side.

Icy fear rushed through me. My heart thudded in my ears. Time slowed.

Each second froze like a frame in a movie.

Each step took the figure farther away from me.

And closer to Kevin.

Kevin would think the other runner was *me*.

He'd be shot in the back.

Panic filled my throat, squeezing my muscles, until I couldn't breathe.

Somewhere above me, a door slammed.

"She's out on seven." Kevin's tense voice echoed through the stairwell.

I barely heard his words over the pounding of my heart. Then, a second door slammed. The second pair of footsteps were gone.

Kevin had left the stairwell, only the dark figure and I remained. The shooter could still follow an unsuspecting Kevin onto the floor.

I had to catch this guy. I had to stop him.

Adrenaline roared through me. I vaulted over several steps to the landing. Skidded. Caught myself.

The dark figure was almost at the top of the next flight of stairs. I wasn't sure which floor we were on.

Launching myself forward, I flew above the steps. My hands snagged the bottom hem of the hoody in a death grip. Laid out flat, I lost my balance and hit off the steps. Wincing at the pain radiating through my right side, I kept ahold of the hoody while fighting to regain my feet.

The gunman struggled against me, throwing me between the wall and the handrail.

I tightened my grip, set my feet, and pulled with all my strength.

The runner's arms flayed. We hung in the balance. With my breath failing me, I hung on for dear life, suspended on the tip of a stair. Slowly, momentum turned. I pushed against the stair. I felt myself falling. Elation filled me.

The dark figure hurdled through the air, following me down.

Panic at hitting the concrete landing set in right before my butt hit. The impact jarred my spine all the way to my brain. My teeth snapped shut. Pain lanced through my jaw.

The hooded figure grunted as he landed on his shoulder. When his hand hit the floor, a gunshot echoed in the stairwell.

Though he wasn't aiming at me, I cringed without thinking. Chunks fly out of the far wall where the bullet hit.

The deafening noise reverberated across my nerves and ears.

The gunman had landed with his back to me. The hoody hid the face and disguised the form. Gloves covered the hands, including the one still holding the weapon. He started to turn toward me.

I kicked his butt, landing a solid blow that knocked him off-balance. Striking out repeatedly, I pummeled the gunman with both feet.

The figure teetered on the top stair. One last kick on his backside tipped the balance. The guy rolled down the flight of stairs.

A second shot filled the confined space as he tumbled out of control.

The smell of gunpowder filled my nostrils and choked my throat. I put my hands over my ears to contain the noise in my skull.

A string of muted curses sounded beyond the renewed ringing in my ears.

I crouched at the top of the stairs, winded, trying to still the ringing in my ears. I was also petrified. As much as I needed to get a look at the gunman, I have an aversion to being shot.

I'd been lucky so far but in this confined space, that wouldn't last long if the guy got his bearings. Should I peek around the bannister or should I not?

A door slammed shut on the level below me.

Raised voices from the hospital floor pulled me out of my haze. Digging up a measure of courage, I scrambled to my feet, wincing at the pain in my side and back. I ran down the flight of stairs, then through the door. I stopped the first person I saw. "Did you see him?"

The young medical student pointed down a long hall. "That way. Slim build. Dark hoody."

"Stay put." I hotfooted it through the corridor. Darkened offices lined the walls. Deep shadows crowded into the corners. Eventually I hit another stairwell. After listening for a nanosecond, I cracked open the door.

Silence.

I looked up the stairs, then down. The gunman could be on the next landing, around a corner, or at my back.

That's when I quit.

By the time I trudged to the location of the shooting, catastrophe mode was in full swing. The hospital units were locked down. The police had been called. Security guards were out in force.

My jaw ached from clenching it. My head was pounding and I smelled like a gun range at the end of the day. I desperately wanted to find a chair and collapse.

Despite my beat-up condition – I was practicing a martyred tone for my report to Crawford - I found the medical student who'd seen the gunman.

He had little to add. He didn't see a face, only the figure from behind. He wouldn't even swear the shooter was a guy.

Neither could I.

The student's height estimate for the gunman was at least two or three inches shorter than his own six feet, which put the attacker between five-eight or five-ten. Average for a guy. Tallish for a woman.

I didn't have anything concrete either. Not one detail to help me eliminate any suspects. Though Liam Weatherington was far too stout to have been the running figure, he might have hired a flunky. Payton was a possibility. Jamie couldn't be the shooter, but she might be in cahoots with the gunman to set up my mother.

Theories and questions chased each other around my brain until I was dizzy. In between questioning witnesses and waiting for the police to question me, I texted Kevin then waited.

Marcus texted me nonstop for an update on Jamie. When I had a moment, I gave him the quick version: "Lost sight of Kevin and Jamie. Found a gunman. Lost the gunman. Waiting for the police."

Though my body wanted to rest, my mind ran full speed. The gunman hadn't attacked my mother. He'd gone after the younger woman. Would Kevin be able to convince Jamie to speak with the police? Why was she at the hospital? Did she want to speak with me? If so, why not come forward?

In between my answering questions from the cops, Kevin finally texted me. "Cheese-frenchie, onion rings later."

The meal was my greasy diner favorite. That meant he'd achieved his goal. Two items of food meant two people. Him and Jamie.

I frowned at the last word. He wasn't coming right back. Evidently, she wasn't willing to return. Since carrying her by force could be construed as kidnapping, it sounded like we were going to be stashing another witness.

I pocketed my phone. This wouldn't be the first time we'd hidden a witness. I hoped that, unlike a previous case, this witness wouldn't run off the first chance she got.

After giving a statement to the police, who were as unhappy with my lack of details as I'd been with the medical student's, I caught a taxi and headed to the resort. It was still early Sunday afternoon. I was ready to take the rest of the day off.

Crawford's ringtone pulled me from my brief catnap in the back-seat. I groaned and turned the phone's volume down.

"You got trouble." His gravelly voice held a note I couldn't decipher.

"Big surprise." I was beyond caring. I leaned back. "What now?"

His hesitation was unnatural for him. "Come to the office."

I opened my mouth, unsure which of a dozen questions to ask. A click in my ear ended my debate. I changed my destination and fought to keep my eyes open. The day was catching up with me.

Fear.

My eyes popped open. That was the emotion I'd heard in Crawford's voice. Now it settled in my gut.

What had happened that had my boss running scared?

15

—•—

20 Across; 9 Letters;
Clue: Put sounds or images on a disc or a tape
Answer: Recording

My tenth call to Crawford was ringing in my ear when I barreled into his office. I'd confirmed Marcus, my parents, and Rickson had arrived at the resort with no problems. Still no word from Kevin. I pointed my phone at my boss like a weapon. "Why didn't you pick up any of my calls?"

"I talked to you once." Crawford, sitting behind the massive oak desk he loved, looked up from his computer. Never shy about raising his voice, his bellow blasted past me like a hurricane. "That was enough."

He was a solid tank of a man who all but dwarfed the chair he sat in. Pale hair shot with gray was combed straight back. The face, like the body, was worn, but the jaw was square and solid. His craggy face and golden-brown eyes held a worry I'd rarely seen.

My worry multiplied. I'm usually fairly stoic, but an adrenaline-fueled chase and two gunshots at close range had undermined my fortitude. I knew Kevin could hold his own against a ninety-eight-pound waif. However, the gunman might somehow have caught up to them.

I slammed the door behind me. "Is Kevin hurt? Is he in trouble?"

"You're all in trouble." Crawford motioned to a chair at his side. "Sit. You need to see this video."

I plopped down at Crawford's elbow and raked my fingers through my short hair.

"Rabi's meeting Kevin. That's all I know." My boss's tone held no apology.

Fear leeched out of my bones. I closed my eyes in relief, opening them a second later. "You could have told me sooner."

"Don't nag." He waved a massive paw in my direction then returned to his two-fingered hunt and peck method of typing. "After Kevin picks up the Caddy, he'll call to see if you're still here."

"Thanks." I barely had the energy to breathe out the word.

The old bear shot me a flat look. "Always a snappy comeback."

I ignored his sarcasm. "What have you got?"

Crawford's private e-mail was open on the screen. The mouse hovered over a message with no sender named and no subject.

The boss man's expression turned grim. "Something that will put your friend away for life."

A sword to the gut couldn't have cut any deeper. I straightened. "What?"

"Watch."

A tap on the mouse started the show. The video opened to a dim view of a dark room. It took me a moment to realize the cone of illumination cutting across the scene came from a flashlight.

Curiosity took hold of me. I leaned closer, studying the details. "This is the library at Rycliffe, after we went lights out so we could look for spirits."

The view was roughly from the height of a man's waist.

Suddenly, the picture blurred, spinning crazily. Darkness replaced the shelves of books and knick-knacks. A couple of bounces later, the picture solidified.

I twisted my head until it was parallel to the floor, the way the screen was oriented. My gut clenched. "Is this a cell phone?"

Crawford nodded. "The dead man's phone. Best guess is he was holding it by his side trying to record the meeting when he was struck."

A close up of maroon carpet popped into view. The shadowy frame of a doorway hung in the background. The beam of the flashlight wobbled crazily just off screen.

I bit my lip. Anticipation was like a knife across my nerves. There was a slight movement on one side of the frame. "What is that?"

Crawford said not a word.

The blurred image solidified into a pair of pink muffs.

My lungs seized.

My heart sank through my gut to my toes, then kept on falling.

The pink muffs shuffled toward the door. Thin, old lady legs did the fast two-step I'd seen more than once in my life.

The video ran for about three seconds, then clipped off. I stared at the screen, numb. I couldn't think. I couldn't speak.

"According to the time stamp, this happened a few minutes before the old lady met you in the hall." Crawford leaned his arms on his desk. His craggy features tightened. "If she goes down for murder, you and Marcus could be charged as accessories. You covered for her. You lied to the police."

"No, I didn't. Well, sort of, but not really." Latching onto my semi-solid version of the facts jump-started my heart. "I didn't tell the police everyone was in the room at all times. Neither did Marcus. We both said we didn't notice anyone leaving."

Which we hadn't, having left the official tour ourselves.

The worry lines etched into Crawford's face relaxed. "Good. When the detective questions you and Marcus again, and he will, admit nothing."

"How could she lie to me? To Marcus?" The facts didn't compute. Mrs. C had known Marcus longer than I had. Well, she'd known of him. She'd seen him on the streets, after dark, running, hiding. I couldn't believe she would endanger the boy.

"The kid won't talk." Relief underscored Crawford's words. "He knows better."

A hard laugh escaped my lips. "Marcus wouldn't admit anything if they had *him* on tape."

Bitterness darkened my tone.

"Was the phone found on the body?" My mouth took charge while my brain was in shock. "If the police had this video from the beginning, why wait until this morning to pick up Mrs. C?"

For pity's sake, she'd been wearing those bedroom slippers Friday night. She always wore bedroom slippers.

"The phone wasn't found at the murder scene," Crawford answered. "It showed up at the police station early this morning. One of the gawkers pocketed it when the body was discovered."

"Oh, that's convenient." I grabbed onto the suspicious circumstances with both hands. "Anyone could have faked that video."

"Are you listening to yourself?" He jerked a thumb toward the monitor. "It's the victim's phone. It has his contacts, his meetings, his notes, his e-mails. Besides, only six people know you three left the ghost hunters group. Your crew of five and me."

If no one else was aware that Mrs. C was on her own the night of the murder, the video could hardly be an attempt to frame her.

Crawford, a friend for years before becoming my boss, shut off the feed and closed his e-mail. He leaned his beefy arms on the desk. "Cut your losses."

Words of wisdom. No doubt about it. Walking away was my best option.

I stole a glance at the monitor, now showing the mountain lake in Canada where Crawford went fishing every year. A shake of my head failed to dislodge the damning video. The scenes were seared into my mind's eye.

"You're going to continue to investigate, aren't you?"

I lifted my shoulders.

"You're too stubborn for your own good." A frown darkened Crawford's forehead. "All you'll do is prove your friend guilty."

"I can't believe she lied to me." I still couldn't wrap my brain around Mrs. C's betrayal. That hurt more than the possibility of me going to prison.

Crawford's chair squealed in protest as he shifted his heavy frame.

"Think it through. Once you're over the shock. You'll see reason." He paused, studying my face. "Though you've never been reasonable before."

A rueful smile flicked on my lips, only to vanish.

My boss pointed a stubby finger at me. "Talk to Kevin. He's a survivor. He'll help you think with your head, not your heart."

His semi-derogatory tone left no doubt which he thought was the smarter stance.

When I remained silent, Crawford continued. "Your mother was stung by a scorpion this morning. Your parents and your son are in the middle of the enemy camp. Everyone knows you and the boy were at the murder scene."

I forced a swallow down my throat. Danger had sunk its hooks into almost every person I loved. "I know."

"If you continue and things go south, which knowing your luck, they will," he fixed me with an intense stare. "You'll lose that boy. You'll lose everything."

The words knifed through my heart. This was from a man I knew was on my side. "Great pep talk. Thanks."

"Rickson can take over the investigation," Crawford offered.

"Rickson doesn't know the Weatherington crowd." I rubbed a hand over my face. "He doesn't have the in that I do."

I was making excuses to continue investigating. I just wasn't sure why.

Crawford didn't respond. He let the seconds tick by in silence.

"I don't believe Mrs. C is a murderer." There. I'd said it out loud.

Crawford's groan morphed into a growl. "You are the stubbornest, most blockheaded person I know."

I stuck my chin out. "Ever look in a mirror?"

He folded his hands across his stomach. "You want to prove she's innocent."

"I want the truth." I slapped the table hard enough to send pain lancing up my wrist. Great. Now I was reduced to quoting old movie lines. Yet, I'd taunted Liam Weatherington with the same question. Did he want a cover-up or did he want the facts? I took a deep breath and struggled to restore my shattered nerves. "Mrs. C was scared when she ran out of that room."

"Because she'd just killed a man." Crawford responded with a roar that had cleared more than one crack house in his days on the force. "She panicked."

"What's her motive?" Raising my voice helped me blow off steam. I usually love arguing with Crawford.

His oversized shoes hit the floor with a thud. "She flashed back to the attack fifty years ago. If she comes clean, the DA may go easy on her because of her advanced age."

I shook my head. "She'll be admitting to the first murder. So far, no one has tied her to that crime. The English courts could charge her."

My retired cop buddy jabbed a thumb in the direction of the monitor behind him. "She lied to you. She dragged you and your son into possible felony charges. How can you defend her?"

"I'm not defending her." With her on the lam from the police, I also couldn't ask her for an explanation. I let out a sigh. I couldn't let go of the case. My gut had made the decision in the first instant. My brain had needed to work through the shock.

I set my jaw. "I told Liam Weatherington I was going to find the murderer no matter where it led or who it hurt, including him."

"You said that to my client?"

I ignored Crawford's protest. Instead, I held on to my one remaining certainty and met his outraged gaze head-on. "If I expect Weatherington to stomach me proving him or one of his associates a murderer, how can I back down?"

How could I explain quitting to Marcus? My parents? Myself?

"Mom and Pop always said not every horse you breed is a winner." My voice softened as I took refuge in well-worn adages my parents were always spouting. "Neither is every person a shining soul. You take the good with the bad in this world."

Had I thrown enough clichés around to buffer me from reality?

"You're naïve enough to believe in happy endings. You think she might be innocent." Crawford delivered the judgment in his version of a stage whisper. "What are you going to do?"

"Stick to the plan." Really, I had no plan. From the amused glimmer in my bossman's eyes, I wasn't fooling either of us. I also had few leads and one more suspect than when I'd stormed into the room. "I have to hook up with Kevin. I have to question my family to find out how Jamie acted after Mom got stung. Then, I'll attend tonight's auction and rattle the Jerrone cages."

Sure, I needed more trouble.

I hadn't gone into detail with Crawford about Kevin hiding a suspect. After twenty-five years on the force, Crawford could put two and two together. Sometimes he came up with four.

Hopefully the police wouldn't ask me about Jamie's whereabouts. Unlike books and movies, the authorities take a dim view of being deceived on an active murder investigation. Since I was already on thin ice, I didn't need to supply the cops with an excuse to take a closer look at my actions.

"I don't know what happened fifty years ago at the first murder scene." Considering what I'd just seen, I'd have to re-think Mrs. C's version of history. "I don't know for sure what happened two days ago."

The realization was incredibly unsettling. From the beginning I'd had few certainties in this case. Now even those slender threads were being ripped away. "I only know I will find out the truth."

No matter who it hurt.

I'd never dreaded resolving a case more. How could I face my son or my friends if I proved Mrs. C guilty of two murders?

Yet, leaving an unanswered question in a crossword puzzle would haunt me. To solve the puzzle, I had to solve the case.

16

19 Across; 7 Letters;
Clue: A series of waves on the water
Answer: Ripples

Hours later, Crawford's dire warnings still circled me like vultures. A long, hot shower and a hot cup of coffee on the quiet patio restored some semblance of calm. A solution remained out of reach.

Kevin joined me in the suite to get ready for tonight's auction. Now, Marcus, Kevin, and I strolled through the resort's rock garden. The scant shade from the palm trees cast a pattern of light and shadow on our clothes and skin.

Kevin scanned the area before continuing his report. "Jamie felt spirits walking the halls the night of Neville's murder."

Luckily, there was no one around to hear my snort of derision. My parents had headed to the auction under Rickson's hawk-like gaze. They wanted time to study the artwork and the bidders.

I'd delayed leaving so I could have privacy to tell my son about the incriminating video, which he'd dismissed out of hand. I also couldn't wait to hear what Jamie told Kevin.

I'd anticipated solid facts, a clue, *something*. "This 'spirits on the loose' story is her explanation for bolting from the police station and the hospital this morning?"

My frustration meter rose to the boiling point. I exhaled noisily as a gust of air swept off the desert. Overhead, billowy, white clouds rolled across the sky.

"She felt the presence of an old evil." Kevin spoke with a straight face, which was more than I could manage.

I rolled my eyes at Jamie's cop out. "Oh, please."

A grin split Marcus's face. He pointed at my expression. "Good thing you didn't question her, T.R."

Kevin smiled briefly, before his tone turned serious. "She said the Jerrone party had been on edge since they arrived. Neville spoke with her repeatedly. Told her about his father's murder and the lead on the killer."

Marcus raised a fist. "He got her on his side and she let him into Rycliffe, where he met the *killer*. Dun. Dun. Dun."

Reports complete with dramatic music.

Kevin, used to the dramatic soundtrack, continued without comment. "They entered around two o'clock. She helped him avoid the cleaning crew, got him into the library, and left him there. No one else was in the building."

"So far as she knew." I built the scene in my mind, complete with a timetable to one side.

A sharp shake of Kevin's head shot down my burgeoning theory about the killer hiding in the closet. "Neville and Jamie waited until the janitors left. According to Jamie, the cleaning crew goes through every room. She doesn't think it's possible anyone else could have been in the building at that point."

"She told Neville he'd be alone in the building." I was as certain as if I'd been there. Kevin's nod confirmed my assumption. "The victim arrived hours earlier than expected. The broken step prevented Mrs. C from being in the library on time. So much for planning the perfect murder."

My son snapped his fingers. "It's like that Grace Kelly movie, *Dial M for Murder*. The husband thought he had everything covered. He was wrong, just like our killer. That's why we'll get him."

Oh, the confidence of youth. Not to mention spending many an evening critiquing movie murders and plots with me and Mrs. C.

"When Neville was murdered, Jamie felt responsible... and scared." Kevin lowered his voice as a foursome dressed in evening attire approached. When they were out of earshot, he continued. "She didn't tell the police any of this."

No wonder the police constantly work under a handicap. No one tells the truth. "Jamie left out a lot of important facts."

"She thought she might be charged as an accessory." Kevin gestured to an open area with a small waterfall. "Ever since Neville's death, she's had bad vibes."

"Murder will do that." Especially when you're neck deep in the details and lies of omission to the police. Unable to listen to the mumbo-jumbo any longer, I opened my mouth to demand facts.

"You want specifics?" Kevin, sensing my frustration, answered my unspoken question. "After the murder, she started noticing doubles. First, Payton. Disguised on Friday night, she came as herself Saturday. Then, a second woman appeared twice."

A dip in Kevin's tone and a tightening around his eyes sent a worm of worry crawling up my spine.

He paused before continuing. "Jamie saw Mrs. Colchester at Rycliffe the night of the murder. She saw her again this morning when your mother was stung by the scorpion."

"That's impossible." Marcus exploded instantly. "I would have known if Mrs. Colchester was at the reptile place."

I jumped on the defensive bandwagon as well. "Mrs. C couldn't have been at Rowdy Reptiles. She was with Rabi this morning."

"Until she took a powder right before the police arrived," Kevin interjected.

I continued without pause. "When was Mom stung? Before or after Mrs. C disappeared?"

"The cops won't take Rabi's word for it." Kevin's firm voice slid between the point, counter-point argument. "He could have driven her there and back without anyone knowing. No one in the neighborhood saw Mrs. Colchester today."

The implications of Kevin's words added another brick to the load on my shoulders. I put my head in my hands. "Not Rabi, too. This case is sucking everyone into trouble."

I straightened, refusing to let worry drag me down. "Jamie gave the ID to the police?"

Kevin nodded. "Gray-haired woman. Colorful muumuu. Pink slippers. Jamie noticed the woman going toward your mother rather than the exit. Marcus and your dad were handling a tarantula. Their backs were to both women. The woman pulled her hand out of her pocket, brushed against your mom, then slipped in among the crowd. Jamie didn't see her after that."

Marcus bunched his fists. "This is a frame."

"A solid frame." A hint of grudging admiration sounded in Kevin's tone. "Mrs. Colchester's distinctive appearance makes her an easy person to recall."

The attack on my mother had been a warning. It had also consolidated the frame against Mrs. C. "Mrs. C has no reason to hurt my mother. Why would the police believe she did this?"

Though knowing the alleged motive wouldn't change things, I had to have the answer. Since the rock garden gave me a clear view of the deserted surroundings, I knew I was safe calling my boss man. A moment later, Crawford provided the supposed reason.

With the volume on low and my two guys crowded around me, my boss's delivery resounded in the air. "Wilson believes your friend is worried because – get this – you're getting too close to unmasking the killer."

I didn't flinch at his skepticism. Honestly, I had to stifle a laugh that *anyone* believed I had the killer pegged.

Crawford, of course, wasn't done. "Not that I know what's going on since I haven't seen one of your elusive reports."

I ground my teeth together. "It's Sunday afternoon. The man hasn't been dead forty-eight hours. I have more suspects and motives than I know what to do with. Don't worry. You'll get your reports."

I cast my son a questioning glance. At his thumbs up, I gave him a conspiratorial wink. "I'll send one this afternoon."

"Thank you, Marcus." Crawford's sarcasm was as thick as molasses. "Belden, get to work."

When he hung up with a final growl, I gripped my phone in a stranglehold.

Kevin chuckled as he put his arms around me. "Don't take it out on the phone. You'll figure it out."

His affection and confidence enveloped me like the warm breath of spring. I took a deep breath and gave a slow ten count. Time to focus on the big picture. "Let's solve our Jamie issue while we head for the auction. Why was she at the hospital?"

"This way." Kevin kept his hand on my waist as we reached the end of the path. An uncharacteristic coolness blew in off the desert as the sun drooped lower in the sky. "Jamie felt the darkness hovering over your parents. That's why she insisted on going to Rowdy Reptiles. She hid in the hospital to watch your mother in case the older woman came around again."

Marcus quickened his pace to get in front of Kevin. The boy turned then stopped on a dime. "Do you believe her?"

"Yes." Though my boyfriend responded without hesitation, he couldn't hide his disappointment. "I was facing her and holding her wrist while she answered. Her pulse remained steady."

My son kicked at the gravel with his sneakers as he fell in step with us again.

I shared his pain. Darn Kevin and his talents. Not only had he been trained since birth to spot the most gullible mark in a crowd, he knew the tricks to be a human lie detector.

The hand on her wrist would be taken as a sign of comfort. In fact, he had his fingers on her pulse, easy to note if her heart rate sped up or if her breathing changed.

"Sometimes I wish you weren't so good at reading people," I admitted. I fell in step on the cobblestones. "Jamie was the perfect accomplice for the killer."

"Not that easy this time, Sherlock." My handsome guy shook his head in mock sympathy. "You and Watson are going to have to figure this out using your brains."

Marcus, with a quicksilver mood shift, straightened his shoulders. "No problem."

"Right." My dejected tone had to climb out of the basement. Unlike my son, I had no false bravado left. "As soon as the murderer raises his hand so I have a way to identify the killer."

"They'll make a mistake." Marcus assured me with a confident tone. "It's only a matter of time."

I looked him up and down. "Are we working the same case? 'Cause I'm not seeing that version."

"Once the big picture comes into focus, you'll see it all." He spread his hands wide and gave me a Cheshire Cat grin. "I'll help, of course. You'd be lost without me and the crew."

Kevin snickered. "In more ways than one."

I drew myself up. "Are you impugning my sense of direction?"

My guy twined his fingers with mine. "Only because you couldn't find your way to the corner store without the street signs."

I kissed Kevin on the cheek. "This is true."

Marcus slapped his forehead. "Enough with the mush. Back to business."

His voice mixed with the classic music drifting on the desert air. A murmur of voices floated atop the notes. Lights and activity drifted out of the French doors that opened into the ballroom.

Time to form a plan. I crossed my arms over my chest and tried to look fierce. "How about we narrow down the suspects for the shooter? The person I chased up those stairs wasn't an old woman. The gunman was young, fairly slim, less than six feet tall. Who fits that description?"

"Payton." Kevin held up one finger. "Barnes, the Jerrone auctioneer. He's bound to move up the ladder with Neville dead."

My son's brow furrowed in thought. "Archie Smythe."

Kevin and I turned as one. Our puzzled expressions matched as well.

Marcus stared at us. "The guy who found and authenticated the sketch."

"How do you know he fits the bill?" I asked.

"I looked him up. This auction is the score of a lifetime." The boy threw his hands in the air. "He's old, forty-three. Kind of skinny. Sandy hair. A couple inches taller than you."

"Did I miss a meeting?" The sun threw Kevin's face into shadow, but his amusement came through clearly.

My boy shrugged. "It's been a busy weekend. I was going to give a report at the auction."

"It's starting soon." I made a herding motion with my hand. "Tell me when Archie arrived in town."

Marcus shrugged. "I said he's the right size. I didn't say he was here. He's not coming to Langsdale. I downloaded a lot of stuff but, with what happened to Gram, I didn't read it all."

Kevin laid a hand on the boy's shoulder. "It's been a busy day. Dig into Archie Smythe. See what you can find out about his movements during the past month."

My hand brushed across the long, soft needles of a fir tree. "Look into his whereabouts last year, before and after he found the sketch. What else was he doing during that time period?"

I blinked as I heard the words come out of my mouth. My mental crossword puzzle was already rearranging clues and the mostly empty grid for this line of investigation. Nothing about Archie struck me as suspicious, but I was willing to go after anyone in order to clear Mrs. C.

Both of my guys studied me. Fortunately, they knew me too well to think I could provide answers. "I have another assignment for you."

Marcus puffed out his chest to make his thin frame look larger. "Do your worst."

"Recheck Gracie Linden's career." With all the threads running through this case, that strand kept reappearing. "Weatherington admitted she had technical skill as an art restorer. Did she have any shows of her own work before the first murder?"

A calculating gleam took hold in Marcus's eyes. He pulled out his phone, a gift from Rabi. His straight, black hair reflected the sun as he gave a sharp nod. "With the publicity on this case, the Internet is flooded with stories about her past."

"Why does it matter?" Kevin put a hand around my shoulders, going into party mode as we approached the buzz of activity ahead of us.

"Mrs. C believes Gracie was the next Picasso." I darted a glance toward the well-lit doors, but no one was close enough to hear my low tone. "Weatherington dismissed her talent for originality as mediocre. My gut says once we know which version is the truth, we'll know who killed Neville."

"Never argue with the gut," Marcus told Kevin in a resigned tone. "You won't win."

"Because her gut isn't logical," Kevin said

I clasped his hand. "My gut may not be logical, but it's usually right. I feel as if I'm spinning in place. Are the Infantino forgeries the motive? Was Neville's position at Jerrone at the heart of his murder? Does the answer lie in the past or the present? Gracie is the thread that ties everything together."

Both of the guys stared at me, obviously wondering where I was heading with this line of inquiry. I didn't blame them. I didn't have a clue.

Kevin looked over his shoulder at the desert falling into shadows behind us. Then he jerked his head toward the building, now painted with a golden hue as the sun started its descent. "Time for the auction. If we're lucky, someone is ready to confess."

"Sure," I said. "We all know how my luck runs."

I work three jobs: a P.I., my and Kevin's contracting company, and creating crossword puzzles to feed my soul and keep me in coffee money. Need I say more about my luck?

When we drew closer to the ballroom, Marcus called my dad. My parents met us at the door.

My mother and I walked in side-by-side. Pop and my two guys sauntered in behind us. Rickson, on full alert, brought up the rear. Unlike Saturday evening, no one met us at the door of the ballroom. Thank, goodness.

"I'm glad that falderal is over." My mother sighed. "Hard to believe it's been less than twenty-four hours since we first stepped into this room."

I gave a rueful laugh. "Between you being stung, me chasing Jamie, then losing a gunman, it's been a full day."

I scanned the large room, searching in vain for any sign of Payton or Holly. Craning my neck toward the podium in front, I noted Liam Weatherington's absence as well. It was early yet. The auction wouldn't start for over an hour.

The Jerrone representatives might be behind the scenes. Holly should be front and center, especially with Jamie, her waif-like assistant, missing in action.

The well-heeled attendees mingled beside the open bars as waiters offered trays laden with an array of finger-foods.

Mom tapped my arm. "The resort switched the color scheme. All new centerpieces and accessories. I like the contrast between the dark blue flowers and the dusky gray ferns."

I'd noticed the switch during my scan. "They remind me of the wildflowers that bloom on the hills at home."

Mom smiled nostalgically. "You and your sister used to bring me bouquets from the meadows when you were little."

The words brought back memories of a childhood spent running through the Kentucky hills with a dog barking at our heels and the sun high in the sky. "You always put our crushed little offerings in vases like they were a florist's bouquets."

The laugh lines around her eyes deepened. "I'd rather have flowers from my children than an arrangement from a high-priced florist any day."

Though the past was clearly etched in my mind's eye, I continued to search the crowd. "Do you remember when we laid out the flowers and ironed them between wax paper?"

My mother nodded. "I still have those arrangements. I put them in scrapbooks for you and your brothers and sister."

I was touched but not surprised. Saving crayon pictures and memories of childhood was right up my mother's alley. Good report cards, pictures of our 4H activities, and sporting highlights were also carefully cataloged.

"I saved Marcus's early gifts. Not wildflowers, but dioramas made from rusty metal and pieces of plastic collected from the streets. They're amazingly detailed."

"You showed me on our last visit. I'd love to see them again." She graced me with a look of pride. Her words reminded me this wasn't the first time I'd waxed on about my son's creations. "He's been good for you. You've forged your own family out here."

Comfort filled me at the welcome realization of my odd but loyal family. "I hope I can do him justice. I worry that surrounding him with criminal cases and leading him into these dangerous situations sets a bad example."

She thought for a moment, then dismissed my concerns with a wave of her hand. "You and your friends look out for him. Your cases show him that there is justice for innocent people."

"You think?" Surprise rippled through me at the spin my mother put on my profession. My main motive for keeping my investigating job with Crawford was to pay the bills until my house painting and fix-it business with Kevin took off.

"Shift to the right, people." Marcus's commanding tone interrupted my moment of pride. "The food is that way."

In addition to the wandering waitstaff, an assortment of hors d'oeuvres graced several tables along the wall. Sparkling fountains of punch sat next to coffee urns.

I gave the boy an arched look over my shoulder even as my mother and I diverted toward the refreshments.

My son shot me an innocent look. "I'm a growing boy. No one's fed me for at least an hour."

My father clapped him on the shoulder. "That's the idea. Go for the feedbag."

A chuckle escaped my mother's lips. "That boy definitely made it to the right family. He is so like you were at that age."

Marcus wiggled his way between us.

Dad put his hand on my mother's spine as he caught up to us as well. "Lighter fare than last night."

The shift gave me the chance to drift to Kevin's side. I took the opportunity to exchange a quick look with Rickson as well.

He gave a reassuring nod. His gaze constantly scanned the crowd in threat assessment mode. His set jaw and determined look made him even more formidable than his behemoth build.

Kevin put an arm around my waist, drawing me closer. "No sign of the main players. Weatherington and Payton should be on duty."

"With Jamie out of action, Holly should be running at full throttle." The words had barely left my mouth when a hard staccato of high heels descended on me from behind.

Nails dug into my shoulder. Before I could react, Holly stepped in front of me. Her hand gripped my arm.

The resort's main PR representative wore a navy-blue sheath dress with a classic cut and a matching jacket. Simple gold earrings and a gold link necklace were her only pieces of jewelry. Her long blond locks had been pulled into a waterfall of curls. She looked elegant and professional, except for her tight expression and the panic in her eyes.

"Thank heavens, I found you." She managed to get the words out without moving her lips, which were locked in a large, toothy smile. "Payton has disappeared. She should have been here hours ago. She insisted yesterday that she had to supervise the arrangement of tonight's pieces."

Holly shifted her frozen smile over my shoulder. She aimed a princess wave at someone out of my view, before she turned to me.

I take pride in my ability to dissemble, but the ability to talk without moving my mouth has always eluded me. I wondered how long she could keep it up. Her frozen gaze made her control look dicey.

In a heartbeat, Holly's false grin trembled then collapsed completely. Her pale, pink nails dug into my upper arms. "What are we going to do? People are dropping like flies. First Neville, then Jamie. Now Payton."

The hysteria train was running full speed. I raised a hand as I opened my mouth to respond, but her frenzy sped on unabated.

Holly drew a quick breath. "What if they've been kidnapped? They may be being held for ransom."

A kidnapper and a murderer in the same case? "I don't think so."

My words had no effect on the panic train.

"They could be dead." She tightened her grip on my arms, ignoring my wince of pain. "Three murders. That means we have a serial killer in the resort, among the guests."

Her high-pitched voice rose with each word, edging toward an all-out screech.

Her words filtered through the murmured conversations. Heads began to turn our way.

I put my hands on her shoulders, while twisting out of her vise-like grip. "Breathe, Holly. Breathe."

She stopped and stared into my eyes as she drew in a trembling breath.

Her hysterical report had taken her only seconds.

Seeing that my parents had stopped a short distance ahead of me, I waved them on toward the food and drink.

Rickson stuck with my parents.

Marcus slipped to my side. With the boy's ability to sniff out mystery, he wasn't about to miss breaking news.

"Jamie and Payton are not dead." In the case of the young PR assistant, I was certain. Rabi had her under his care. As for Payton... that was more of a gut feeling. The murderer never gets killed, okay, rarely gets killed, and not until the end. Either way. "I'd stake my reputation they'll both show up alive and well."

Since I had no real reputation to risk, that bet was totally safe.

Holly's long blond curls bobbed as she clutched her heart. "What a relief. You wouldn't risk your impeccable reputation unless you were certain."

Marcus turned what sounded like a chuckle into a cough, thumping his chest and pointing to his throat when I gave him the eagle eye.

I didn't waste time looking at Kevin. With his icy control, his guffaws would be on the inside.

How could I chide them? An impeccable reputation? Seriously. I forced what I hoped was a reassuring smile. "I assume Payton is not answering her cell. When did anyone see her last?"

Holly flashed a professional and sincere looking smile at a passing couple. Older, stiff, and self-assured, something about his attitude screamed a politician with matching spouse. Someone the PR rep would know by sight and would want to stay on their good side.

Once the pair were past, Holly's mask gave way to concern. "Payton was organizing the pieces in order of presentation. She took a call, lost all color, and bolted. That was... "

Holly's gaze darted to her phone. "It's four now. That was right after two o'clock."

"Two hours." With a murderer wandering around, I had to admit that was long enough to be concerned. "Did you contact Mr. Weatherington?"

Holly smoothed her dress. "He's looking into it. He'll get back to me if he has news."

I exchanged a glance with both the males at my side. Liam Weatherington's response was not that of a worried man.

Kevin shifted. "Did you notify the police? With Neville dead and Jamie missing, they'd take Payton's no-show seriously."

Holly took a steadying breath. "Mr. Weatherington said if it came to that, he'd call them."

No need to let a small thing like a disappearance and another possible murder ruin a night of heavy money.

I didn't think she was in danger, because she was my front runner in the suspect race. Weatherington should have been concerned. I put a hand on Holly's arm. "It sounds like Mr. Weatherington may have sent her on a private mission for the company."

"I should have thought of that." A rush of air escaped the woman's parted lips. Color returned to her cheeks. The perky meter was rising in her eyes. "You're so smart. That's why you're the professional."

That and a continuing need to pay the bills.

My peripheral vision caught Marcus and Kevin exchanging a skeptical glance. I stuck to reassuring Holly. "I'll follow up with Mr. Weatherington to confirm Payton is safe. Do you know where he is?"

"He hasn't answered my calls. I'm certain you'll be able to locate him." The lights reflecting off Holly's toothy smile almost blinded me. She clasped her hands together. "What a relief. I'll leave the matter in your capable hands."

"You do that."

Holly's attention shifted to the room at large. When her eyes darted toward the food and drink stations, alarm tightened her features. "That display is in the wrong place."

Without another word, she swiveled on her stilettos to weave through the shifting masses. A woman on a mission.

As was I. It was time to hunt down my buddy, Liam Weatherington.

17

——— ✲ ———

6 Down; 8 Letters;
Clue: Regarded as more important
Answer: Priority

I left the ballroom filled with a sense of purpose. I had clues, suspects, and crimes, but how did they fit together? With questions swirling in my brain and blanks in my crossword puzzle, the need for answers consumed me.

Kevin and Marcus followed me as I swam against the tide of last-minute arrivals. Out in the corridor, I quickened my pace. "This doesn't make sense. What could be so important that Liam Weatherington would skip his high-stakes auction?"

"Covering his tracks in a murder," Kevin suggested.

I'd called Weatherington's cell with no luck. Not that I'd expected him to answer.

Marcus's fingers were flying on his phone, no doubt searching for information on Gracie's background. He looked up. "Bet I find factoids about Gracie's career before you find your guy."

Why had he thought of that now? I'd forgotten my earlier request, but the boy loved competition. Happy to have his attention diverted, I answered his evil laugh with a mock glare. "Game on."

As soon as I spoke, I knew I stood a good chance of losing.

"He wouldn't be in his suite." I intended to find Weatherington if I had to track him all night. "I'm betting he's in the offices assigned to Jerrone. With the rest of the team at the auction, he'd have the place to himself. A good place to hide."

Judging from Kevin's expression he obviously realized I was trying to convince myself. "You're the card-carrying P.I.."

Marcus cast Kevin a sidelong glance. "It's the gut again."

I just hoped the gut was right.

Kevin led the way through an annoying maze of twisting halls.

Marcus walked and talked with his gaze glued to the phone. "Gracie did jobs for her family's art restoration business while still in her teens. The article says: 'her technical expertise was brilliant.'"

"That's old news." I strode down the corridor, wondering whether Gracie or Liam held the key to Neville's murder. "Your assignment was to find out her plans for the future."

"I'm closing in on the goods." Marcus swiped a thumb across the screen. "Kevin, walk slower."

Despite my son's stage whisper, our steady pace carried us through the quiet halls in no time.

Though Kevin hid it well, his attitude had grown edgier. He carried himself with the air of a panther ready to pounce.

Only our long friendship helped me recognize the tension simmering below the surface. My fingers brushed his hand. "What are you thinking?"

He glanced over his shoulder at the boy he'd spent almost as much time raising as I had. "The killer is building to a big final act."

Though I knew Kevin hadn't meant to add to my burden, I felt the pressure of trying to out-think a murderer. After all, I was the one who had led my family and friends into a dangerous situation.

"I have the killer right where I want them, confident they're going to get away." Which might well happen since I had more theories than I needed, coupled with absolutely no proof. While my light-hearted tone may have covered my uncertainty, Kevin knew me too well to be convinced.

"Got it." Marcus's triumphant tone rang out as we turned into the corridor leading to the Jerrone offices. "I think."

Kevin turned with the air of a hunter. "What'd you find?"

My son's eyes flicked over the phone's screen. "Her sister said in an early article that Gracie's absence left a hole in the family business of art restoration. Gracie was the most talented in the family and planned to take over the business when their dad retired. Gracie wouldn't do that if she was a great painter."

His comment fed into my idea that Gracie's future as an artist hadn't been as bright as Mrs. C believed. "Any mention of her building a career or having her own shows?"

Marcus read for another minute before looking up. "Nothing about her selling her own stuff. Staying with the family business was her plan. I win."

My son held up his phone while his confident gaze turned to Kevin, pushing for my boyfriend's vote.

Kevin winked and nodded. "I agree."

A ding drew the boy's attention back to his device and saved me from conceding defeat.

He tapped the screen. "Results on my Archie Smythe search."

I glanced up and down the corridor as if Weatherington might be eavesdropping, but there was no sign of life. "See what you can find, maestro."

The boy chuckled. "I got this."

Kevin and I shared a smile. Marcus had changed so much in the three plus years he'd been with me. With his confidence and skills, the future lay open before him. If he'd remained on the street would he even be alive?

Kevin read my somber mood with an eagle eye. "I see you're still delegating the hard stuff."

Glad to be diverted by his teasing, I slid my gaze sideways. "I have to save myself for theorizing. Not everyone can come up with an unending string of half-baked ideas."

"Focus, people." Marcus's command cut through our banter. "I found something on Archie. This is strange."

His words piqued my curiosity, but we'd reached the office door. I waved the ID card Holly had provided to get past the electronic reader. A flashing green light and a soft click confirmed our entry. Marcus pocketed his phone.

The silence of the offices settled around my shoulders. Empty. I clutched the plastic card until the edges dug into my palm. I'd guessed wrong. I'd have to start over.

As I sought for another avenue to explore, Kevin tensed, then he pointed toward a corridor leading to a rear office.

I heard nothing. However, he'd never led me wrong. I marched down the hall. When I was two feet from the door, I heard a noise from within. I threw the door open without knocking.

Liam Weatherington stopped in mid-stride in front of a large oak desk. His hands were clasped behind him. He spun around. Hope lit his gaze. As soon as he recognized me his expression fell like a popped balloon.

I planted myself in front of him, fisting my hands on my hips. "Why aren't you at the auction?"

He stared at me as if I'd pole-axed him. "I... I'm... "

"Has Payton returned from her errand?" I changed my tone to curious rather than suspicious. "I have more questions for her."

"I... " Weatherington gestured toward the desk covered with papers. "She's... "

His square face settled into a glare. He collected himself with an effort. "I should never have hired you."

"Probably not." I felt a twinge of sympathy for his plight. "It's going to look awkward when I prove you guilty of the murder you paid me to investigate."

His eyes bulged out of his head. "I didn't kill my brother."

"And you evidently don't care who did." My voice rose in anger. "Because you've been withholding information from day one."

He drew himself up. "I never lied."

"Quit splitting hairs." While telling half-truths is one of my favorite tactics, it's not something I appreciate in clients. "I know the truth."

I stared him down, letting the questions and uncertainty build in his mind.

His eyes narrowed, trying to read behind my mask. How much did I know? What secret should he confess? In the end, he said nothing.

"Payton lied." About practically everything if my suspicions were correct. I made a mental note never to play poker with the woman. "Where is she?"

My erstwhile client wiped a band of sweat off his forehead and half-stumbled to a chair by the desk. "At another meeting."

Shock rippled through me. "Not with the murderer?"

"You let her go alone?" Kevin's tone was incredulous. "She could be killed."

"Not if she's behind the scheme," Marcus's murmur was too low for anyone but me to hear.

I gave him a quick nod. Suspicious soul that I am, I thought the same thing. She could be tying up loose ends; find Jamie, finish what she started at the hospital. Of course, if Payton *was* murdered, she'd prove me wrong. Then I'd have to find another suspect.

Weatherington rose to his full height like a stung bear. "I didn't *let* her do anything. She got the call. She agreed to the meeting. She called me after she left."

Whether Payton was guilty or innocent, I needed to know the cover story. "Who is she meeting?"

Weatherington drew on a mantle of arrogance to hide his flustered emotions. "She's meeting Gracie Linden."

"No, I'm not." Payton's sharp tone caused my heart to do a stutter-step. The younger woman stood in the doorway, her face tired and drawn. "Whoever called me was a no-show. I don't know why they dragged me out there, but at least I'm still breathing."

18

27 Across; 9 Letters;
Clue: Double dealing
Answer: Duplicity

"Gracie Linden didn't show?" Liam Weatherington managed to look both relieved and disappointed.

I was simply relieved even though I knew Gracie was never going to show up. She was dead, and innocent of both murders. It was Gracie's relatives - sister, brother, niece, nephew – who were pulling Payton's strings.

"I don't know who called me." Payton took a steadying breath. "The voice was filtered through a computer. My contact said they had information that could expose Gracie."

"That's how Neville got killed." Kevin smacked one hand into another with a resounding clap. His action interrupted Weatherington and Payton's sidebar conversation.

"No one has seen or spoken with Gracie in fifty years." I spread out my arms. "Yet she has you crossing continents and jumping at her commands. Come to Langsdale. Have an auction. Meet me at a haunted house. Why would you or Neville agree to these bizarre demands?"

Because of the forgeries, of course. But I needed to get that out in the open without revealing that Mrs. C had already told me their secret.

"Only one reason." Kevin started walking forward. "A threat to the Jerrone reputation would make you jump like puppets on a string."

Weatherington held his breath. His shocked gaze followed Kevin's every move.

Payton's expression tightened, but she revealed nothing.

His spot-on guess, seemingly coming out of nowhere, laid bare their darkest secret.

Kevin came even with me, stopping slightly to my left. "Your contact threatened to reveal that Jerrone knowingly authenticated Infantinos forged by Gracie Linden."

The older man barreled onward. "How dare you accuse my company of misrepresentation? Our reputation is flawless."

"Which is why you'd do anything to protect it." I infused my tone with absolute certainty. Attitude is everything in a bluff. "Any fact can be uncovered with a bit of computer savvy."

Not *my* savvy, but he didn't need to know that detail. I pointed to Marcus. "Tell them."

"The Internet is your friend. It has everything." Marcus wiggled his fancy phone. "I downloaded old photos of the original murder scene. Lots of blood."

"Don't." Weatherington raised a hand, palm out. "Finding my father's body traumatized my mother. She never entered his office again."

His words tripped a trigger in my brain, but nothing came into the light. I wished my brain would communicate better. Until it did, I brought my scattered thoughts in line.

"That's not all I found." Marcus paused, building the tension. "In the past four years, you bought back three of the Infantinos your father authenticated during the year he was with Gracie Linden. The fourth Infantino sold by Jerrone is in a museum on the east coast."

Weatherington scoffed. "The purchases were a marketing ploy to drive up the price after the sketch was sold."

A world-weary expression played over Kevin's handsome features. "Archie Smythe discovered the sketch a year ago."

"I... " Weatherington sputtered to a stop. His brow furrowed as he thought through the sequence of events.

"It's okay." I felt for the man, even if he was a conspirator. "I know how hard it is to come up with a flawless story under pressure. Trust me, I've been caught out a time or two myself."

"She's had a *lot* of practice," Marcus assured him.

I shot my son a look before turning to Weatherington. He stared back with fire in his eyes. "We know Gracie forged those paintings. Quit wasting my time or *I'll* go to the media."

The man's jaw stiffened. Looking ready for a brawl, he eyed Kevin, but my guy stopped him with a look.

Spoiling for a fight, Weatherington stabbed a meaty finger in my direction. "You've been working with that murderess all along. That's the only way you could have known."

Unlike Kevin, I was happy to step into the boxing ring. "I am not working with Gracie Linden."

No way to collect cash from a corpse. Unless my suspicion that Mrs. C was actually Gracie proved to be true.

I poked Weatherington in the shoulder. "If you'd been honest with me, I wouldn't have had to waste so much time unraveling your and Payton's lies."

My attack put him on his heels, but only briefly.

He thrust his big head closer. "How did you know about the forgeries?"

I searched for an answer that wouldn't unveil Mrs. C's existence. To buy time, I pulled on my best snarky sneer and rocked on my heels.

"We didn't know." Despite the boiling emotion in the room, Kevin's voice remained non-confrontational. "You just confirmed our theory. Three Infantinos found in two years? Add in a talented art restorer. It was all there."

Thank God for Kevin and his clear head.

Weatherington's jaw tightened.

"Would you work with me?" I spread out my hands and lowered my voice. It was time to defuse the situation. "You want to know how I knew? I guessed. It's what I do in these cases. I take bits and pieces and I add them together."

I paused to give the man a chance to calm down and think.

"Your father had an affair with a superb art copyist the same year he miraculously discovers a lost Infantino? That story is the epitome of why police don't believe in coincidences."

Payton gave me a hard stare through lowered lids. Her lips curled in disgust. "Liam, I hate to admit it, but we need her help."

"And another thing." I don't know why I never shut up when I'm ahead. "I don't appreciate that you've been in contact with the killer. Neither will the police."

"If only you'd lived up to your reputation." The man's solid fist smacked the desk as he strode past it. "You find the murderer. The forgeries remain a secret. Why didn't you stick to the plan?"

As if I ever had a plan.

Payton's jaw tightened. "If this comes out, it will destroy the company. You have to help us."

"It would be easier with all the facts." I didn't like her belligerent attitude. "When did this person first contact you?"

She looked like a deer caught in the headlights. Then, her expression turned to one of grudging resignation. "Yesterday. Saturday. The caller said Gracie was in the area and they were willing to provide information."

I took a step back in the opulent office. I needed cooperation. Giving her more space, should lessen the antagonism on both our parts. "Did they mention the forgeries?"

She cast a quick glance at Weatherington.

He stared down his nose for a moment, then nodded.

Payton pressed her lips together, then relented and let the words escape. "I laughed when the caller told me about the fakes. Then, she said to talk to Liam."

"I knew the caller could only be Gracie Linden." Weatherington sounded more resigned than angry. "She swore she'd reveal the truth if we didn't follow her instructions."

This didn't sound like what I knew of Mrs. C. But did I know her at all? The video from the victim's cell phone seemed to prove she'd killed him. Yet, the caller could still be one or both of Gracie's siblings who knew of the forgeries.

My pulse jumped at the possibility of another explanation. Or Payton could be making up the call to cover her own guilt while she gets a hefty blackmail payoff.

Pick a theory. Any theory.

"Who else knows about the forgeries?" Kevin inserted the question seamlessly.

Weatherington's haughty attitude returned. "My mother told my brother and me. She didn't want us taken unawares if someone discovered one of the three paintings were fakes."

"Four," I corrected. "You sold one ten years later, the one that matches this sketch."

Weatherington's brow furrowed. Then, his expression stiffened. He raised his chin. "That is an original Infantino. Its provenance has been verified by more than one expert."

Kevin studied the man with an intense gaze.

I didn't stop to think. My mouth took off. "The signature block on the painting doesn't match the one on the sketch that you're selling. One of them is a fake."

The older man's confident attitude didn't waver. He shook his head. "The sketch was made before the artist developed his style. None of the signatures from that year match the paintings."

Why didn't anyone tell me these things? I exchanged a glance with Kevin, who gave an infinitesimal nod. Shock rippled through me. Weatherington was telling the truth? "You're saying the painting in the museum and the sketch it matches, the one being auctioned off, are both originals?"

"Yes." The Jerrone owner spoke with a ring of authority. He threw in a patronizing tone for good measure.

While my brain ran around in circles, I fought to wrap my mind around the concept. "They're the real thing? Both legit?"

Weatherington exhaled slowly. "Yes."

Marcus gave a high-pitched whistle. "I did not see that coming."

"Neither did I." The ground beneath my case, already shaky, crumbled beneath my feet. I'd believed knowledge of the forgeries was the motive for Neville's murder. I kept up a brave front as one corner of my crossword puzzle simply evaporated.

Where did I go from here?

Payton looked to her boss before facing me. "Infantino gave the sketch away long before completing the painting. He didn't remember how he signed it."

"That makes sense." Marcus cast me a quick glance then, he tapped his phone. "Infantino was a starving student. His landlord accepted paintings and drawings for rent money from a lot of students. The landlord kept some, but he gave away a lot of them. He only had Infantino's sketch a few months. The buyer moved to the States and opened an antique store in Arizona where Archie Smythe found it."

All tied up in a neat package. Dang it.

"Let's return to Gracie." Kevin stepped forward, taking control of the conversation. "What was her explanation for contacting you?"

"She's dying." Payton's cut-glass tone chilled the air. "She says she's innocent and wants the world to know the truth."

Despite the sinking feeling in my stomach, I can't say I was surprised. Gracie's family had lived the past fifty years with her publicly condemned for a murder she didn't commit. Fearing the worst, I pretended ignorance. "Why would you help her reveal the truth about the forged paintings?"

"That's not it." Weatherington snorted. "She claims she had nothing to do with my father's death. She wants to restore her good name before she dies."

I hid a wave of bitter disappointment. The caller knew the truth about the first murder. Gracie must have told her siblings she hadn't killed Weatherington's father. "Did this person say who murdered him? Does she have proof of her innocence? What was the plan? An announcement at the auction?"

Weatherington sneered. "She didn't invite discussion. She issued ultimatums followed by threats."

Kevin's brow furrowed. "What would have prevented her from revealing the truth about the forgeries?"

Weatherington's face flushed.

That was answer enough. "You intended to silence her before she had a chance to talk."

The older man's expression stiffened even more. "Nothing of the sort. I am not a common criminal."

"He's an uncommon criminal." Marcus chuckled at his own joke.

Weatherington glared at the boy. "No one would have listened to that woman."

Exchanging an amused glance with Kevin, I could have told Weatherington he needn't have bothered. Marcus is far too impressed with his weird sense of humor to be drawn into an argument with someone he barely knows.

Marcus never looked up from his phone, where he was thumbing through articles.

I cast an eagle eye toward Payton. "Did the caller have an accent? Did she say anything odd or distinctive?"

"She said if I didn't show up, she'd destroy the company." Fists clenched and voice shaking, Payton marched straight at me. "A company I've dedicated my life to."

Kevin walked on as if in thought. Stopping in her path, he interrupted the woman's progress and her angry rant.

"Why hasn't your contact done anything to further her supposed goals?" Kevin looked from one Jerrone rep to the other. "Despite her threats, her deadlines, her demands for a meeting..."

"Two meetings." Marcus held up a pair of fingers.

Kevin gave the boy a nod. "In spite of your compliance, she hasn't come forward. She hasn't contacted the media. She hasn't given you any additional instructions. Why not?"

Restrained energy simmered in the air.

The answer was obvious, at least to me. "Her threat to reveal the forgeries was a smokescreen. The killer has an ulterior motive."

"The killer could be a guy." Marcus wiggled his phone in the air. "Computer programs can disguise a voice."

"What else could the murderer want?" Frustration squeezed Payton's voice to a tight shriek. "We're stuck in this backwater corner of the world."

That was rude. Langsdale was an upscale resort town. It was also my adopted home.

Weatherington flung his arm in my direction. "It's that Colchester woman. She's behind this. Find her and figure out what she wants."

I wish I *could* talk to her. "I told you before, her background checks out."

"Mrs. Colchester has no motive to bring you here or kill your brother." Marcus's steady certainty contrasted with the high-strung emotions of the adults. "This mess has gotten her accused of murder."

Something jelled in my brain. I stared at him as if hearing the words for the first time. Crawford had mentioned more than once during our friendship that he always looked at the end result of the crime. Cut out all other factors and focus on who profited. Who lost? What changed?

As Marcus spoke, my mind flipped his words. *What if this mess was designed to get her accused of murder?*

The spin left me speechless. My brain was evidently becoming desperate. No one would construct these elaborate plans to get an old woman charged with murder.

Except... my gaze swung to Kevin's profile. He'd also commented about the endgame in a scam. The two undeniable facts from the weekend stood out in stark relief: One man dead. One old woman accused of murder.

That was the result. Had it been the intent? Was I being paranoid? Someone had lured Mrs. C to the library where Neville had been killed. The video from the phone haunted me. Had Mrs. C told me the whole truth, even now?

I was on a carousel of suspicion. My brain spit out questions faster than I could think of answers. Time to get on with the present conversation. "How do you hear from this contact of yours?"

Payton clicked her tongue. "Phone calls."

"Has anyone else been in contact with this person, the alleged Gracie?" I didn't bother to hide my skepticism.

"You think I'm making this up?" Payton's anger permeated the air.

I refused to back down. She'd kept her share of secrets. "Did anyone approach you Friday night at Rycliffe?"

She shook her head. "When I heard your friend's British accent, I was convinced she was the one. She's the right age, coloring, and height."

Marcus scrunched up his face. "If Gracie wanted to stay hidden, she'd speak with an American accent."

"I waited until I could barely breathe." Payton continued. "No one approached me."

"When did you realize Neville was at Rycliffe?" Kevin asked.

She swallowed hard and pressed her lips together. "Only when I saw his body. I couldn't believe it was him."

When her voice broke off, Weatherington eyed her with an uncertain air. He started to reach out then his hand fell to his side.

I used their distraction, to glance at Kevin with a raised brow. "Lying?" I mouthed.

He flicked a glance at Payton, then gave an infinitesimal shrug.

Typical guy, refusing to commit. In this case, I didn't mind. I'd covered this same ground earlier with Payton, with the same result. For now, his waffling left Payton at the top of my suspect list.

Of course, there were holes in my theory the size of a cement truck. I had no proof. I couldn't tell anyone without exposing Mrs. C to the fifty-year-old murder charge. And, given Payton's acting ability, she wasn't a good candidate for confessing.

Other than that, I was on my 'A' game. Not. I decided to throw another question into the mix. "What about the gunman who tried to kill Jamie at the hospital?"

I used a bit of license with the last statement. The gun wielder had come closer to shooting me than anyone else, but Payton and Weatherington's dropped jaws and wide eyes were worth my creative license.

A flurry of astonished questions and answers filled in their supposed gaps of knowledge. Unfortunately, neither betrayed the slightest hint of foreknowledge of the attack.

"Jamie must be in on it." Weatherington was obviously ready to believe anyone guilty of complicity. "She must have arranged for Neville to be at Rycliffe. The murderer is tying up loose ends, killing the accomplices."

The man might be a broken record, but his idea was feasible. I waded in before we lost sight of the real objective. I pointed at Payton. "Have you told the police about your mysterious caller?"

"I'm trying to keep the forgeries a secret." She clipped off the words as if I'd missed the first act. "Telling the police would negate everything I've done up to this point."

"I've had enough of your accusations." Weatherington shifted to stand shoulder to shoulder with her. "Payton and I have acted to protect the Jerrone reputation. Since you work for me, I expect you to adhere to the law and keep any information you have obtained about this matter confidential."

Kevin didn't try to hide his snort of laughter.

"Client confidentiality applies to lawyers, not P.I.s." I didn't bother to add that I prefer to think of rules as suggestions rather than binding oaths. "I told you before that if I discover you're involved in your brother's murder, nothing will protect you."

A vein throbbed in his neck. "I wish your skill matched your reputation."

For once the man and I were in agreement.

"I follow the facts," I retorted. "If you're innocent, the time I've spent chasing this trail would have been better used pursuing other leads."

If I'd had any other leads.

Weatherington's response was a harrumph. He took Payton's arm. "Time to get to the auction. For all we know, that murdering female is even now destroying the family's good name."

By telling the truth? I shook my head. "She won't do anything without you in attendance."

The stout man stiffened, turning to me with a suspicious look. "How can you be so sure?"

Kevin crossed his arms over his chest. "The person who arranged this scheme is building to a big finish. They want an audience."

"I just hope everyone survives the climax," I said.

After a final glare, Weatherington departed without another word.

Marcus's chuckle cut through the tension in the room. "You really pissed him off, T.R."

I smiled at his infectious laughter. "I have to go with my strength."

Kevin crossed the room and opened the door. "We better get back to the auction. It's a cliché, but I have a bad feeling about tonight."

19

—— · ——

14 Down; 7 Letters;
Clue: Dress in a particular set of clothes
Answer: Costume

Kevin's ominous words reverberated through me as I walked from the room. My mind whirled like a gyroscope on steroids until I could barely think straight. "I'm going to freshen up before I make my grand entrance."

I threw out the comment in an upper-crust tone, adding an arched eyebrow for effect. What I really needed was a chance to collect my thoughts.

Marcus and Kevin slowed as I headed for a women's lounge.

I walked by a maid, pushing her cart at an unhurried pace. The brassy tint of her hair contrasted with the black uniform. She was one of the rare maids I'd seen in the evening. Until now the cleaning crew had been like elves who come at night only to disappear in the full sun.

Returning her nod, I walked into the women's lounge.

A fancy place like the Silver Mountain had a sitting room adjacent to the restroom. Mirrors. Tables with chairs. Padded benches. The place was furnished with more style than my apartment. Too bad I couldn't take the furnishings home.

I faced myself in the mirror. The woman looking back appeared more confident than I felt. But she had no answers. I ran a hand through my spiky brown hair, took a deep breath, and closed my eyes.

I needed a moment of silence to marshal what was left of my wits.

Where to begin? Three forgeries, not four. The sketch was real.

That all but eliminated Weatherington as a suspect, but Payton still had her blocked promotion and possible blackmail as motive.

Then there were Gracie's relatives. One of them had to be involved. They must know the truth about the first murder, Mrs. C's involvement and her identity. They had either fed Payton the information or... they could be acting on their own to clear Gracie's name.

I tossed that idea around. They could have lured Neville here promising to lead him to Gracie, all the while intending to expose my friend.

Expose her? I tossed that thought around. Gracie's family gained nothing by killing Neville. What if the murder hadn't been planned?

A feather light touch on my arm roused me. I opened my eyes to the lighted mirror. The brassy hair and black uniform of the maid was reflected by my side.

"Hello, ducks." A sing-song British accent sounded at my side. "Feeling all right, are we?"

A blinding shock jolted my brain. I didn't faint or black out. However, a few thousand synapses did go belly up.

Mrs. C's concerned gaze stared at me from a pair of horn-rimmed glasses.

I studied her from her brassy wig to her black shoes. Surprise zapped my brain. "You're wearing shoes. Real shoes."

"Ver-ry uncomfortable things they are, I can tell you." She confiscated the chair I'd ignored and plopped down. "Feeling more the thing?"

"What are you doing here? How did you get here? How did you elude the police? Who's helping you?"

She smiled, apparently unfazed by my rapid-fire questions.

"Never mind. I don't want to know who else is involved." I circled back to my first question. "What are you doing here?"

She wiggled her feet out of her slip-on shoes and curled her stocking clad toes in the plush carpet, then sat back with a look of relief. "I can't think with those on. They constrict the blood flow something awful."

The blood flow to where? Her brain? What was she thinking being here?

I grabbed another chair. I'd need all my strength to get through this interview.

"How's your mother? On her feet, I see."

I didn't even ask when she'd seen my mother. My nod confirming my mother's health barely gave the other woman pause.

She clicked her tongue. "I hate to say I told you so."

Somehow, I doubted that.

"I did warn you this would be dangerous."

It seemed odd to hear a British accent, usually associated with high tea and county estates, speaking of danger.

"I've come to tell you something." She leaned in. "There's more to this affair than meets the eye."

"I caught on to that fact." She didn't think I'd figured that out by now?

What a vote of confidence.

As Mrs. C eyed me expectantly, I chased the new theory down a winding path. Had the murder resulted from a confrontation gone wrong? The frame-up for murder... what if it was a panicked reaction? Neville wasn't supposed to be at Rycliffe that early.

A knock on the door interrupted my thoughts.

Marcus wiggled through, constrained by Kevin's hand on his shoulder.

"Told you she wasn't a real maid." Marcus flashed a know-it-all smile over his shoulder. "Hi, Mrs. Colchester."

Mrs. C folded her hands in her lap. "Hello, gents."

A moment later Marcus was circling the room, taking in the furnishings, the flowers, and all the little extras. "We don't get benches in the guy's bathroom. What do women do in here? Hang out?"

"It's their home away from home." Kevin eyed me with a reassuring expression, that shored up my confidence. "This is where they confer, compare notes, plan strategy."

"Sounds like a war-room." My son cast a glance my way. "Which means I'm behind enemy lines."

I rolled my eyes. Commandoes had nothing on this snap team.

"Stay on topic people." I pointed at Mrs. C. "We have a witness and I have a new tangent to explore."

We updated Mrs. C on Weatherington's oath that the fourth painting and the sketch were both originals. Then I tossed out my latest theory.

"Think about it." I spoke to no one in particular, except perhaps myself. "Nothing went as planned Friday night. The broken step delayed Mrs. C's arrival in the library. Neville had been in hiding for hours by the time his assailant arrived."

"If he jumped up without warning..." Marcus's black eyes sparkled. A smile played on his lips. "Whoever he was meeting might have panicked."

Kevin stood by the door. He wasn't one to agree without thinking through the scenario. After a moment, he nodded. "A man of his standing would have been annoyed by the game playing. Crossing continents. Secret meetings. Impatient with waiting, he would have demanded answers."

Mrs. C's expression turned sour. "The Weatheringtons are an arrogant lot. They're used to being lords of the manor, aren't they? Giving orders, not taking them."

Kevin raised a brow at the woman's bitter tones. Then, his gaze grew thoughtful. "If Neville blew his cork, his contact might have grabbed the paperweight and struck him without thinking."

"A single blow to the head." Marcus repeated the line used in so many of the news stories over the past two days.

Something tapped at the edge of my brain, but the connection remained in the shadows.

Mrs. C's expression grew somber. "He looked so much like the scoundrel who ruined poor Gracie."

I was beginning to doubt poor Gracie was the victim Mrs. C had painted her.

Kevin glanced at the door. Fortunately, the offices in this wing were closed, reducing the chances of anyone walking in to discover guys in the women's bathroom.

The thought pricked me to action. I had to get to the auction. Best to make good use of this time. "Marcus, can you find out if Gracie's relatives traveled here? Maybe see if they're still at their business?"

"You don't ask much." Kevin put a hand on the boy's shoulder. "He's an eleven-year-old boy with a smartphone, not Interpol."

"Before I check out the Lindens, I have an update for Kevin." He looked up at my boyfriend. "You wanted to know about Archie Smythe's movements."

I folded my arms across my chest. "How is that different from my request?"

Kevin dismissed my objection with a wave of his hand. "Archie's been in the news over the past year."

"Yeah, right." I couldn't win against these two. I turned to my son. "What did you find?"

"Nothing on his recent movements." Marcus strolled to a padded chair. He made a show of sitting, then paused. He was such a showman. "Archie lied about where he was last year."

"Last year?" My mind spun like a top, searching for a connection. After Marcus's build up, this wasn't the big reveal I'd anticipated. "How does that play into a murder two days ago?"

"I don't know." My son faced me with cheerful aplomb. "But his lie involves the *Ponzers*."

He emphasized the name as if it should mean something.

I stole a glance at Kevin, who returned my puzzled look.

Mrs. C sat forward. "The Ponzers, you say? Well well, that's something isn't it?"

"Exactly." Happy with the recognition, Marcus's grin widened. The boy eyed me and Kevin with no sign of remorse for his drama. "Ponzer is the guy Infantino traded the sketch to in the first place. Eighteen months ago, his family sold some of his art books and old diaries."

I made a rolling motion with my hand for him to get to the punch line. "Still not seeing the connection."

"Because while you've been running around, I read all kinds of articles." The boy shot back. "Dozens. Hundreds. Thou--"

"All right." Kevin interrupted him with a chuckle. "We get it. You're a martyr to the case. Move on."

Marcus laughed, then he sobered. "In one of the interviews about the sketch, Archie said he'd been in North America for the past two years. He missed a friend's wedding and a funeral in England. He said he was 'mining the treasures of the New World'. Blah blah blah."

Marcus ran down, but his triumphant look remained.

Kevin tapped a rhythm on a marble countertop. "He could have flown back for a weekend to finalize the sale or they did it online."

"Nope." The boy, unable to sit still any longer, jumped to his feet. "The paragraph about the sale said the Ponzer family and Neville sealed the deal over a pint at the local pub in true English fashion. Archie lied. People don't lie for no reason. He has something to hide."

My gut tightened. Marcus was right. Distracted by this new puzzle, I didn't even wince at his wording. "What is he hiding?"

Mrs. C rubbed her hands together. "He got the sketch off them, didn't he? That'll do it."

"That wouldn't matter." Deciphering her meaning sometimes made me wonder if we spoke the same language. "Anything the Ponzers sold to Archie belongs to him. If he bought the Infantino, he has the right to resell it."

"No, he doesn't." Marcus jumped up. "One of the articles told how the family remodeled the old guy's house thirty-some years ago. The workers found old sketches and a few paintings hidden behind panels in his office furniture and in secret drawers in his desk."

"I read that bit." Excitement rang in Mrs. C's voice. "The name caught my eye, it did. The old landlord told his wife he had insurance for a rainy day. He never would explain."

Marcus popped to his feet, all aquiver. "He died in a freak accident when he was fifty-three. He left his wife in debt. She thought he sold all the artwork he'd been given, but he kept some."

Now, I was getting interested. "How does this tie in with the Infantino?"

Enthusiasm shone from my son's black eyes. "The family tore everything apart. They found a bunch of stuff, but ever since then, when they sell anything, they put a... what do you call it? Special wording in the bill of sale."

"A clause?" Kevin's narrowed eyes betrayed his growing interest in this new information.

"That's it." My son snapped his fingers. "The family has a clause that the purchase is only for the specific item sold. Anything extra reverts to the family."

As his ringing tones faded, the silence seemed deafening.

My interest meter was climbing steadily. Crossword clues and answers vied for attention, but did this connect to my case?

Kevin drummed on the counter.

I puzzled over the possibilities. "It's intriguing, but even if Archie did find artwork in one of those books, there's no way to prove it was the Infantino."

Marcus's jaw tightened. When he shook his head, the light reflected off his glossy, black hair. "Then why lie about not being in England at that time? He's hiding something."

Kevin studied the boy's intense expression. "The Ponzers know by now that Archie discovered the Infantino sketch. If they were suspicious, they would have come forward to challenge the sale."

The boy pounded his fists on his thighs. "They think it was sold years ago."

It was time to take a mental step back and look at the big picture. "I'll grant you Archie lied about his movements. He may have acquired some artwork illegally, but the Ponzer family hasn't had the Infantino sketch for decades. I'm curious, but I have to focus on who has a motive for murdering Neville."

"What if they had the Infantino and didn't know it?" Marcus stood before me arms spread. "Neville could have discovered the truth about where the sketch came from, like I did."

Kevin shook his head. "He'd have killed the sale long before this weekend if he was suspicious."

I met Marcus's determined gaze. Despite myself, his new information had wormed its way onto my mental crossword puzzle. Now I'd have to find answers to the boy's questions. "I'll look into it. However, my priority is finding the killer."

My son threw both arms up in the air and did a victory dance. He knew he had me on the hook.

I shook my finger at him. "Whoever murdered Neville knew Mrs. C lived in Langsdale. That information had to come from Gracie's family. My money is still on them as the killers."

Surprise crossed Kevin's face. "Payton slipped out of first place?"

I tapped a finger to my lips. "I think the death was the result of Neville surprising his contact. They argued. He died in the struggle. I'm not sure the frame-up wasn't part of the original scheme. If the murder was an accident, the killer had a huge problem with Neville lying dead at their feet."

Some of that explanation I was semi-confident about. Most of the details were shaky or completely missing.

The wrinkles around Mrs. C's mouth deepened. "Gracie's family might be involved. She was close to her sister and brother."

Despite feeling like an outsider among my own family, I knew that if the world turned against me, I could always find refuge with them. "She probably contacted them after settling in the US, perhaps after the notoriety of the murder faded."

"Gracie would never have told me she'd spoken with them." The other woman seemed to look into the distance as if trying to view the past from a different angle. "She knew I'd object. Of course, I left no one behind. To me, our escape was a grand adventure. Over the years, the new identities became a game."

You were the one who attacked and killed Daniel Weatherington. I bit off the comment. If the two women had been found, Mrs. C was the one who'd have been charged with murder.

Though Gracie had been convicted in the court of public opinion, she had less reason to keep hiding, except for loyalty.

I put myself in her position and wondered how far friendship would extend, realizing, as each year rolled into another, that I had sacrificed my family and future to protect someone else from their own mistake. I wasn't so sure I would have remained silent over the long haul.

Gracie never returned home. She'd gone to her death without publicly declaring her innocence. I needed a fuller picture of her. "Was Gracie ambitious?"

Mrs. C clicked her tongue as she nodded. "She wanted fame and fortune. She could have done so much more with her career. Gallery space and shows with a bit of a push. She did nothing thanks to that man."

The same tune Mrs. C had sung before, but talent could be found in many people. A career requires drive and dedication. Nothing I'd heard made me believe Gracie had those qualities. I threw up my hands in momentary defeat. "We're not going to find answers here. We need to get to the auction."

I pointed at Mrs. C. "I assume you have a plan to get away from the resort."

She put the horn-rimmed glasses on. "No one looks at the help."

Marcus cocked his head to one side, studying the disguise. "Jamie might not even recognize you in that outfit."

Mrs. C's brow furrowed. "Should I know this Jamie? You mentioned her before."

It took under two minutes to bring her up to speed on the young PR assistant who'd gotten embroiled in the case.

The details failed to clear the puzzlement from Mrs. C's face. "I remember seeing the young girl on Friday, from a distance, not face-to-face."

"She saw you," Marcus confirmed. "She remembered your outfit when someone copied it this morning at Rowdy Reptiles."

Bells clanged in my head. A picture formed as several pieces finally fell into place. My gaze sought Kevin's. "Was Jamie facing the woman who approached my mother this morning?"

Kevin's eyes narrowed in thought, then he nodded. "She mentioned the calculating look in the woman's eyes."

The world froze except for a new set of clues and answers for my puzzle, spinning in my mind like a roulette wheel.

"That's why Jamie was targeted." The words popped out of my mouth. "She was at both locations. She saw Mrs. C. She saw the other woman."

I was babbling. There were too many she's.

Mrs. C cast a puzzled frown at Kevin. "She's lost me, she has. Can you follow this lot, then?"

He nodded slowly. "I'm beginning to see."

I flipped the facts around, testing the strength of my latest theory.

"Distinct outfits are easy to copy." A knowing gleam lit Kevin's gaze. "Faces aren't."

Marcus looked from one to the other. "What are you talking about?"

"Rycliffe was planned. The murderer had the pieces in place." I spoke hurriedly. My mind was still putting the picture together. "The attack on Mom was off-the-cuff. It was a last-minute scheme to warn me off the case, but they didn't have time to account for variables."

"Jamie's intuition drove her to stay with your parents and Marcus." Kevin took up the story in a calmer tone. "That's why she went to the Rowdy Reptile Ranch at the last minute."

"No one could have foreseen that. Jamie saw Mrs. C on Friday. This morning she was facing the woman who put the scorpion on my mother." My thoughts jumped out of the fast lane. This filled in a few of the blank squares in my puzzle. "Jamie is the one person who saw both of their faces. She knows there are two different women involved."

Now, so did I. I felt almost buoyant. Even if Mrs. C and Gracie were one and the same, this theory would mean Mrs. C hadn't killed Neville. This strengthened the argument that the video on the phone had been faked.

"Jamie must have told someone that she was going to the hospital." Marcus's body tightened like a coiled spring. "That's how the gunman found her."

"You're right." My brain shifted into high gear. "She confided in someone."

By the time I finished speaking, Kevin had his cell phone out. "I'll find out who Jamie called."

Time was short. I felt it crowding around my heels. At any minute some woman might come in the bathroom. As much as I wanted to stand by Mrs. C, I couldn't afford for my son to be found with a fugitive from the law.

"The call isn't going through." Kevin gritted his teeth in frustration. "I'll keep trying."

I flashed back to the short time I'd grappled with the gunman. The dark hoody. The slim form. I gritted my teeth in frustration, if only

I'd seen the face, but no amount of wishing would change that fact. "Who's the most likely person Jamie would call?"

"Jamie trusts Holly." Marcus shot out the name instantly.

Kevin eased the door open. Evidently satisfied, he turned to face us. "You need to track down your number one fan."

Mrs. C looked up from rubbing her feet. "As usual, people know more than they're telling."

This from her? She'd kept more than her share of secrets for several decades. I shook my head. If only answers would multiply as quickly as the unknowns. "We're past due for the auction."

As I stood to go electricity seemed to charge the air.

Tonight's the night.

I jumped as if the words had been carried on the current scurrying over my skin. I rubbed my arms to dispel a feeling of a looming catastrophe.

Not tonight. I wasn't ready. I had no safeguards in place.

Kevin's brow furrowed. He aimed a challenging look at me. "We're missing pieces, puzzle master."

"Don't I know it." I had no answers. Then again, what else is new? I put a hand on Mrs. C's arm. "You need to leave the resort. Get away from here."

"I can't leave you to face the danger, now can I?" Mrs. C's jaw jutted out at a dangerously stubborn angle. "Someone set me up for murder, and after all me hard work of hiding."

She sounded more outraged at her cover being blown than being framed for murder.

"We're in this together." Marcus slammed his fist into his palm. "One for all and all for one."

I bit back a groan. Sacrificing everyone for a cause is only romantic in ballads. In real life, I prefer "retreat is the better part of valor". If only I was in charge of the world.

Mrs. C struggled into her shoes then stood with a wrenching groan of agony.

Kevin helped her up then turned toward the door.

A sudden suspicion had me staying his hand as he grasped the handle. I turned to Mrs. C. "Did you get another message? Is that why you're here?"

"I'd have told you, now wouldn't I?" A hint of reproach mixed with the innocence glimmering in her gaze. "I wouldn't let you go into a fight without the facts."

Her, keep secrets? What was I thinking?

"Try to stay out of sight and out of trouble." I knew I was wasting my breath even as I spoke.

"No one will know I'm around." A flawless American accent came from her lips. She put on the horn-rimmed glasses. "If naught else happens, I'll text Marcus then slip away."

It wasn't the reassurance I'd hoped for, but, as so often in life, it was the best I was going to get.

20

22 Down; 7 Letters;
Clue: Bizarre qualities; like a dream
Answer: Surreal

The Sunday night auction was in full swing by the time I slipped in with Kevin and Marcus to rejoin my parents. Rickson was sitting at a small table with his back to the wall. His position gave him a wide view of the room.

The painting on the dais showed a yellow dot inside a black circle. The bidding was mid-six figures... for a picture of a yellow traffic light.

By the time we sat, Marcus had loaded a plate full of goodies with the efficiency of an expert. He was now wolfing down finger food while he researched Gracie Linden's family on his phone.

After the item sold, my dad nudged Kevin's arm. "Couple of shills in the audience, bidding up the price."

"Always." Kevin's knowing response spoke of long experience.

My parents were aware Kevin had left his family of con artists for the cushy life of owning his own painting company and barely getting by.

I munched on an hors d'oeuvre topped with salmon and listened with half-an-ear as Mom and Pop launched into a review of the highlights so far.

"Two matched paintings sold separately." My dad warmed to discussion of the auction, familiar ground for him. "That's the way to ensure interest in the second piece."

Though my mind spun scenarios on the violent episodes of this weekend, none of my results made a coherent whole. Instead, details of the table talk drifted in and out of my mind.

Something about a consortium of bidders pushing up the price on items by one artist, then managing to grab an antique print from the same school of art at a steal.

Kevin instantly grasped the point my father was making. Feints and maneuvers were the very air he'd breathed during his first eighteen years of life.

"The old print was the target all along," Dad continued.

Mom's eyes shone with excitement. "The other bidder was too close to the situation to see the maneuver."

"You two have experience in the planning that goes into high-stakes sales like this auction." Kevin leaned closer, obviously impressed by their analysis. He popped a marinated olive in his mouth. "My mother always said planning was ninety percent of success. Lay the groundwork, execute, and you won't go wrong."

I smiled, momentarily diverted from thoughts of murder. Horse breeders from Kentucky and a con artist from L.A. Who knew they'd find common ground at an art auction? Funny how people interpret the same circumstances based on their viewpoint.

"Building toward a big finish tomorrow." My dad's expression lit with anticipation. "The final day."

Mom speared a piece of fresh pineapple. "With the publicity from the murder, the Infantino sketch may go for double the expected high of fifteen million dollars. Several people have asked how close you are to solving that poor man's murder."

"Not as close as I'd like." Which was a huge understatement. "The motive is sketchy and currently unprovable. I only have half of my squares filled in, and a lot of clues seem to belong to a completely different crossword puzzle."

"We know lots of stuff." Marcus gestured with one of the tiny sandwiches. "TR likes to play it cool 'til the end."

Though I didn't share my son's confidence, I was touched by his unswerving loyalty. Conversation quieted as the auction resumed. A detailed history of the provenance of the next piece delayed immediate bidding.

Marcus nudged my elbow. "I found something."

When he leaned in on my right side, Kevin put his arm around my shoulders and leaned in on my left.

"Linden Art Restoration isn't taking any new projects." Marcus eyed his phone screen. "New commissions from current customers only. No deadline guaranteed. No new clients."

"Interesting, but not conclusive," Kevin mused.

"I know." Marcus concentrated on the readout. "They could be busy or short staffed."

Fortunately, I hadn't expected anything conclusive. "No help there."

The auctioneer's voice over-rode our conversation. During the next several minutes of bidding, I concentrated on a few of the many questions that bothered me. "Why not name Mrs. C in the note? Why leave it to the police to connect her with Gracie Linden?"

I wasn't aware I'd spoken aloud until Kevin turned to me. "What did you say?"

"Thinking out loud," I admitted, waving away any need for an answer. "The killer knows Mrs. C's identity. The note and the video prove that much."

Amusement tinged Kevin's steady, sapphire gaze. "Give me a sign if you want me to break into this one-sided conversation."

I was too consumed to come up with a snappy response. "The killer didn't expose Mrs. C to the cops."

Kevin leaned in until his breath fanned my cheek, unperturbed at the repetition. "Why not, Sherlock?"

I sighed in frustration. "I have no idea."

The staccato calls of the bidders and the auctioneer drummed through the air. A going, going, gone call preceded the rap of the gavel. An efficient choreography brought the next presentation to stage.

The Jerrone representatives looking pleased.

Holly floated along the wall, orchestrating details in the background.

My gaze flowed to the auctioneer. Front and center. Look at the item. See what I want you to see.

The whole weekend had been crafted as carefully as any scam Kevin's family had ever arranged. What was I *not* seeing?

"She's thinking." Marcus leaned across my line of sight to whisper to Kevin. "I can smell the wood burning."

While I fought to nail down a revelation that taunted me from the shadows, relief for my mother's safety wafted across my mind like a whisper of smoke. Across the table, my parents presented a double profile as the action on the dais captured their attention. Two profiles. Two murders. Two women. That was the key.

Applause washed over the room. I sat up, startled. For an insane moment thinking I had spoken aloud and the response had been for me. Thankfully, only Kevin and Marcus had noticed my reaction.

The auctioneer gestured toward a painting being carried off stage.

Tucking away my questions for later dissection, I shared a chuckle with Kevin while Marcus's laughter cut through the sudden silence.

Dad eyed us with a raised brow. "What are you three rogues plotting?"

"I'm planning what to get for dessert." My son responded with a cheeky grin. "I'm a growing boy."

He aimed the sentence at me, his sharp black eyes full of silent pride for his quick save.

I rewarded him with a nod and a smile. "You'll have to wait for the next break."

Two sharp raps of the gavel announced that very thing.

Marcus shot to his feet, a smile on his lips. "I need some cake."

Mom scooted back her chair. "Why don't we stretch our legs on the balcony before hitting the sweets? Are you two coming?"

Kevin and I declined. Marcus fell in step with Mom and Pop as they walked toward the row of French doors with Rickson on their heels. His sharp, assessing gaze warned away any who dared to saunter close to his charges.

Still seated, I did a quick sweep myself. Holly, near the front door, was deep in conversation with two people in resort colors. The Jerrone reps, Weatherington and Payton among them, had their heads together at the front table.

Kevin drew his buzzing phone out of his pocket.

The soft tone that filtered from the incoming caller told me it wasn't Rabi. I listened unashamedly to Kevin's side of the conversation. "Just the one? Okay."

"Was that about Jamie's phone call?" I barely gave Kevin time to disconnect. "Who knew she went to the hospital?"

"Her one call was to Weatherington."

I was momentarily taken aback. I'd just eliminated him as a suspect. This case was maddening.

"He'd have hired a professional. The gunman I wrestled with in the stairwell was an amateur." I stewed over the possibilities. "I wonder if Weatherington told Payton that Jamie called. It could have been her in the stairwell."

"When things go wrong, amateurs panic." Kevin's voice carried a tone of disapproval for the lack of professionalism.

"Where to go from here?" I wasn't sure whether I spoke the words or thought them. Just as I didn't know whether it was my idea to stand up or Kevin's. I only knew we were both on our feet.

Kevin caught my hand in his as we sauntered between the tables.

I didn't know about him, but I freely admit I had no plan. Images and clues roiled below the level of conscious thought. As the voices and movement flowed around me, a certainty settled in my gut. "Tonight's the night, not tomorrow."

Kevin's features sharpened. "Letting Jamie get away was a blow to the killer. He's lost containment. He has to finish."

Our steps slowed several yards from the Jerrone table. I considered whether confronting Weatherington in public would throw him off-balance enough to force a fatal confession.

As I weighed my options a white-haired woman with a shuffling gait approached the man.

Kevin squeezed my arm. "She didn't leave."

I buried my panic behind a stiff mask. Without conscious thought, I increased my pace.

Weatherington bent to hear what the woman was saying.

A flick of her wrist deposited what looked to be a slip of paper in his jacket pocket.

"What is she doing?" Kevin's sharp tone betrayed surprise rather than anger.

Little things, minutiae I couldn't catalog, came together. "That's the imposter."

The woman kept her back to us the entire time. She moved with amazing spryness into the audience mingling among the tables.

Even as I thought to nudge Kevin toward the departing figure, he was gone, slipping past tables, chairs, and people with a seemingly unhurried air.

As I started to follow, Weatherington headed to cut me off. Though logic said I'd witnessed a meeting of conspirators, my gut wasn't convinced. Nothing about this weekend was what it seemed on the surface.

A buzzing came from my phone. I pulled it out and read an incoming text from Rabi. "Onsite with Mrs. C."

Rabi was here? Why hadn't he...

Then I noticed the time. The text had been lost in the ether for an hour and a half.

My jaw clenched. The information would have been nice to know earlier. Mrs. C hadn't mention that detail. No doubt, she thought I knew. I shelved my irritation, telling myself to be grateful for more backup.

Weatherington's gaze hardened. The curl of his lip signaled his contempt of me and my efforts more eloquently than his earlier words.

My gut and brain both agreed I was about to be fired.

I don't care. I shot a silent rebuttal toward my client.

Payton called his name.

He glanced at her, then continued his march toward me like a cannonball fired at a target. Another soft, but urgent call from his assistant drew a raised hand of acknowledgment. His path to me remained steady.

I quickened my pace. Though my peripheral vision registered the well-dressed people as I wove between them, I was unprepared when a figure stepped directly into my path. I drew back.

"I'm glad I found you." Holly, breathless as usual, grabbed my arms. "It's your son. You have to come."

The words were like a sucker punch. The air left my lungs. The thought of confronting Weatherington vanished. I vaguely noted Payton catching up to my erstwhile opponent, then my vision, my world, narrowed to Holly.

"What happened?" I choked out. "Marcus was with my parents."

And Rickson, I added silently. It was unlike the boy to indulge in horseplay on a case. He took his role as a detective seriously. His years on the street had made him more mature than most children his age.

"I got a text." Holly waved her phone in the air while she dragged me toward the exit. "I don't know details. There was an accident. He's hurt. Your parents and that man are with him."

I opened my mouth, but I never stood a chance of interrupting her rapid-fire delivery.

"He was taken to a small meeting room just down the hall. The hotel doctor has been called," she continued. "No ambulance. I don't think it's serious, but I knew you'd want to know."

Part of my tension eased. An attack was all but impossible with Rickson on the scene. I wondered what could have happened. Marcus had the grace of an alley cat, with more than his share of nine lives.

As Holly and I hurried toward the main doors, I glanced over my shoulder. Though most of the crowd had settled into their seats, I couldn't spot Kevin's tall figure. He must have followed the imposter from the room.

I dismissed the notion of contacting him or Rabi, unwilling to pull either of them from their stations. The thought flitted through my mind as I followed Holly into the corridor.

My long stride almost bypassed her. I put a hand on her arm, urging her to walk faster.

A minion in resort colors stepped into Holly's path. "There's an issue with-"

She brushed the man aside. "I have an urgent matter demanding my attention."

Her breath came faster. Whether from worry, like me, or just trying to keep up, I couldn't say.

"I don't know how he could have been hurt." She noted in a worried tone. "We have extra personnel in the room and on the patio. There are even some plainclothes police."

She shot me a sideways glance.

"No one is supposed to know," she whispered.

I didn't tell her both Marcus and Kevin had spotted them. Or that Crawford and I had discussed them being on-site. The police had been covering the auction all weekend. We'd all followed the same breadcrumbs. Crawford had kept them updated with the information I'd uncovered. They had been less than forthcoming in return.

The police had the principles under surveillance.

So far, no one had a solid answer.

"Where's the meeting room?" I asked.

It seemed as if we'd been walking forever. Perhaps that was just my perception.

"Here." She quickened her pace with me hot on her heels. "It's around the corner on the right."

She reached the door first. I crowded at her heels. Together we burst into... an empty room. A medium sized oval table filled the center. A smaller table with a water pitcher half-full of melting ice sat in one corner.

Holly advanced slightly. Her brow furrowed. She leaned to the side and peered around the door before turning to me with a look of wide-eyed shock.

I arched a brow. "Where is my son?"

She spread out her hands. Her expression reminded me of a lost lamb.

"Never mind." I regretted my cutting tone. "Is this the right room?"

"Yes." Her sharp retort betrayed her own short temper. She raised the phone and pointed at the screen.

"It's the correct room." A cultured male voice, complete with a British accent, spoke behind me as the door clicked shut. "You are exactly where you are supposed to be."

I clenched my teeth at the arrogant tone. I'd been had. I hated it when that happened.

Holly pivoted. "Obviously not. Where are Marcus and his grand-parents? Has he been moved? Did the doctor arrive?"

I studied her indignant profile, realizing, not for the first time, that my number one fan was not the sharpest knife in the drawer.

When the mystery man didn't answer, she stomped her stiletto. Too bad the plush carpet absorbed the sound. "Where's the boy?"

A flurry of emotions sped through my mind - relief that my son was safe, followed by annoyance at my gullibility. I put a hand on Holly's arm, wondering when she'd catch on. "I'm sure Marcus is at the table with my parents."

Fighting a growing fear at our situation, I turned to face the mysterious Brit head-on.

21

— ※ —

16 Down; 7 Letters;
Clue: No knowledge of a situation
Answer: Unaware

Blocking the doorway was the missing player that I'd known had to exist.

Sometimes I hate being right, especially when still I had so many questions about the *current* players.

This guy was slim, with thinning blond hair above a disdainful expression. British accent. Payton's accomplice? Archie? I wasn't sure. I regretted too late not asking Marcus to pull up a picture of Archie.

I settled my hands on my hips. It didn't take much effort for anger to fuel a belligerent attitude. "You are?"

"Archibald Smythe, what are you doing here?" Holly's demanding tone cut across my words. "This is no time for games. I'm worried about Marcus's safety."

And mine. Thanks for asking.

She started forward; fists balled.

She'd barely taken one step when he raised his right hand from the pocket of his suit coat. A flat, square gun complete with a silencer was pointed straight at us.

"Holly." I grabbed her arm and jerked her to a stop, edging in front of her. "Let me handle this."

I don't know whether my warning tone alerted her or if she caught sight of the gun. Either way, she stopped.

It was like watching an avalanche in slow motion. Her eyes widened, then her skin went slack, right before her mouth dropped open.

"Are you..." Her voice failed. She turned to me in a jerky movement reminiscent of an old-time film. "Is he threatening us?"

I stared at her, stunned. "Yes."

I underlined the word with a hard tone, hoping to bring her up to speed.

Holly held up her phone. "The message was a ruse?"

Our kidnapper eyed her with an increasingly incredulous expression. "Are you serious?"

I held out a faint hope Holly was putting on an act. If so, this was an Oscar-worthy performance. For the first time in my life I felt a sense of camaraderie with the person holding a gun on me. But it would be wrong to switch sides at this point.

"I should never have involved you," he said to Holly.

Again, he and I were in total agreement. As much as I'd hate to wish anyone into this situation, I'd be so much better off with Kevin beside me. Or Rabi. Or Mrs. C. Or even Marcus.

"Drop the phone," he ordered. "We're at our quota for guests."

Her grip tightened around the device.

When she pulled it close to her chest, I smacked it out of her hand--hard enough to sting my palm.

From her anguished look, you'd have thought I'd killed her pet kitten.

"And yours." He jerked his chin at me. My phone joined Holly's on the floor.

A gasp came from Holly's perfect pink lips. "Is he involved in the murder?"

Seriously? She was just now getting around to that realization? I nodded. "Definitely."

How - I wasn't sure. I knew Marcus would never let me forget this turn of events. The boy's suspicions about the art dealer had scored a direct hit.

Archie *had* lied regarding his movements. That he'd discovered the Infantino sketch hidden in one of the Ponzer family art books was the only explanation for him being here.

Had Neville stumbled onto the truth regarding the provenance of the sketch? Had Archie killed the other man to protect his payout?

Time to rattle his cage. "So, Archibald. By the way, what kind of a name is that?"

"It's a family name." He drew himself up as stiffly as an English butler. "Heritage and honor and all that rot. Things you Yanks know nothing about."

"Blah blah blah." I made a rolling motion with my hand. "Tell me how the murder of an innocent man protects your heritage."

His shoulders relaxed. He slipped the gun into his pocket. The extra weight pulled down the fabric of his tailored jacket.

I told myself his smugness was a good thing. The more confident he felt, the more careless he might become.

"No time for explanations," he said. "You have an appointment to keep."

"You're taking us somewhere?" Holly's voice rose to a squeak. She squeezed my arm. "He's kidnapping us."

Oh, goody. A crisis complete with cue cards and a narrator.

I clamped my lips together and fought to maintain my composure. To get through this was going to require all my strength.

From the way his right hand tightened in his pocket, I got the distinct impression Archibald's self-control was being tested as well.

"There had to be another way," he muttered.

If only he'd thought of that before texting Holly.

"How do you expect to get us off the grounds?" I asked. "We're in the middle of the resort, near a ballroom full of people."

He smirked again. "The guests are thirty yards away and by now the auction has started. If you're thinking of trying anything, I have a silencer on my pistol."

He stared me down, letting the words sink in before continuing. "If either of you attempt to alert anyone, the resort will need a new PR person. Holly will take the first bullet."

"It's not fair to shoot me if she tries something." Holly's complaint ended in a wail.

So much for my fan club.

She was right, but life's not fair. Besides, she had a better chance trusting my judgment than I had trusting her decisions.

Archie shrugged. "You've served your purpose. She still has a use."

Not for long, I'd wager. I was under no illusions that the mastermind behind this scheme could afford to let either of us live through the night. I only wondered what my use would prove to be.

"Not my decision, Holly." Evidently that absolved him of all responsibility. "You're excess baggage. Be good and you can stay that way a bit longer."

In the long run, both Holly and I were disposable. I had to stall - and hope. For a change in fortunes. For a moment of inattention on Archie's side. For a rescue attempt.

Scratch that last. Even when Kevin realized I was missing he'd have no idea where to find me.

Holly made a noise that sounded like the whimper from a drowning cat.

I stepped between her and Archie's gun. "We'll cooperate."

"Good show." He spoke in an encouraging tone. "Spoken with the voice of experience."

"I've been taken hostage before." I'm not sure what that said about my skill. Fortunately, my arched tone hid my nerves. "*I'm* still here."

"Thanks for the warning." His oozy, patronizing tone indicated his lack of concern that I might escape. He squatted without taking his gaze or the gun off of us. Picking up both phones, he turned them off. He tossed Holly's aside. He pocketed mine.

Another mystery. He not only wanted me. He wanted my phone.

That fact worried me more than the former. An arctic chill lanced through my heart. The sole reason to keep my phone was to contact someone and have them believe the call or text came from me.

There was only one possibility.

Mrs. C.

Another weight descended on my shoulders. Seconds ago, I only had to worry about getting Holly out of here. Now, I had Mrs. C to save.

Need I mention, I'd also like to get out of this alive? I gathered my wits. "You haven't explained your role in this affair."

Time to stall and maybe see what I could find out. Archie had no way of knowing Marcus had uncovered a good deal of his background.

"He's the art dealer who found the sketch." Holly spoke quickly, the words tumbling out. "He was supposed to be in Europe, unable to attend this weekend. He *lied*."

Surprise still underlined her tone. I kept my expression neutral only through long practice. Would the woman never catch on? Lying was hardly the worst of his crimes. Theft. Murder. Kidnaping. All to ensure he got the biggest slice of the money for the sketch.

As Holly had said yesterday, the owner of the piece gets the largest payout from an auction. Due to the clause in the sale, Archie didn't legally own the sketch. Instead of returning it, he'd found a stooge in Arizona so he could walk away with most of the fifteen to thirty million dollars the Infantino was now expected to bring. Money that should go to the Ponzer family.

Should I hit him with what I knew now or wait? At this point, what was the use of saving knowledge for the future? "This isn't the first time he's lied about where he was, is it, Archie? You made a trip to England eighteen months ago. I believe you attended an estate auction."

His eyes widened. The depths of his gaze held a glimmer of fear. "You've done your homework."

Not really or his presence wouldn't have been such a total surprise. Was the Arizona connection on-site as well, to protect their interests? Was he working with Gracie's relations? Someone who knew about Mrs. C's past? "Care to tell me who you're working with, Archie?"

His jaw tightened. "You may call me Archibald or Mr. Smythe."

"Or what?" I asked. "You can't shoot me. I have an appointment to keep. Remember?"

He gestured the gun hand toward Holly. "She doesn't."

I twisted my mouth to one side. Anyone who knew me could have told him how little I liked playing by rules not of my own making. "I don't think you'd shoot her over a bit of name calling. You don't want to risk losing your payout now, do you?"

My bravado scored a glare from him.

Holly paled even more.

"Seriously?" Her shaky whisper was a hair short of tears.

I gave her what I hoped she would see as a reassuring smile. I'd have to find a way to throw him off-balance without scaring Holly to death.

Archie stepped several feet away from the door, no doubt to ensure neither of us could jump him or grab the gun.

Not that I intended to do anything to endanger Holly.

She wadded up the back of my dress in a two-handed grip that reminded me of going through haunted houses with my friends in high school.

I reached back, loosened her hands, and linked arms with her.

Her nails bit into my arm.

"Holly, I promise we'll be fine." As a rule I don't make promises unless I know I can keep them, but I had to go out on a limb. Desperate times and all that. "Trust me."

"Let's go, ladies." He stepped to one side, then gestured toward the door with his gun hand. "Out the door, turn right. End of the hall, turn left."

Still linking arms with Holly, I gave her hand a squeeze. "Do what he says. It'll be okay."

"I get it." Her shaky jaw stiffened. "You're playing with him."

Again with the cue cards. Though playing with him was a bit overconfident, I gave her a wink. Anything to ease her fear.

I opened the door. The once spacious hall seemed to close in on me.

Archie pressed next to Holly on her other side. "Do let's act like we're all friends."

I held my breath as we walked the corridors. Though I couldn't believe he'd shoot me in plain sight, I didn't want to test him.

Despite the steady beat of fear that ran through my veins in an icy mix, curiosity was rising like a tide. My half-filled crossword puzzle nudged me. At least I might finally get some answers.

Holly and I followed directions exactly. I saw no one except a flash of another maid at the far end of one hall. After the last turn, we walked toward an exit. An outdoor patio stared us in the face. I beat back a rising panic.

"Stop," Archie commanded. "Call the elevator."

He smirked at the shock I couldn't hide. Another surprise came when we went up instead of down. Don't ask me what I expected. The laundry room, a deserted furnace room, a dungeon. I don't know.

Nope. Fourth floor here we come.

I hadn't seen any of this coming. I hoped the tide would turn my way and I'd find a way out of this mess. While I tried to puzzle out Archie's plan, Holly stood by my side with the expression of a plastic doll. Despite her earlier recovery, she'd zoned out again. She may have gone into shock.

I couldn't tell for sure. I only knew she didn't deserve to be treated as if she were disposable.

Fury at the callousness behind this scheme burned away everything except the need for action. Time to go on the attack.

The mastermind wanted my phone to trap Mrs. C.

How had the bad guys known the older woman was on-site? Had they seen her? Recognized her?

Hard to believe.

Had they expected her to come here?

While I'd been stunned to see her, in hindsight, I should have expected her to show up. Anyone who knew her, would know that laying low was not her style.

Anyone who knew her.

The phrase circled in my mind. Knowledge of Mrs. C's traits had to have come from Gracie's family.

New scenario. Gracie had grown increasingly bitter over sacrificing her life for the friend who'd killed her lover. She'd been in contact with her family for decades. She told them the truth about her old friend and what really happened fifty years ago.

"So, Archie." I deliberately baited him with the nickname. He needed me, at least for a short time more. If he planned to kill me anyway, I was going to get some digs in first. Besides, I'm at my best when I'm annoying people. "You never answered my question about your trip to England."

No comment.

The elevator dinged our arrival.

"Let's go," Archie said in a too-calm tone. "Turn left. End of the hall."

An undertone in his carefully controlled voice told me I'd gotten under his skin.

Holly was already moving when I put my arm around her waist. She appeared not to notice my attempt at comfort.

I had to protect her. Though I'd probably missed several calls or texts from Kevin and Marcus, a rescue was not happening. I was on my own.

The hotel corridor stretched out before us. The seemingly endless series of doors marching down the hall reminded me of a horror movie I'd watched years ago.

"Archibald travels extensively due to his job. He's ambitious, checking leads on artwork, following trails." Holly came to life with no warning. "When we were putting the show together and I thought he was coming, I had Jamie authorize him in our system."

I swallowed my surprise and gave the woman a silent bravo. Relieved beyond measure that she'd overcome her paralyzing fear, I struggled to match her matter-of-fact tone. "That's interesting."

She flashed me a sideways look. The tight edge to her jaw and the fast pulse beating in her throat were evidence that she wasn't blind to our situation.

My admiration for her shot up several notches. It takes guts to fight through fear.

"Keep moving," Archie growled.

Holly took a deep breath. "Archibald worked at the Metropolitan Museum of Art for several years before branching out on his own. He's been an art dealer for well over a decade. I noted his short trip to England eighteen months ago. I didn't realize it was pertinent to this case."

"How do you know that?" Panic underscored Archie's voice.

Good thing he asked because I was wondering, too. A glance over my shoulder showed his white-knuckled grip on the gun.

Holly's mouth flattened to a straight line. Her narrowed eyes sparked with irritation. The jab roused her to full fire. She evidently took her professionalism seriously.

"We do extensive background checks on everyone connected with the pieces we auction." She shot him a look over her shoulder. "Our guests visit from all over the world. We don't give access to our offices to just anyone who walks in off the streets."

Go, Holly. I was dancing on the inside as I stole a look at the man behind us.

His eyes drilled a hole in Holly's head. "Shut up, both of you."

Holly's comments had definitely stuck a nerve. Archie had left more of a trail than he'd thought. How could I use the knowledge against him?

22

24 Down; 6 Letters;
Clue: Show publicly for the first time
Answer: Unveil

With Archie's gun at our backs, Holly and I walked into the sitting room of a small suite. A perfectly made king-size bed was visible through an arched doorway. The cinnamon and beige furnishings were spotless and the cool, stale air had the feel of an uninhabited room.

A stage set for this moment.

A lot of planning had gone into this weekend.

"Keep moving, ladies."

The ominous situation coupled with a James Bond accent reminded me of a thriller the gang and I had watched on movie night last week. The comforting memory paired with possible death twisted my insides like a giant corkscrew.

I drew a breath and pivoted on my heel, careful to position myself between Holly and Archie. "What now?"

"We wait." Archie walked to a round table in the corner. Taking the gun out of his pocket, he pointed at the sofa with the barrel. "Sit."

The PR rep and I had barely hit the couch when a knock sounded on the door.

"Right on time." Relief sounded in Archie's tone and the tight line of his shoulders eased.

Uncertainty. It was a thin reed to build on but my quiver of arrows was empty, so I stored his reaction away for later use.

He backed toward the door. "Don't move."

I put my hand over Holly's where it rested on the sofa. In case she got a wild idea to bolt, I wanted a chance to grab her before she gained her feet.

"You're doing great," I whispered.

Her attractive face was still pale, but she managed a wobbly smile. "I know you'll get us out of here."

At least one of us had confidence in me. I squeezed her hand to save myself from responding out loud.

Archie opened the door a crack, passed my phone through, then shut the door without a word.

Which of Gracie's relatives was his accomplice? Another unknown. I chewed my lip, then forced myself to stop. Attitude is everything in showdowns. Yet I'd never been so maddened or frustrated. I couldn't do anything. I didn't know anything.

Why kidnap me and Holly? At worst, this could only result in two more murders. I also didn't see the profit in using my phone to lure Mrs. C out of hiding. Archie and his conspirator had her set up as the murder suspect. Why not let the police find her?

The man in question walked to the leather chair next to the black and chrome table and sat. He put the gun on the glass top, resting his hand on the weapon.

I raised a brow. "You're evidently settling in for a long wait."

"We'll see." He shrugged. "The gun can get heavy. If my hand gets tired, I might miss and only wound."

I clicked my tongue in mock sympathy. "That would be a shame. A misfire could ruin your plans."

A muffled noise that sounded like a giggle erupted from Holly. Her eyes sparkled.

I was relieved to see her color had returned, but the hint of mischief in her expression gave rise to a new worry.

Hoping she wouldn't do anything crazy, I returned to harassing Archie. "You do have a plan, right? I'd hate to think I'm involved with amateurs, which is how it's been shaping up."

The skin across his cheeks tightened. He raised a brow in a stiff upper lip expression.

"Neville's murder was perfectly executed." I deliberately used the harsh word to smack Archie in the face with his crime. Annoyance by pinpricks and paper cuts.

Anger simmered in the air around my target.

"Full marks for the advance planning." I exchanged a look with Holly, who obliged with a nod. "Since then, there are indications of an over eagerness. The scorpion episode especially smacks of desperation."

Archie's gun hand twitched. The cinnamon-colored wall behind him darkened with the shadows of the dying day.

"You don't have to say anything." I assured him in the face of his silence. "Loyalty among thieves and all that. Or should I say murderers?"

His hand spasmed on the grip of the automatic. "Do you ever stop talking?"

I hid my jangling nerves behind a careless flick of my wrist.

"If you're going to kill me anyway, the least you can do is assuage my curiosity." I eyed him with a skeptical expression. "Do you know the whole story? Are you part of the inner circle?"

His jaw clenched.

The response was slight, but it was enough. My dart had struck home. His accomplice was pulling the strings. If Archie were in charge, he'd have outed Mrs. C immediately. The last thing he wanted was for the police to keep poking into this case. Someone wanted to play games with her, to see her twist in the wind.

Now it was time for me to rub salt in his wound. I turned to Holly and put a hand on her arm. "Bear with me. This may take some explaining."

"Don't worry about me." Her pink cheeks and shining eyes looked out of place in the room's dark atmosphere. "I find this fascinating."

I quelled a geyser of fear. Her enthusiasm and his twitchy trigger finger were a bad mix. Unfortunately, I had no other option but to forge ahead.

"Correct me if I'm wrong," I paused to draw breath.

Archie leaned in ever so slightly.

I had my fish on the hook. Now to reel him in. "The person who planned the murder seems to have lost sight of the reason you started this scheme."

He shifted in his chair, made a show of hooking one ankle over his other knee. "You don't know anything."

I knew I was on the right track. He hadn't scoffed. He hadn't sneered. The rigid set to his body hadn't relaxed.

"I know people." I glanced at Holly again. I tried not to notice the shadows creeping into the bedroom behind her. Tried not to wonder when she and I would no longer be necessary. That would mean the ringleader had Mrs. C.

That would mean I had failed everyone.

I squashed the dismal thoughts and focused on Archie. "If all your boss wanted was a patsy for Neville's murder, they could have turned in Mrs. Colchester that first night. Saturday morning at the latest."

Archie opened his mouth only to clamp it shut with a snap so hard he could have cracked a tooth. Perhaps he'd argued in favor of that option.

"The only reason she wasn't exposed the night of the murder was because the person in charge wanted to toy with her. Jab her with little pins."

Like I was doing to Archie.

"The attack on my mother proved especially dangerous for you." Derision added a sneer to my voice. "That's how Jamie realized two different women were involved. Mrs. C at Rycliffe on Friday and the imposter at Rowdy Reptiles Saturday."

Good grief. Had my mom really only been stung a day ago? Would this weekend never end?

"Now, you have Jamie to worry about." A tiny note of sympathy sounded in my voice. I tried to go big, but I could only muster a sliver of false concern. "No matter what you do with us, you still have to silence her."

"She has no proof." Archie's silence ended abruptly. "By the time she comes out of cover, her confused version won't matter."

After enough pinpricks even the toughest balloon pops. Good thing. I was nearing the end of credible guesses. Now to make the most of his slip.

His reference to timing implied a deadline. Only one looming finish line came to mind...

"Selling the Infantino sketch was your goal all along." I eyed him through a narrowed gaze. "Due to the clumsiness of the operation, your payout is in danger."

Alarm clouded his stiff expression before he concealed his emotions.

Holly, fortunately, decided to join the conversation. "How do you know the sketch is the key?"

I shrugged. "If Archie and his pal aren't worried about Jamie's testimony, their endgame is soon. The sketch goes on the block tomorrow. The payoff for that one piece is enough to justify any risk to a greedy person."

Archie sniffed at my explanation. "Jamie will be ferreted out."

I made a harsh buzzer sound. "Too late."

He snatched the pistol off the table.

I'd gone too far. Panic clutched at my heart. Hiding my fear, I spoke quickly. "Jamie won't be found."

Not when Rabi and Kevin had hidden her.

That was the one detail I could be certain of in this case.

Comprehension dawned in his gaze. "Your buddy from the hospital caught up with her."

His words puzzled me for an instant. Then, it was my turn to put the clues together. "You were the gunman in the stairwell."

His slim build. His height. It all fit.

He glared as he rubbed his head. "I took a bad spill thanks to you."

Though I worried about his itchy trigger finger, I wasn't about to let that go unanswered. "You were planning to shoot my boyfriend. In the back, most likely."

He snorted. "I only intended to shoot *Jamie*."

"Oh, that makes your attack excusable." A heavy dose of sarcasm underscored my words. "Next time I'll stay on the sidelines."

"You should have stayed out of the whole affair." His voice rose before he caught himself and fell silent.

"I'm being paid to solve this crime." I reminded him. "I have to earn my money."

Which I hadn't done so far. I had a dozen facts. Lots of clues. One clear villain, but his accomplice was unknown.

Though Payton was still in the running, Weatherington as a conspirator had lost its allure. Yet only Weatherington knew that Jamie was going to the hospital.

What would he have done when Jamie called babbling about conspiracy theories? Who would he have gone to?

My head turned slowly toward Holly. Her blond hair was the one bright thing in the room's dark atmosphere. "Did Weatherington tell you about Jamie's phone call?"

Holly nodded. "We were in the gallery getting ready for tonight's auction."

I stared at the PR rep in stunned shock. "Were others there?"

Furrows marred her brow. "Mr. Weatherington burst into the gallery when I was giving several patrons a tour. He thought Jamie was on drugs. They all heard."

I barely managed to stop my groan. After one murder, Holly hadn't been concerned enough to contact the police? Or me? "Why didn't you tell me?"

"I tried to call her, but she didn't answer." Holly's lips trembled. "I didn't know Jamie was in danger. I was so relieved she was safe. I thought once she settled down, she'd call me."

I tried not to roll my eyes. Instead, I patted her arm. Her reasoning wasn't all bad. One or more of the attendees must be Gracie's relatives. "Don't worry. She's safe."

Safer than us.

Archie shot me an arrogant, know-it-all expression.

I ground my teeth and fought to align the facts. Instead, Mrs. C's image forced its way into my brain. With the sands of time running out, I gave my subconscious free rein. Hopefully my brain knew more than I did.

The first death, fifty years ago, had started Mrs. C and Gracie running. They'd spent decades hiding, creating new identities, searching for a new life.

Mrs. C, with nothing to lose, considered it an adventure.

Gracie lost her family and her future. She left her art behind. No more drawing or painting. She lived off the grid, knowing all the time that due to her skill as a forger she had a potential fortune at her fingertips. What had Mrs. C said? Gracie wanted fame and fortune.

What if she took a shortcut to achieve her goal?

My thoughts skidded to a stop. A white-hot burst of lightning reduced my seemingly random thoughts into one question.

"What are you thinking?" Archie's sharp tone intruded as if on cue.

I slammed back to the present with dizzying speed. My hands hurt from their death-like grip on the couch cushions.

"I'm thinking..." Unclenching my hands, I let a knowing smile tip up the edges of my mouth. "An ambitious person like Gracie might have chosen to supplement her income. She had a gift for copying great artists, but she would have needed help selling the pieces. Too many finds from the same person would look suspicious."

Archie's body jerked as if my words had delivered an arrow straight to his heart, or his wallet.

"Holly," I cast the blonde a sideways glance. "Has Archie found other valuable pieces of art over the past... say fifteen years or so?"

A thoughtful expression drove the vestiges of worry from her face. She studied him with a narrowed gaze. "He's had a string of successful finds spaced throughout the last twenty years or so. Nothing like the Infantino, but added together, he had an almost unbelievable string of luck."

Blood drained from Archie's face, leaving him with less color than the ghosts we'd hunted at Rycliffe. "I have a gift."

I love it when I'm right. "Sure, a gift for fraud."

Though I was smiling on the inside, I kept a business-like expression on my face. Let them think I was a professional with all the answers. "No wonder killing Jamie is worth getting your hands dirty."

Archie's fingers curled over the handle of his gun, still lying on the table. His grip alternated between going slack and a white-knuckled grip.

"You need this sale to go off without anyone asking questions." I had to keep talking. If he focused on my words, hopefully, he wouldn't think to use the gun. "Once the sale is made, the profits will be sent to the *owner*, your accomplice in Arizona."

My breath caught in my throat. The accomplice. Wouldn't it close the loop nicely if Gracie's relatives were involved in the sale, getting their cut? Who else would he trust in so delicate a scheme? That would give them an excuse to be on-site for the sale and – more importantly – for killing Neville and framing Mrs. C. Was that part of their deal for cooperating?

A loud ring erupted from his cell phone.

I jumped at the jarring noise, relieved to see the other two jerk as well.

Archie recovered first. The tight lines around his eyes eased. He snatched at the phone with his free hand.

I swallowed my disappointment along with a wave of worry. Just when I was finally putting pieces together, I was out of time.

Holly's touch on my arm left shivers in their wake.

A knock on the door froze Archie with his thumb hovering over the phone. He stared at the door with a puzzled frown.

For the first time since I saw him, I felt a bit of hope. Whoever was at the door was obviously unplanned. Perhaps, Holly and I had a chance to survive.

23

30 Across; 7 Letters;
Clue: A source of help in an emergency
Answer: Cavalry

Archie's tension returned full force at a second rap on the door. His narrowed gaze remained riveted on the door.

A second blast from his phone burned its way through my veins and brought the anxiety level in the room to DefCon Three.

He brought the gun to bear on me and Holly from the other side of the suite's sitting room, then answered the phone with no greeting. "Someone's at the door. From you?"

Holly's fingers dug into my hand.

Adrenaline pumped through my blood with the help of my heart beating double time.

The sharp knock sounded again. "Hotel maintenance."

The low drawl zapped my heart into a dizzying triple beat.

It was Rabi.

Though relief spread through my body, I kept my attention on Archie. I couldn't imagine how my little band of detectives had found our trail. Thankfully, what they lacked in numbers, they made up for in cunning.

His expression tightened even more. "I can't move them. A janitor is at the door."

Holly's fingers tightened around mine. "A reprieve."

I had no way to tell her the cavalry had arrived. Perhaps it was just as well, I couldn't risk Rabi's safety by giving the game away.

The squeal of a walkie-talkie sounded through the door.

"No answer at four seventeen." Pause. Static. "Want me to go in?"

I wasn't sure maintenance people were allowed to come into a hotel room if the person didn't open the door, but Archie looked as if his heart had dropped to his shoes, along with every ounce of blood in his body.

He bolted to his feet. Momentum carried him halfway to the door. He stopped, spun, and pointed the gun at us. "Not. One. Word."

I shook my head. I put a hand in front of Holly as a warning for her to remain still as well.

Rabi wouldn't need our help.

"Hold on. I'll get rid of him." Archie clutched both phone and weapon in twin white-knuckled grips. He lowered the phone before facing the door. "You have the wrong room. I didn't call the front desk."

"Maybe your wife called," Rabi answered. "Is the air-conditioning working now?"

"I'm not married." Archie's voice rose as he wiped sweat off his upper lip with his phone hand. "The AC is fine. There's no problem here."

Rabi's voice sounded through the door as he supposedly reported to the front desk. He argued as "they" insisted the problem existed.

On our side of the door, Archie was engaged in his own disagreement. "Send someone to get rid of him."

He pressed the phone close to his ear. His eyes hardened to rocks of coal. He flicked a glance in my direction, weighted with a significance I didn't understand. Then I realized he hadn't told his caller that I'd guessed a good portion of their scheme.

Rabi's murmur continued in the hall.

"I haven't been compromised." Archie clipped each word off with the precision of a surgeon cutting off an arm. "You're the one with a missing witness."

He hung up without waiting for a response, frowned at the phone then pocketed it.

Trouble among the conspirators was a good thing for my side, but his "I haven't been compromised" comment didn't bode well for me and Holly. He'd have to kill us both to avoid leaving a trail.

Archie raised the gun again, then started toward the door with a grim expression.

For the first time, my throat closed with fear for Rabi.

"Sorry for the interruption." Rabi's apology held a disgusted note. "It's the fifth floor."

His voice faded on the final words.

Archie, gun aimed at the door, didn't move.

I fought to draw air into my starving lungs.

Archie stared at the door for a long moment. Then, he walked over and peered through the spyhole. When he pivoted and sauntered toward us, his easy stride telegraphed his returning confidence.

Murder in a locked room. He could cut his losses and walk away. It wasn't as if the bad guys would be dumb enough to rent this room in their own names.

I raised my chin against a new and growing fear. A few minutes. That's all my peeps needed.

"Let's get back to the plan, Archie." I hid the thudding of my heart behind a cavalier grin worthy of Marcus at his best. "How did you find the sketch? Hidden in one of the art books you bought from the Ponzers? You must have had heart failure when you realized what you had."

"Nice try, but you'll never know." He stood over us, the weapon held in an easy, confident grip. "I see no need to unburden my soul."

I crossed my legs and casually draped my arm over the end of the couch. My mouth tipped up in a sly smile.

Our captor clicked his tongue. "Too bad you're not as good as your reputation."

That seemed a constant refrain this weekend.

"I'm good enough, Archie." That's all I needed to be, I told myself. Good enough to keep him guessing until the time was right.

However long that might be. I buried the uncharitable thought. My troops would come.

"Good enough," I repeated. "To know you'll be the one charged with murder. You're the one who has to pull the trigger. You're the one who escorted us through the halls."

"No one saw us," he countered.

It was my turn to sneer. "You can't know that. It only takes one."

"It doesn't matter." Holly's voice had a breathless undertone. She tossed her head, possibly to hide her nerves. "There are cameras, newly installed in the halls and elevators."

Archie rolled his eyes. "This fabrication is the best you two can muster? We're done."

Though he dismissed it, my heart vaulted in a somersault of hope. This wasn't the type of thing Holly would make up.

Holly leaned closer, cheeks flushed a bright pink. "We host auctions worth millions of dollars with international guests from the highest levels of society, including foreign dignitaries. The surveillance system was upgraded due to the increase of global violence. Do you think we tell anyone outside of our own personnel?"

Nice touch. Very believable. My hope rose with each word.

Uncertainty flickered in his eyes.

I crossed my arms over my chest. "Believe her or don't, Archie. Either way, with three deaths, this case will never grow cold."

His hand tightened on the weapon. "The police have the killer. She's on-site. You got too close and she shot you. It's elegant."

"Hardly." I furrowed my brow. Actually, it was fairly believable, except the police and Crawford knew me and Mrs. C. "I expected better from a Brit."

He simply shrugged. "I'm done talking."

I sensed the guillotine about to fall. I poured all my certainty into my gaze.

"This will never be done." That much I knew to be true. "My friends know Mrs. Colchester would never hurt me. They'll follow the trail as long as it takes and that trail leads to you. Not your ally. You."

I paused for one precious moment, relishing the feel of my heart beating in my chest.

He hoisted the gun.

"No one knows your associate." I pointed to the phone. "They have nothing on the line."

An infinitesimal shake of his head caught the light reflecting off the sweat on his brow.

His gaze revealed nothing. I'll give him that.

He started to shrug. A click from the door turned his gesture into a full body shudder.

We all turned and froze.

The door was flung open. A mindless humming sounded.

Archie pocketed the gun. Stepped forward. "Who's there?"

I leaned forward. My pulse picked up speed. A maid's cart sat in the open doorway. A quick flick of a uniformed arm stuck a rolled-up towel in the top corner to keep the door from closing.

A slim brunette faced her cart in the hall. Her quick hands grabbed supplies as she jived to music only she heard. Wires from earbuds draped over the shoulder of the black uniform.

My chest seized. Another innocent in the fray?

No. This couldn't be a coincidence.

Archie stormed forward. "This room is occupied."

Keeping my eyes on the main action, I shifted toward Holly. "Be ready. Follow my lead."

To do what, I had no idea. My teeth clenched.

Were these my peeps?

What was their plan?

Did they have a plan?

Archie blocked my view of the woman. "Get out."

The mindless tune continued. Her white sneakers turned toward the room. When she faced him, an ear-splitting scream bounced off the walls, reverberated down the entryway, and into the suite.

Behind me, Holly started to rise. "This is our chance."

I pushed her down without looking. "Not yet."

Archie had his hand in his pocket, on the trigger, no doubt.

"What are you doing here?" The woman's New York accent tone sounded accusing. "This floor is empty. The Saudi prince is due tonight."

Ignoring my own warning, I half-rose. I didn't recognize the woman's voice. Archie's tall frame blocked her face.

The man advanced steadily. The outline of the gun was clear against the fabric of his jacket. "I have this room reserved for the weekend."

He continued toward the woman, forcing her back.

I found myself on my feet.

"I'm sorry, sir, but you can't be in this room," the maid protested. "Let me call the main desk."

Putting his hands on her shoulders, he propelled her to the threshold, then beyond. He flung out his left arm, pointing behind her. "Get out."

Archie was suddenly pulled forward. His body crashed into the housekeeping cart. A second later, he shot back into the room.

24

13 Across; 6 Letters;
Clue: A surprise attack
Answer: Ambush

Shock held me in place even as adrenaline pulsed through my veins. I breathed a sigh of relief when Rabi and Mrs. C followed Kevin and Archie into the sitting room of the suite.

Sixty seconds of sound and fury ended when Kevin pushed a battered Archie into the chair he'd just left. Our erstwhile captor massaged his throat where my boyfriend's elbow had connected with satisfying force.

Rabi stood over him like a sentinel on guard. His face stern. His eyes hard as granite.

Kevin's hard expression softened as his dagger-like gaze swept over me.

I threw myself into his arms. A surge of relief spread through me like a warm river as he gave me a tight hug. I was stunned that he and the others had been able to find me and Holly. Though, in hindsight, I should have had more faith.

They're a great group of sneaks.

Rabi, ever vigilant, had pocketed Archie's gun and frisked him. His black eyes settled on me for a moment, then he gave a silent nod.

"You all right, ducks?" Mrs. C's worried gaze studied me from beneath a brown wig. An artful makeup job had taken a good fifteen years off her age. "Thank goodness I was here to help."

I was too happy to do anything but grin at her cheeky attitude. "Absolutely."

She was already settled into the tan leather chair next to the sofa and had slipped off a pair of loafers. An exaggerated sigh of relief followed. Then, with an exclamation, she reached into her oversized pocket and pulled out a tangle of plastic strips. "I thought these might come in handy this weekend."

I couldn't believe my eyes. Zip-ties?

Of course, who doesn't carry a few zip-ties at all times? I arched a brow at Kevin before helping him secure Archie's hands behind his back.

Holly had shrunk as far into the sofa as she could get during the brawl. Her nervous gaze took in my friends before settling on me. "Friends of yours?"

"You know Kevin." Taking a man prisoner is no reason to forgo good manners. I put my arm around Kevin's shoulder for a quick hug before completing the introductions. "I don't understand how you knew where I was... we were."

"You left." Rabi took up station by the door. "I followed."

I'd forgotten Rabi's text that he was on-site. I hadn't noticed him in the ballroom or in the hall. The man had a knack for being inconspicuous.

Kevin clamped a vise-like grip on Archie's shoulder. "Who's this guy?"

"Archie Smythe, the art dealer. Marcus was right. He and his nameless contact are the hidden villains of the piece." I gave a quick update of what I'd learned. Then, I cast Mrs. C an apologetic look. "It's time to bring in the police. You'll have to duck out."

I'd kept Jamie under wraps. I hadn't turned in Mrs. C, who was wanted for murder. Now, we had a man handcuffed in a chair. Even with Crawford's influence, this would take some tap dancing to explain to the authorities.

The older woman waved away my concern. "Tch, don't mind me. Of course, you have to give him to the bobbies. I'll make myself scarce."

Archie perked up. "Who's the old bird? Somebody important?"

Kevin smacked him upside the head.

A buzzing noise cut across their interaction.

Mrs. C pulled out her phone. One eyebrow rose. "It's a text from Tracy."

Rabi's eyes narrowed.

I nodded as the puzzle pieces fell into place. "That was their plan."

"What does the message say?" Kevin demanded.

Mrs. C glanced at the phone. "'Come to the gazebo past the tennis courts now. K and I are waiting. Hurry.'"

I listened objectively. "That sounds like me."

"You're always running toward trouble." Mrs. C pressed her lips together as she studied the message. "It's well done. No need to check with Kevin. He's mentioned."

"We can't lose this opportunity." The chance to nab the murderer shot a fresh jolt of adrenaline into my blood. I was ready to bolt now. "If Mrs. C doesn't show up, the mastermind might take off."

"No time to coordinate a grab with the cops." Determination and anticipation mixed in Kevin's tone. He exchanged a glance with Rabi. "Someone needs to watch the stooge. I'll text Rickson."

"You could help yourself." I eyed Archie. "Tell us what you know."

A bark of laughter burst out of the man's mouth. "I'll make my deal with the authorities."

"What if your friend slips away?" Mrs. C's British accent was laced with undercurrents. With her ankles crossed, she was a perfect picture of etiquette. Interrogation in an English manor house. "If you're the only one we've got, you'll be convicted of murder."

Archie's mouth thinned. "I didn't kill Neville."

I jumped on the opening. "That won't matter. The city needs a scapegoat and you'll be it."

Minutes were ticking by. Time we could ill afford.

I bent over until Archie and I were nose to nose. "You were set up from the beginning to take the fall."

"This was meant to be a victimless crime." Self-serving regret underlay Archie's bitter tone. "The sketch is real. The provenance is flawless. The art houses know me in Langsdale. I've been coming here for a decade. If Neville had looked the other way, he'd be alive."

"Don't be naïve," Kevin jeered. "The man was meant to die."

I glanced at my boyfriend, struck by his statement. Then I turned to our captive. "Neville was murdered in the same manner as his father. The note targeted Gracie Linden. Those aren't coincidences. You were a pawn. Yours is the only face we've seen."

Archie frowned. Uncertainty crept into his expression.

I tried a new track. Pulling back, I shrugged. "You know what? Your cohort getting away isn't my problem. I turn you in to the police and get paid. You rot in prison. The murderer plans another art sale with another stooge."

Archie strained against the plastic ties. His arms shook with the effort. "I did the work. I took the risks."

I stepped away. "We have you for two counts of kidnapping. The Infantino sketch ties you to Neville. Your accomplice set you up. If they leave before we get to the meeting, you'll go down for Neville's murder, but go ahead, keep quiet. Sacrifice yourself."

His gaze darted from the windows to the wall like a trapped animal looking for a way out, a way to win. Finally, he slumped in the chair. "What do you want to know?"

Electricity zapped through my nerves. I sat. "Who is involved? Who's your accomplice?"

The firm clamp on his jaw lasted several more seconds. "Lisa Carmichael."

My resolve to keep a know-it-all mask in place dissolved. Life is so unfair. All my clues. All my theories. For this? "Who is she?"

"No doubt it's an alias," Mrs. C observed, calm in the face of my frustration. "Names aren't meant to be taken literally."

Well, she would know. I ran a hand through my already savaged hair. I'd rarely had such an irritating, frustrating, annoying case. "What about Payton? Or Weatherington?"

Archie looked at me as if I'd lost my marbles. "They're clueless."

Evidently, so was I. I had wanted one of them to be guilty. I tossed aside the self-pity. My parents hadn't raised a quitter. I was going to get answers, even if it meant starting from scratch. I faced Archie head-on. "Who's Lisa? How did you and she get together?"

"I could have been in Tahiti and you'd still be searching for answers." Archie spat the words at me. Self-recrimination fueled his anger. "You're no private eye."

"Yes, I am. I have a license to prove it." I upped my tone to full snarky mode. "And I'm not the one strapped in a chair."

Kevin, standing at the man's shoulder, allowed himself a smug smile.

I gave Archie a searching stare. "Your partner could be catching a plane right now. Talk or I'm leaving. Who's Lisa?"

His defense crumbled. "She's an antique dealer in Arizona. I met her several years ago when she was traveling in England. She agreed to go along with my story that she found the Infantino."

"I'll bet this isn't the first time she's gone along with one of your schemes." A flash in his eyes told me I'd scored a hit. But where did that lead me? I cocked my head to one side. They'd met in England? "Is Lisa related to Gracie Linden?"

"I don't know how this Gracie person got involved." Exasperation colored his retort. He scowled at me. "Lisa's an American. She's in it for the money. So, am I."

Kevin snapped his fingers. He shot me a triumphant look. "At last night's gala, the manager said the art dealer insisted the sketch had to be sold in Langsdale."

"Thank goodness one of us was paying attention." The importance of his words hit me instantly. "You couldn't set Mrs. C up for murder anywhere but here."

I thrust myself in Archie's face without hesitation and without warning. "Which means, you're lying."

Archie reared backward, trying to retreat from my attack. "No, I'm not! It wasn't me!"

"Enough!" I grabbed the sides of the chair with both hands and tipped it back. "You brought Neville here with notes taunting him about finding his father's killer. You brought Mrs. C to Rycliffe to frame her for murder."

The art dealer tried to escape. He pushed at the floor. The chair slanted at a precarious angle. "I didn't do it! I didn't. It was her. I swear."

I grabbed his shirt with both hands. "Quit lying."

Just as the chair passed the tipping point to send Archie crashing to the floor – and I was going to let him go – Kevin grabbed the frame, pulled it from my grasp and righted it.

Feeling like a child who's had her cotton candy pulled out of her hand, I cast him a questioning look.

He looked slightly disappointed as he shook his head. "He's telling the truth."

I stomped my foot. Why did my suspects keep turning out to be innocent? Well, he was innocent of murder. "Coming to Langsdale was Lisa's idea?"

"Yes." Archie nodded so fiercely it looked as if his head would fall off. "We've sold several items here over the last decade. She thought it would be a good venue. No big deal."

Mrs. C shifted in her seat. "Ooooh, that was well played, then, wasn't it?"

"Reconnaissance." Rabi's low drawl confirmed Lisa's deft handling of setting the scene in Langsdale. She'd had years to confirm Mrs. C's location and identity.

"She must be working with Gracie's family." I heaved a sigh, then pointed a finger at Archie. "Why was Neville in town? Lisa's idea?"

Scowling, Archie shrugged his thin shoulders. "Neville called her a few weeks ago with questions. She got worried. I told her if she stuck to the story, we were good."

I stepped back, puzzled. That didn't add up. "Why leave the note by Neville's body? Who sent him and Mrs. Colchester the notes to come to Rycliffe on Friday night?"

"I don't know." Archie reared up, pulling the chair off the ground. Frustration fueled his anger. "I never heard the name Colchester before. I didn't send Neville any notes, and I didn't kill him!"

Kevin pulled the chair down.

Archie's chair slammed to the floor with a resounding thud.

I didn't need to check with Kevin to know the art dealer spoke the truth. He was in this scheme for the money. Neville's death only complicated the sale. A sale that would have gone through if he and Lisa Carmichael stood by the make-believe provenance.

The only player I had left was this Lisa person. Could she be Gracie's sister or niece? A family acquaintance in the world of art dealers? "How old is Lisa?"

Irritation flashed in Archie's eyes. "I didn't check her ID. Mid-to-late-fifties."

"That's all you know?" I'd hoped for more. Raising a brow in query, I glanced at Kevin, asking for his profiling judgment.

My boyfriend gave a grudging nod.

My puzzle had gaping holes where answers should have been. "Who did you give my phone to?"

"A messenger." Archie's muscles bunched, straining against the ties, evidently tiring of the interrogation, surly at having been caught. "They had instructions to pick it up here and drop it off at another room."

"What room?" I asked.

"I don't know." He snapped off the words, disgust clear in his tone. "It wasn't important."

My sense of uneasiness grew like a balloon on steroids. "What's the plan?"

"I don't know details." A sneering note crept into his tone and his manner. His supercilious smile spoke volumes. "Lisa said she could get the police off our backs with one phone call."

"This is to get Mrs. C out of hiding." Kevin's voice hardened. "If the police get their suspect, the case will be closed."

"An arrest would bring notoriety to the sale of the sketch." I stood, suddenly impatient to be gone from Archie. "I'm done with you."

His shoulders slumped. A long exhale escaped his clenched teeth. "How could you have ruined over a year of planning in only days?"

I shrugged and gave him a mocking grin. "It's a gift."

A tap at the door signaled an end to the interview.

A moment later Rickson lumbered into the suite. He took up a quarter of the living area, not to mention a good deal of the oxygen.

"Marcus and your parents are in our suite." Kevin answered my unspoken question. "Crawford sent extra guards when you went missing."

"I got this." Rickson's advance seemed to crowd out even the lengthening shadows. He nudged my shoulder in a playful punch that knocked me off-balance. "Go get 'em, Tracy."

"I can't believe I'm in on one of your cases." Holly clasped her hands together. "Except, this time, I'll stay behind."

"I agree." I was relieved she'd be safely away from any further action. "You were brave, but we'll take it from here."

"Come along, ducks." Mrs. C's gaze shown with the light of battle.

While Kevin and Rabi followed the older woman, I marched toward Rickson. With every step, I had to wonder why I wasn't walking in the opposite direction.

I bounced my fist off Rickson's broad chest. "Remember Marcus's strategy for winning checkers - cover the corners and watch all the pieces."

It was also my son's code to warn against treachery from a supposed ally. Evidently, my brain didn't completely trust Holly. Or perhaps being kidnapped had made me paranoid.

His broad, plain face didn't so much as twitch. But a glimmer sparked in his eyes. "I got things here."

Out in the hall I breathed a sigh of relief. A mountain's weight of worry lifted off my shoulders. "Now, I'm ready."

"What was that about?" Kevin asked.

I met his gaze and admitted. "I have no idea."

Kevin hugged me to his side. "That's what I love about you."

"That I don't have a clue?" I asked. "Or that I admit the fact?"

"You're not *totally* clueless." Mrs. C studied me with her pale, but shrewd, eyes. "You leap in with your heart. Your head catches up, eventually."

I wasn't sure if that was an insult or a compliment. Though I had to admit, it sounded like my MO.

Rabi, loping ahead of us, glanced over his shoulder. His quick wink held a gleam of admiration.

Kevin glanced over his shoulder. He cast me a puzzled glance. "You're suspicious of Holly?"

"I must be." If only the back half of my brain would tell the rest of me what was going on. "I've been blindsided in this case more than once. She's had as much opportunity as anyone else to work behind the scenes. Besides, she's young, blond, and perky. What's to like?"

Kevin chuckled.

Mrs. C did a fast shuffle ahead of us, half-leaning on and half-pushing the maid's cart. "Gracie and I were several years younger than her when we left England."

Her words brought to mind an impression that had been growing all weekend. The feeling that Gracie and Mrs. C had two different views of their shared past.

Though I hadn't said anything, my gut told me the heart of the case revolved around that schism, plus Gracie's skill as a forger as well as the fifty-year-old murder.

However, with Gracie long dead, Mrs. C's memories were the only version I had of the past.

A moment later, we poured into the elevator.

While my nerves revved up, my mind whirled. "Are Payton and Weatherington accounted for?"

"Until ten minutes ago, we were rescuing you." Kevin straightened his navy jacket, appearing unconcerned by the missing players. "By the time Rabi texted me that you were being kidnapped, the auction was over and everyone split."

I shifted to the upcoming confrontation. "That gazebo is isolated."

"No cover." Rabi growled.

"The lights cast a halo on the bushes around the gazebo." Kevin's tone was equally disgusted. "We won't be able to get close."

"The murderer set you up from the beginning." I cast a worried glance at Mrs. C. "Maybe you shouldn't go."

"I'll not have them endangering the only family I've ever had in me life." A new timbre echoed in the older woman's tone. Her jaw hardened. "I've run for the last time in my life. Here, I stand and fight."

I gazed at the irascible old woman. "I'm going with you."

"We all are." A fierce look lit Kevin's eyes. "We're family."

"Damn straight." Rabi's low voice put a period on the decision.

The thought of Mrs. C walking into a trap was more than I could stomach. There had to be another way. Besides, I like to keep an ace in the hole. "I hate playing into the murderer's hands by giving them what they want."

"I know you love confrontations, but you can't play this time." Kevin tapped a rhythm on the elevator wall. "No one would mistake you for Mrs. C. Besides, everyone in the resort has seen you."

I eyed Mrs. C's wig. "That doesn't mean they'll recognize me."

Rabi followed the direction of my gaze. His attitude sharpened as his attention lit on the maid's cart Mrs. C had hauled into the elevator. "Leaning on the cart will disguise your height."

Mrs. C's jaw tightened. "This is my fight. I can't let you go."

"I'm not the one they want." I tried to placate her. "The cart will give me protection if Archie's partner tries anything. If running is called for, I'm quicker than you. And Rabi has Archie's gun."

"Belden's right." Kevin put a hand on the older woman's shoulder. "Rabi and I won't let anything happen to her."

"All I need is a few minutes," I said.

Kevin talked through the details. "A hooded sweatshirt would hide your face. A phone in your pocket dialed into us so we can hear you. Rabi and I will get as close as we can."

"Whoever shows up will be incriminated. What other excuse could they have for being at this meeting?" And I might be able to finish off my crossword puzzle with the name of the killer.

25

3 Across; 8 Letters;
Clue: To conceal one's identity
Answer: Disguise

The housekeeping cart rattled over the pathway as I made the final turn toward the gazebo. Careful to stay hunched over and to keep my youthful hands hidden in my sleeves, I slowed my gait to a crawl.

I'd circled around to enter from the shadier. Wearing the hooded sweatshirt Rabi had liberated should buy me another minute or two. I shuffled into the fringes of light and peered through the hood I had pulled up to cover my face.

"Where are you, ducks?" My best English accent whispered forward. "What's afoot, eh?"

I'd always wanted to use the word Sherlock Holmes made famous. I could almost see Kevin rolling his eyes. He and Rabi were listening on the open line of the cell phone stuck in the breast pocket of the maid's uniform.

Silence answered my query. I edged forward. My heart thumped with anticipation to see who had framed Mrs. C for murder and exactly what they had planned for her now.

"The place is deserted." Leaning forward on the cart had the added benefit of giving me closer access to the cell phone. "Wait. A figure is entering the gazebo from the other side."

I hung back, which would only be natural. "Tracy, luv, is that you, then?"

"She's not here." A female form advanced from the darkness on the opposite side of the gazebo.

The familiar voice was followed by a face I knew well.

Payton.

A victory march played in my brain. I'd been right. Neville's assistant was the murderer.

Remembering my role, I looked around with a wary air.

Mrs. C would not have been expecting the Jerrone administrator.

"Thankfully, Ms. Belden is nowhere around." Payton's tone held a cutting edge. "I've seen enough of that self-styled investigator to last a lifetime."

The Belden charm strikes again, though I took exception to that self-styled crack. I was getting paid for this gig. I had a P.I. license. Why did I have to keep reminding people I was a professional?

Perhaps I should have T-shirts printed up. Marcus would do it, but he'd charge me.

I quickly refocused on Mrs. C's response.

"Who are *you* then?" I laid the English accent on a bit thick I admit. "How'd you get Tracy's phone? Where is the girl?"

A frown furrowed the other woman's brow. "I don't have her phone. I came in response... "

Her abrupt silence shot my worry meter into the red zone. A response meant there had been a summons. Had she been brought here, too? This didn't sound good.

Payton stepped forward boldly. "Why did you murder Neville? You couldn't even have known him. Why kill him?"

I stared at her, speechless. As the murderer, Payton was the one person who knew Mrs. C had no reason to confess.

Increasingly wary, I froze. This meeting wasn't adding up.

She sounded like a wounded innocent, which didn't jibe with kidnapping me and stealing my phone.

Payton stepped closer again. Her hands reached out in a pleading gesture. "Are you Gracie Linden? Did he confront you about your past?"

My thoughts whirled at warp speed as she pressed for a response.

"Did you plan it?" Her voice broke in a convincing manner. "Tell me it was an accident."

I gripped the handle of the maid's cart, grateful for the support. I shook my head to clear it.

"You were in the room while he lay dying." Her tone sharpened with accusation, evidently misinterpreting my gesture. "I need to know why you killed him."

My certainty of Payton as the murderer crumbled like a sandcastle in a tsunami. I shored myself up against the disappointment and waited as my brain flipped to what she'd said about responding.

To a call? A text like Mrs. C received?

On the night of the murder, the mastermind had pulled Mrs. C into the library with a note. Perhaps Neville had come in answer to a summons as well, not knowing who or what to expect.

Had this meeting been arranged with two blind messages? Mrs. C expecting me, while Payton came expecting - no, demanding an explanation.

Epiphany hit me like a solid blow to my sternum, knocking the breath out of me.

One call. Archie had said one call would double the price of the sketch. Kevin had pointed out that an arrest would spike the public's interest.

A groan escaped my lips. How could I be so stupid?

The woman was wearing a wire. Even if she *were* guilty, she could have contacted the police and claimed she'd received a message summoning her to this meeting.

"Tell me the truth, please." Tears filled Payton's thickening voice.

I put my head in my hand. The gesture brought my lips closer to the phone in my upper pocket. "She's wired. The cops must be close. There's no way for me to get out."

I took a deep breath, straightened to my full height, and threw back the hood. "Can the act, Payton. Mrs. C isn't here and she's not coming."

When I stepped into the light, the young woman paled. She grabbed at her throat, gasping for air.

I rushed around the cart, convinced she was having a heart attack. "Are you okay?"

She held up her hand as if to ward me off. "What are you doing here?"

Her screech stopped me in my tracks even as her hands clenched into white-knuckled fists. "Everywhere I turn you're in my face."

"Your boss hired me to solve this case." Leaving the phone on, I decided attack was the best option. "Why did you consort with Archibald Smythe to murder Neville? Why did you have me kidnapped and arrange this trap for Mrs. C?"

She glared at me silently.

Running footsteps forestalled any further questions. Two men in rumpled suits burst out of the trees and into the gazebo.

Victor Wilson and Tom Rhoden were the detectives on this case. Wilson, Asian and older, was tightly wired and had wrinkles on his forehead, possibly due to his current frown, which looked to be permanent. Rhoden was a younger white guy, with a round, chubby face that made him look too gullible to be a cop.

Lesson in life, when in the wrong, go on the attack. Say or do anything as a distraction.

"What's going on?" My mouth formed an 'O' of surprise. I turned to Payton. "Someone kidnapped me and stole my phone. His partner texted Mrs. Colchester pretending to be me and arranged this meeting. Now I find you here with the police?"

I made a show of looking around wildly, backing up, and generally acting in fear of my life.

"Did you get that?" I jerked the phone out of my pocket. The hysterical fear in my voice was pure Oscar material. "The police are in on this murder cover-up. They framed Mrs. C."

"I got it all." Kevin stepped out of the shadows. He raised his phone. "So did our associate on the other connection. It's on record."

"There's no conspiracy." Wilson, the older man, stepped nearer, arms raised. He aimed an eagle eye at me. I'd spoken to him several times during this case and previously when I'd met Crawford at the local cop hangout. "As you well know."

"I know nothing of the kind." I certainly wasn't going to admit it. I fisted my hands on my hips. "I come here to help a friend who's being framed for murder."

"I don't believe you're here." Payton suddenly came to life, spitting the words at me. "If I *were* guilty, I'd confess just to get away from you."

"Thanks. A confession will make my job a lot easier." I pointed at Payton. "Detectives, get out your notebooks."

They stared at me, equal parts annoyed and frustrated.

I don't think they appreciated my humor.

Kevin hid a smirk behind his hand.

Wilson crossed his arms over his thin chest. An angry red flush started to creep up his neck. "How did you learn about this meeting? Why are you impersonating a suspected murderer?"

I glanced at Kevin, whose gaze telegraphed a warning. Keep it simple. I took another breath and tamped down my inner diva, who was struggling to rise to the occasion.

As much as I like a good scene, now wasn't the time to antagonize the police, not when the proverbial ice was cracking beneath my feet. After all, Archie and Holly had both witnessed me and Kevin talking with Mrs. C.

I couldn't afford to incriminate myself, not to mention Kevin and Rabi. Thankfully, Lisa Carmichael gave me a way out. Archie's co-conspirator provided an alternate suspect to Mrs. C.

At least that's how the scene played out in my mind. Hopefully, the detectives would buy my version. Several minutes later, I wrapped up a replay of the meeting with Archie.

"Obviously, Mrs. Colchester is the target. She's being framed." Followed closely by me I wanted to say. However, since Wilson's stern gaze hadn't thawed, I kept that bit to myself.

"You should have brought her with you." The older detective declared. "Where is she now?"

"I thought the murderer would be at this meeting. I was trying to get evidence to clear her." I spread out my hands in a gesture of innocence. "I told her the law required her to turn herself in. I'm sure that's where she headed."

No one present had taken me seriously, but I did say it. "I could hardly force the woman to come with me."

Wilson raised a brow. "You didn't hesitate to tie Archie Smythe to a chair."

"He kidnapped me." I'm the victim. Why didn't anyone see that? "He held me at gunpoint. He planned to kill Holly and me so he could sell a sketch he kept from the rightful owners."

"That's basically what happened." Kevin's calm, steady tone was in direct contrast to my higher pitched, more colorful version.

I knew from past similar scenes, that his confident manner and guy-next-door quality was a calculated appeal to get the detectives on his side. It usually worked. Compared to me, authority figures love to deal with Kevin.

"Mrs. Colchester left us ten minutes ago," Kevin continued. "She said she was leaving the resort."

"She could still be on-site." Wilson turned to Rhoden. "Have the uniforms and resort security be on the lookout. Check on Smythe."

The younger detective nodded and walked away, talking into his radio.

Impatient, I leaped in again. "If Lisa Carmichael was worried that Neville might expose her and Archie's fraud, she has a perfect motive for murdering him."

"Tracy, you'd make up any story to save your friend." Wilson said. "There's a lot of evidence implicating Mrs. Colchester."

"She has no motive." I had to tread carefully. So far, Mrs. C's real identity remained unknown to the authorities. "Mrs. Colchester could have been framed. Her manner of dress is distinctive."

The detective rolled his eyes. "To say the least."

"That makes her an easy target for identification." I parroted Kevin's earlier observation. "Once she discovered the body, the murderer had a perfect patsy."

I opened my mouth to lay out how the video could have been faked. After all, the phone wasn't turned in until this morning, more than a day after the murder.

Fortunately, every once in a while, my brain and my mouth communicate. This was one of those times. I remembered that no one outside the police force was supposed to know about the incriminating recording.

Wilson eyed me expectantly, waiting for me to continue.

I snapped my jaw shut and pulled up my best version of innocence. "My friend didn't kill Neville."

Air hissed out between the detective's tight lips.

Trying to convince Wilson was doing me no good. I'd be better off listening in on Detective Rhoden's interview with Archie. I gestured toward the resort. "Perhaps I could show you the room where I was held prisoner?"

Wilson grunted. "My partner can find room four-seventeen by himself."

I hid my disappointment. "Holly is easily startled. How about I go and make sure she's all right?"

The man gave me the death stare.

I edged backward. "I'm not under arrest, am I? I won't leave the property. I think I need to comfort Holly and sit down. Being kidnapped put me under such a strain."

Payton gave an unladylike snort. "Can you arrest her for being an annoying busybody?"

Fortunately for me, that wasn't a crime.

Wilson looked disappointed as he shook his head. His skepticism of my fragile condition was palpable.

Kevin, with perfect tag-team timing, stepped forward as I continued my retreat. "I'd be happy to answer any questions regarding what I know about the kidnapping and the aftermath with Mr. Smythe."

"Fine." Wilson ground out the word.

His icy glare tracked me as I backed out of the gazebo onto the closest path. I felt like the Cheshire Cat as I faded into the shadows.

Worried he'd call me back, I didn't turn around until I was completely out of his sight. Then I put on my running shoes and took off down the trail. I jogged for half-a-minute, taking several turns before I slowed to a stop.

Darkness. The elaborate landscaping blocked the horizon. A few lights flickered through the trees. Too bad I was farther away from those taunting lights then when I'd left the gazebo.

I bit my lip. A slow circle made me no wiser. Ornamental grasses and desert shrubs all look alike in the dark. A familiar feeling came over me. I was lost. I didn't even know how to find the gazebo.

Perhaps the sound of voices would point me in the right direction. Kevin and Wilson had to be close. I stood still and listened.

Taunting silence rewarded my efforts.

"Where are you headed?"

I spun to face the feminine voice. With my hand over my thudding heart, I admitted the truth. "I don't know where I am. I'm lost."

The woman's low chuckle held a dark note of triumph. "You made this far too easy."

I didn't have time to wonder at the dark-haired woman or her words. I was too busy staring at the gun she pulled out of her pocket.

26

32 Down; 6 Letters;
Clue: A feeling of having experienced a situation before
Answer: Deja Vu

"This can't be happening." I stared in disbelief. A second kidnapping? In the same day? "You're taking me hostage?"

Great, now I was starting to sound like Holly.

Archie's co-conspirator, Lisa Carmichael, in the flesh. She'd obviously sent both me and Payton the texts for tonight's meeting. Then, she'd waited on the sidelines to see who she pulled in.

She must have done the same thing to Neville and Mrs. C the night of the murder. The method worked once. Why not try it again? Like them, I'd fallen into her trap. I fought the urge to grind my teeth. Nowhere to go but forward.

"Evidently, the old adage is true." She walked out of the shadows with measured steps. "If you want something done, you have to do it yourself."

A menacing tone sharpened her husky voice. Despite her smooth skin, age lines showed around the artfully made-up eyes. Brunette. Early fifties. She matched Archie's description to a tee. "Lisa Carmichael, I presume?"

She stopped in a patch of moonlight well beyond my reach and set her feet. "You're a snarky, pushy broad."

"You make that sound like a bad thing." I was too numb to think, so I resorted to mouthing off. Other than Holly, no one appreciated me this weekend. "Those are my best qualities."

"You had to keep poking, jabbing."

"Speaking of jabbing." My brain came to life, fueled by indignation. "What is Mrs. C to you? Why paint a bull's-eye on her back?"

Lisa's mouth flattened. "She deserved everything she's gotten."

"You're connected to Gracie." My revenge theory returned full force. "What was she to you? A relative?"

The other woman's nostrils flared. Fury rolled off of her in waves. She lowered her head, reminding me of a bull getting ready to charge. At the same time, she hunched her shoulders.

The move multiplied the wrinkles around her neck and upper chest. The full moon highlighted her thin, parchment-like skin.

My gaze flipped to her face. Tight and unlined.

Too tight.

Her thin, wrinkled neck was far too old to match her face. That skin belonged on an older woman. Say, someone about Mrs. C's age.

Thunder roared in my ears as the world spun on its axis. What if the one thing I knew to be true, turned out to be a lie?

I stared into her eyes, bitter and hard. Their color was brown, contact lenses no doubt, to mask the pale eyes that matched Mrs. C's. "Gracie."

She jerked as if the whispered name was a knife and I'd cut open her heart.

She recovered quickly. "You may have a bit of a brain behind that mouth of yours after all."

"You lied." The surprise in my tone didn't begin to match the shock roaring through my veins. "You lied to Mrs. C all these years. You let her believe you died."

"How could I die?" Her voice rose to a crescendo. The gun wavered as her hand shook with fury. "The person I was pretending to be never lived. She was made of paper. She didn't leave behind a family or a mother she might never see again."

Her bitter words barely registered.

"Move." She jerked the gun toward the graveled path.

She'd lied. The phrase repeated in my brain. For some reason, that fact seemed to offend me more than the murder. She'd lied to Mrs. C from the beginning of their acquaintance.

I zeroed in on that last, unexpected nugget.

"I said move." Lisa... Gracie's grip tightened on the now steady gun. "You think I won't shoot? I can pull on a new face and disappear into the night. I have other names, but soon I won't need them. I'll be able to go and live with my mum and see my family. Soon Daniel's murder will be solved."

My adrenaline-filled body was screaming at me to do something, but my brain was still coming to grips with the fact that Gracie was alive.

She raised the gun. Her head nodded toward the eastern, most deserted area of the resort. "Start walking or else."

I turned slowly and started forward, taking position slightly in front of her.

"Not too fast," she warned.

Though I intended to follow her order, my body and brain weren't in sync. My feet tangled over each other.

"Don't try anything smart." The sharp command carried a wealth of warning.

I didn't feel too smart at this point. I threw out my arms, hands up. My peripheral vision caught a flash of the gun. "I stumbled."

With my heart thudding in my throat, I started walking again. My lungs strained against the steel grip of fear encasing my chest.

One step. Two. I forced my arms to my sides and filled my lungs with air. Where was Kevin and Rabi's cool savoir-faire in a crisis? Back at the hotel with them.

Determined to regain some measure of control, I focused on the new puzzle pieces. Gracie and Archie had made a complete jumble of my theories. Now that I had more information, I could find a pattern in this mess of lies and illusion.

In the meantime, I decided to resort to the tactic that never fails - mouth off and agitate. "You can't win. The cops have Archie. The sketch will be returned to the Ponzers. Your payoff is gone."

Her unladylike response had a hard edge to it. "You let me worry about that."

"This was your big strike." I flicked a glance in her direction. My dart had barely drawn a response. What was wrong with this picture? She'd just lost millions. "This prize fell into your lap after a lifetime of lies."

"Left."

Busy with my thoughts I followed her directions.

"You were overconfident." I threw in the note of derision that had wheedled its way under Archie's confident exterior. "Planning gave you an edge initially, but your emotions got the best of you. Hurting my mother to warn me away was a pointless risk."

The path led out of the ornamental landscaping. A flat vista met my gaze. We'd walked off of the resort property. I faced a stretch of emptiness so vast not even the combined light of the stars and the moon could pierce the darkness.

Endgame.

A large stone lodged next to my heart. Gracie had no further use for me, but if I was going to die, my snarky attitude was going to be with me to the last breath.

"Why didn't you turn Mrs. C into the cops when she slipped away from Rycliffe? Didn't you expect that contingency? How could you underestimate her like that?" I clicked my tongue in mock sympathy, then forced a chuckle. "Having Archie kidnap me was obviously one of your off-the-cuff ideas. They're going to be your downfall."

A tight laugh broke the silence and dissipated into the darkness that surrounded us. "You act like I'm going to be caught."

I sucked up my courage. I was going to badger answers out of this hag if it was literally the last thing I did. I might get shot, but I refused to die with my crossword puzzle incomplete. "The money for the sketch is what you're after. The big strike to ease you in your ancient years."

A hiss sounded behind me. "I'm younger than Delia. Mrs. C as you call her."

Finally, a crack in her facade. I should have guessed from the plastic surgery that vanity was Gracie's failing.

I tossed my head. At least I had her attention. "Mrs. C hasn't spent her life trying to steal money she doesn't deserve."

"She's an old fool." Gracie's voice trembled. "She treated our escape as an adventure. My life was a shambles. I left my mum behind. She's grown old and sick worrying about me, hasn't she? I didn't see my sister or brother for years. Always sneaking around, hiding. The world owes me. I want to live in the sun."

A sliver of an idea pierced the darkness surrounding me.

"You've been busy since you supposedly died." Pieces started falling into place. "Archie made a good living finding lost masterpieces. How many of those pieces were yours?"

Another glance behind showed her smug smile.

A clearer picture was taking shape. She surely had money stashed away. She'd traveled to England to visit her family. She'd said that her mother was alive, but the woman had to be in her nineties. Little time left to be together. Not to mention the upcoming documentary.

When Gracie didn't respond, I glanced at her.

"Time's running out for you isn't it?" I slowed my steps as unobtrusively as I could. "Your mother only has a few years left. Neville was cooperating on the documentary about the first murder."

"A murder I've been blamed for all these years." Venom laced her bitter tone.

I scanned the vast desert before and came to a decision. I spun to face her.

My about-face brought her up short.

Her hand tightened on the gun, tensing at my sudden confrontation. Her hard gaze glittered like the frozen heart of a dead volcano.

"You sent those notes to Neville. You lured him to Langsdale deliberately." Facing possible death brings amazing clarity. It also helps when you finally have all the players identified. "With him dead and Mrs. C convicted of both murders, you'd be in the clear."

Her expression didn't change. Decades of choosing the path of least resistance had robbed her of whatever morals she'd ever possessed.

She raised the gun and gestured behind me with it.

I remained where I was, facing her. "You sacrificed an innocent man to betray a woman who considered you a friend."

"She wasn't supposed to survive Friday night." The older woman shook the gun at the sky. Anger, then frustration crossed her face in waves. "He was there, attacking me. Me! Then, they blocked the stairs, didn't they? It all went against me. She was late. She ruined everything, as usual."

I couldn't believe the venom spewing out of her mouth like acid, burning and destroying everything it touched. "You blame her for how your life turned out?"

"She destroyed my life." The plastic face screwed up into a mask of hate and fury. "Leaving our homeland didn't cost her anything."

"Leaving England was your choice." I stabbed a finger at the woman. "Running, hiding, staying away all these years was the path you chose. She gave you the option to return. To give her name to the police. You refused."

A flicker of emotion swept over her face. Too quick. Too elusive to pin down. Her structured jaw tightened. "I was a fool."

So much for friendship. But the question that had bothered me for days refused to go away. Why had Gracie run away with Mrs. C and stayed away for fifty years?

Call me cynical, but I don't believe loyalty was a character trait Gracie had ever suffered from, even in her youth.

The other woman pointed behind me again. "Keep moving."

I was tired of being pushed around. I dug in my heels. "I'm not taking one more step."

We were already too far from the resort for help to come. At least, my body might be found quicker here than in the desert.

A calculating gleam sparked in her gaze. "I thought you wanted answers. Are you conceding defeat?"

I folded my arms over my chest. My heart thudded against my forearms. Walking farther would only lead to my death. "You want a question? Why are we here? Why risk taking me? Your trap for Mrs. C failed. You don't have her and neither do the police."

Her cackling laugh sent shivers sliding over my skin. "She might not go to prison. But your death will haunt her for the rest of her life."

The hate-filled eyes met mine. She aimed the gun at my heart.

For a throat clutching instant, a parade of the faces I might never see again flashed through my mind. My son. The man I loved. My parents. Then a cold anger against Gracie ignited a fire in my chest. A furious calm descended on me.

I refused to make this easy for her. Vanity was her weakness. Exactly how much did she want to talk? How far could I push her? "I know the lies you've buried over the years."

I had no idea where that jab came from. What the heck? Letting my brain do the talking might avail me something.

Her brittle laugh burst between her lips. "You're stalling, wasting time with a bluff."

"Tracy rarely bluffs." The British accent held a weary tone.

My heart leaped - in fear, in hope? I couldn't say for sure.

A slim gray-haired woman wearing pink muffs shuffled up the gravel path on my right. Several years of sand and shrubs were laid out behind her. She'd snuck up on us in plain sight.

I swear she hadn't been there a second ago.

Gracie spun as if a puppet master had pulled all her strings at once. Her hand held the weapon in an unwavering aim at her former companion. She backed up to keep us both in her line of sight. "Delia, you're just in time."

"Mrs. C." If my landlady had been a ghost, I couldn't have been more surprised. I wasn't completely convinced my brain hadn't conjured up a mirage.

Though if that were the case, Kevin or Rabi would have been a better choice for the cavalry. Actually, I'd have preferred a whole troop rather than any single individual.

I scanned the open view behind the two women. The resort grounds Gracie had marched me through looked impossibly distant. From the high grasses to our present location, the area was flat and empty.

No hiding places.

And no hint of a rescue party.

Despair gnawed at my stomach. "You came alone?"

27

29 Down; 7 Letters;
Clue: To come apart; undo
Answer: Unravel

The fading moonlight silhouetted the two women against a landscape of pewter gray. The scrub brush, sand, and sky framing the resort formed a still-life as cold as the breeze that slapped my cheeks.

"Mrs. C, are you okay?" It was an inane question, but I wasn't thinking. I was too busy squinting past her slim, gray-haired profile in the vain hope of seeing reinforcements. "You're alone?"

I should have played it cool. I'd asked once. My friends were cunning. Surely, they'd cooked up a scheme.

Mrs. C didn't answer. She didn't even blink. Her attention was locked on the brown hair, brown eyes, and smooth face of the curvy woman holding the weapon.

Gracie, upscale chic, faced off against the familiar muumuu. Hard to believe they'd passed for each other in their youth. No one would mistake them now.

"The clues were all there, nice as you please. But I refused to see." Though Mrs. C's skin looked sallow and drawn, her voice was surprisingly strong. "Tracy was close to the truth. Time and again she mentioned the old ties, the original case, revenge."

For once, I didn't feel like taking credit. I'd been clueless until Gracie pulled a gun on me. I felt removed from the current crisis. Despite the melodrama playing out in front of me, my attention shifted toward the seemingly distant resort.

Gracie's narrowed gaze swept the area as well. Suddenly wary, her grip tightened. "Where are the others? You must have told your friends."

Mrs. C's wrinkles deepened. A heavy moment of silence stretched out before her downcast eyes shifted toward me.

"I didn't tell anyone." Regret weighed down the words. For the first time in our acquaintance, her voice bordered on tears.

A chasm of disappointment opened at my feet. No cavalry? "No one?"

My voice sounded reedy and thin. So much for a brave front. I tried to gather my faculties, but this was my second kidnapping in two hours. Between fear and adrenaline, I was getting a bit worn around the edges.

Gracie raked Mrs. C with a searching gaze. "You're wearing a wire."

My hopes rose. I should have thought of that myself.

"Search me." Mrs. C threw her arms out to her sides. She pulled the square cut top of her muumuu down to her faded bra, showing off thin, wrinkled skin.

Gracie raised the gun and inched closer. She ran a hand along Mrs. C's stomach through the dress then around her back. Apparently satisfied, she resumed her distance.

"This is your fault." Mrs. C's chin jutted out as she stabbed a finger at me. Her sudden antagonism didn't hide a flash of guilt in her eyes. "I couldn't get your wild theories about Gracie out of my mind. I followed you out here so that when she didn't show, I could throw it in your face."

Though taken aback at Mrs. C's uncharacteristic blame game, I rationalized that her friend's resurrection had thrown her off-balance. After all, like the faultless provenance of the Infantino sketch, Gracie's death had been a truth we all believed.

Mrs. C slowly faced her companion. "Only you would have known to find me in Langsdale, but I told myself it had to be your family. My old friend wouldn't have let me believe she'd died."

Gracie's mouth tipped in a chilling smile. "What better way to hide than by being dead?"

The byplay whirled around me. Fighting to gather my wits, I asked Mrs. C the first thing that came to mind. "How did you know where to look for her? For us?"

"The easternmost corner of the hotel where we were staying was our meeting place in case we were separated. If Gracie was alive, she'd be here." Mrs. C clicked her tongue. The narrowed gaze that targeted Gracie looked more like the woman I knew. "I told you the way to stay hidden was to shed your old ways. I was always better at this game than you."

Gracie's expression hardened as the taunting words hit her like a slap in the face. She raised the gun.

"It wasn't a game. My mum is sick. I want to be by her side." The words were torn from her throat. "Go stand by your private investigator. Both of you, head for that path."

Mrs. C walked over and hooked her arm through mine. She patted my arm with her bony fingers. "I'm sorry you're in this mess."

"It's not your fault." I took a deep breath. Was it wrong to be grateful Holly wasn't by my side? Mrs. C was a crafty old gal. "Kevin says my superpower is finding trouble. I like to prove him right."

"Get moving," Gracie commanded.

Without warning, Mrs. C spun on her heel, pulling her arm loose from mine. "After all we shared, why did you make me believe you were dead?"

"Everything was going according to plan. I had a private studio. I had a network of buyers. I was twenty-one and richer than any of my family." Gracie's face turned a deep red. Her hand tightened on the gun. "I worked on Daniel for months to pass off my painting as the real thing. You destroyed years of planning."

So much for betrayed innocence. Gracie had been looking out for herself and lining her own pockets from day one.

Mrs. C's eyes narrowed. A weary look deepened the wrinkles on her face as the truth hit home.

Gracie wasn't finished cataloging her woes. She shook her fist. "I was labeled a murderer."

Now she's the victim in all this?

"You could have stayed in England." Mrs. C stood her ground like a small, fighting rooster. "I told you to go to the bobbies. You came with me willingly."

"What choice did I have?" Gracie all but choked on the words. "Who would have believed me? You were a nobody, a nothing."

Mrs. C raised her chin. "I was never a nothing. I was your friend."

Accusations continued to be thrown like poison darts. The two women were so lost in their own versions of the past, neither noticed how the vast ocean of sand swallowed up their voices. The seemingly endless desert made our problems seem fleeting.

I looked for a way out, an opening to overpower Gracie. But she stayed beyond my reach with a clear line of sight to both of us.

If this had descended into a free for all, I might as well go down swinging. "Back off, Gracie. You set her up for Neville's murder."

Well, I'd set out to find the murderer. I'd done that. My new goal was to live and save Mrs. C. "Why the elaborate ruse? Why kill Neville?"

"She always looked back." Mrs. C supplied the answer before Gracie had a chance to respond. "She refused to move on or make a life for herself."

"At least I had a past." Gracie drew herself up to her full height. "I had a family, a future. I want to walk the old neighborhood as myself. To do that, I need the authorities to find Daniel's killer and close the case."

"You didn't like being broke, so you wished for a rich man." Ignoring her friend's self-serving words, Mrs. C sniffed. "No matter where you were or how much you had at your fingertips, you were never content. Always wishing you were somewhere else."

Gracie swung the gun toward Mrs. C in a white-knuckled grip. Her arm trembled. "I've lived under the cloud of being a killer for fifty years. You can't know how it felt."

"How could I not know?" Mrs. C's desperate tone knifed through the air. "I lived with the guilt of killing that man every day since I struck the blow. I saw him die."

The raw passion of her anguished guilt froze the very air.

"The blood trickling on his forehead." Her breath stuck in her throat. "His pale face lying on the carpet. I didn't even try to help him. When I heard a noise in the hall, I panicked and ran, never looking back."

Wait a minute.

I thought I said the words aloud, but neither woman reacted so my brain and my mouth were evidently not talking to each other again. That was okay. I was sorting out questions and crossword clues that had gotten lost until now.

Mrs. C's gut-wrenching confession set off all kinds of bells and whistles. I stared at my friend as if seeing her for the first time. "Tell me, Mrs. C, what did you and her lover talk about that night?"

Gracie blinked at me as if she'd forgotten my presence.

"I tore at him for using Gracie, for lying about their having a future together." The British accent shook with her old anger. "I knew he had no intention of marrying her."

"What did he say?" I prompted, determined to keep the other woman listening to the pivotal scene in her life.

"He admitted marrying Gracie would be pointless." Mrs. C waved a dismissive hand at her friend. "The only reason he'd stuck with her was to save the family company, to provide for his wife and children."

"That's what you overheard, isn't it, Gracie?" I shifted half-a-step, moving slightly in front of Mrs. C's slim form. "You followed her. You were in the hall when you heard Daniel dismiss you as nothing more than a tool to be used and discarded."

"You're wrong this time, luv." Mrs. C shook her head. "She wasn't there. I struck the blow."

"*She* killed my love, my Daniel, my future." Gracie pointed at Mrs. C while glaring at me. "I was nowhere near his office that night. She was hysterical by the time she reached the flat."

"Enough!" My full-throated scream rose into the night, unfettered by walls. The facts I'd absorbed all weekend had coalesced to form a whole picture. "You might get away with killing us, but you're going to admit the truth. You murdered your lover fifty years ago. Mrs. C is innocent."

Gracie flipped the gun in my direction with a flick of her wrist. "You can't rewrite the past."

"Neither can you," I retorted, stepping forward. "I've wondered all weekend why you left with Mrs. C that night. Why you stayed on the run for fifty years. Who has that much loyalty? I don't, and I'm a nicer person than you ever were."

I wanted that on record before she shot me. "Even now, you could have called the cops and given them her name and address."

Mrs. C reached toward me. Her arm barely covered half the distance. "Tracy. Ducks, what you're saying is not true."

"Bear with me," I said. "To begin with - none of the details of the original killing match Neville's murder scene from two days ago."

Mrs. C put her hand on her chest. Sorrow drew her face into a frown. "Neville looked exactly like his father did when I left him."

"When *you* left him, but not when he was found." I watched Gracie, but her plastic facade left little room for real emotion. "Mrs. C struck him once and only to save herself. He fell. She ran. In all the years since, she's never been able to read or look at any pictures from that night."

Her white hair shimmered in the moonlight as she shook her head. "I couldn't bear to see what I'd done."

After all the scenarios I'd dreamed up this weekend, this time I was right. I knew it. "Marcus read every detail of the first murder. He mentioned the amount of blood at the original scene. One of the articles noted the closed casket."

"That's not right." Despite her words, Mrs. C's voice had lost its certainty.

My gaze remained riveted on Gracie. "When Kevin and I interviewed Weatherington, he told us the entire room had to be cleaned. His mother was so traumatized by the blood she never set foot in the office again."

Mrs. C slowly turned to her old friend. Disbelief was etched onto her expression. "That can't be true."

"That much violence requires a fury fueled by passion." I stepped toward the weapon. "You made the noise Mrs. C heard in the hall. When she ran, you finished the job. Isn't that right, Gracie?"

The other woman's sculpted jaw slackened. Her gaze darted to Mrs. C then to me. "Shut up!"

"You were furious, hurt beyond all thinking at how Daniel dismissed you. He planned to throw you aside. No more sales of your forgeries." I drove the truth home relentlessly, inching nearer. "You confronted him. Did he laugh? Is that what pushed you into a killing frenzy?"

Gracie shook her head. "I was home all evening."

She punctuated each word with a jab of the gun.

I shook my head. "Mrs. C stumbled through the streets in shock. You ran back to the flat and cleaned up. That's how you could be waiting for her when she came home."

Mrs. C's gasp sounded at my elbow. "How could you do that to me?"

Gracie swung the weapon toward her former friend.

"You destroyed the only good thing in my life." She drew a trembling breath. "Afterward, I had to get out of the country. I was afraid of being caught. I didn't want... "

"To admit the truth to yourself." I finished the sentence when her voice failed then turned to Mrs. C. "You stepped forward as the perfect scapegoat. Over the years, she told herself that you *were* the guilty one."

"You let me believe I killed that man, that I orphaned his children." Anger crept in and hardened Mrs. C's voice. "You were my best friend. I'd have stood by you. I'd have helped you escape if you'd told me the truth."

The sad fact was Mrs. C's loyalty probably would have extended so far as to leave her homeland behind to help her friend.

Too bad Gracie had never been worth the sacrifice.

I reached out a hand to console my friend. "That's why she left England with you. If she let you surrender, you'd have known the truth at your first police interview. She couldn't let that happen. She didn't have the skills to get past the blockade that was set up within an hour of finding the body."

Mrs. C's slippers scraped across the gravel as she stepped to my side. "You killed Neville to clear yourself? You were planning to kill me as well?"

Gracie's jaw tightened. An icy glint of determination shown in her eyes.

"Answer me." A steely tone sharpened Mrs. C's voice as she pushed past me.

I threw my arm out to block her.

Gracie raised the gun

As I stared down the barrel of the weapon, a voice blared out of the darkness. Bright lights pierced the night. "Police!"

My heart clutched, then stopped, frozen. After catching my breath, I forced my dazzled eyes to peer beyond the glare of the ring of uber-bright flashlights.

Several figures coalesced out of the shadows at the edge of my sight. The fact that the authorities had been so close and had remained unnoticed testified to how absorbed Mrs. C, Gracie, and I had been in our conversation.

Mrs. C had done a bang-up job of distraction.

"Put down the weapon." The command thundered over the desert.

A wild, desperate look came over Gracie's expression. She kept the gun pointed in place, ready for the kill.

28

15 Across; 5 Letters;
Clue: In a nervous or edgy state
Answer: Wired

Gracie's trembling finger struggled to find the trigger. Thankfully, she hit the trigger guard instead. Her gaze darted to the shadowy forms, then her attention swung to me and Mrs. C.

The sudden lights and thundering voice sent a jolt to my heart that could have powered the space station. There's a reason I don't play poker for anything but pretzels or chocolate.

One look at my shocked expression evidently satisfied any question she had concerning *my* involvement. Between the blinding lights and my pounding heart, I was still trying to figure out which was worse - being kidnapped or being rescued.

"Wearing wires is so twentieth century." Mrs. C sniffed. "The current technology allows listening devices to work from incredible distances."

On a good day her aplomb left me feeling two steps behind. Tonight, the gap was more like a dozen. As I stared at her in the heart-stopping silence, I realized my hands were raised in the sign of surrender. Feeling a little sheepish, I lowered them.

I should have known better than to buy her story of coming alone. Fifty years of skulking had obviously not been wasted.

She *was* good at this game. Better than me and definitely better than Gracie, which brought me to the woman holding the gun. Though relieved at the rescue, I didn't need fifty years of experience to tell me no one was close enough to get the drop on our captor.

"Gracie, this is Detective Thelen. I want to talk with you." Thelen's figure formed out of the darkness. Walking slowly toward us, he spoke in a calm, even tone. "No one else has to get hurt."

Or killed, I added silently. Unfortunately, Gracie showed no sign of having heard the police detective.

"Stop or I'll shoot." Gracie's guttural tone brought Wilson to a stop. Her jaw was clenched so tight she was in danger of cracking a tooth. Finally, she forced more words out. "You set me up."

Hypocrisy at its finest. Gracie had put these events in motion. In the end, the two had set each other up. However, Mrs. C definitely got the prize. She who laughs last and all that.

Of course, I still wanted to survive our rescue.

Since the police had evidently been listening since Mrs. C appeared, Gracie didn't have a leg to stand on by way of defense. She'd not only alluded to murdering Neville, she was on record for killing his father fifty years ago.

"Gracie, you can walk away from this." Wilson spoke again. Other figures formed in the shadows behind him. "Lower the weapon and talk to me."

Gracie's expression hardened. She raised her chin. An aura of resolve emanated from her.

Sure, the police had her confession on record. Sure, she had no chance of escape. She also had nothing to lose.

Why not double up and make it four deaths?

As the barrel of the gun loomed ever larger, my brain spun through ploys like a roulette wheel on steroids. Amazingly, with everything on the line, calm descended. I might not be able to out-sneak Mrs. C, but I could out-talk anyone.

I dredged up the conniving skills developed over a lifetime and leaped in with both feet. "You can still have revenge, Gracie."

Surprise and curiosity played across her features, but her finger remained firmly against the trigger.

"There's no need for more death. Yours or ours." Especially not ours. I swallowed a rush of fear. Focus on the moment. No telling how long Wilson would let me take the lead.

Gracie's eyes narrowed, the question in them clear.

"Think about what's best for you." Don't mind us. You're what matters. "Surely you don't believe the police set up this confrontation without a marksman in position?"

In all honesty, I wondered if the police had time to call in a sniper. Fortunately, a showdown allows little time for logic. The only rule is to grab your opponent's attention and hold on for dear life.

At the mention of a sniper, Gracie's too-smooth face tightened even more. When her gaze slid sideways, her gun hand trembled.

For once, Mrs. C drifted into the background and remained silent. Any comment from her might re-ignite Gracie's fury.

"You can walk away from this." Not walk away *free*, but I thought it best not to mention the handcuffs, trial, and imprisonment that lay ahead.

Gracie's grip tightened on the gun. Obviously, she was not convinced freedom lay in her future.

"No one has to die." The fact bore repeating, especially when I would be on the receiving end of any bullet. "If you surrender, you can tell the world your story."

A spark lit her eyes. She focused on me fully for the first time.

Judging by the continued silence, Wilson had decided to let me play out the hand.

I summoned all the sincerity I could muster. "If you drop the gun, you'll be on the front page."

Come on, Gracie, I pleaded silently. Where's the vanity that brought you through your plastic surgery?

"Your lover was a cad." Ignoring the weapon, I laid out points sympathetic to Gracie. "He exploited your talent. Surrender and you could tell the world that he sold forgeries."

I doubted that fact would force Jerrone to close its doors. After all Daniel was long dead. The family could truthfully say they'd tried to rectify the matter. They'd already recovered the forgeries.

I doubted Weatherington would see the beauty of my plan, but that was his problem. He and his family would have to spin the publicity as they saw fit. I'd found the murderer.

Gracie's fake brown eyes narrowed. Her trigger finger slipped onto the grip of the gun. "He said he loved me."

"He preyed on your innocence." Which might not be the truth. They used each other. I pressed my advantage. "After all these decades of silence, you could tell the world how you hid. You were so smart to figure that out all by yourself."

Lesson in life - when talking to a crazy person, don't shrink from altering reality.

The woman shot Mrs. C a triumphant look.

Be my guest. Take the credit. "There'll be articles about you, documentaries, maybe a movie. Surrender and you'll be famous."

I held my breath, praying no one behind those floodlights did anything stupid, praying Gracie was vain enough to sacrifice revenge for fifteen minutes of lurid fame.

Seconds ticked by, marked by the booming of my heart.

Gun in hand, her arm descended as if it were moving through molasses.

When the weapon finally dipped too low to shoot anything but the ground, I took a shallow breath. My lungs were too knotted to allow for more. "Put the safety on and drop the gun."

Without warning, Gracie's arm shot up.

My lungs seized, refusing to work. Just when I thought I'd won, I found myself staring at the business end of the automatic.

Her knuckles turned white as she clutched the gun. She stared at Mrs. C with a venomous look that seemed to come from the depths of her soul. "You stay out of my life this time."

I realized I'd flung my arm in front of Mrs. C. A useless gesture if ever there was one. My hand would hardly stop a bullet.

The cold light from the moon emphasized every wrinkle on Mrs. C's face, deepening them as if they were carved from stone. The regret weighing down her expression as she stared at her onetime friend would have wrung tears from the most hardened soul.

"I don't even know you." Sorrow dripped from Mrs. C's voice. She caught a trembling breath, then steadied herself. "Evidently, I never did."

29

12 Down; 7 Letters;
Clue: Reactions to questions; responses
Answer: Answers

Monday morning had never looked so good. The day dawned clear and cool, typical for mid-January in Langsdale. The ring of mountains, purple and lavender in the distance, seemed especially vibrant against the sky of cornflower blue.

With murder and mayhem behind me, I sat on the patio outside our suite and reveled in the clear sky and the bright sun. My gaze drifted from the resort's carefully landscaped grounds to the wider view of the desert and the distant ring of purple mountains.

Kevin resumed his seat next to me and slipped an arm around my shoulders. "Ready to leave all this luxury behind?"

I looked across the glass-topped table to the breakfast dishes that had been filled with Eggs Benedict, croissants, cheesy hash browns, sweet rolls, tart orange juice, and coffee that tasted like snickerdoodle cookies. This was my last chance to have a catered meal for the foreseeable future and I had enjoyed it to the fullest. "The life of the rich and famous is too violent. There are kidnappers around every corner."

Across from the table, Marcus's black eyes sparkled above his set jaw and crossed arms. He ignored the eggs on his plate. "If I'd been there, the bad guys would never have gotten the drop on you."

I fought to suppress a smile. I'd listened to variations of his claim all through breakfast. He was lucky I'd let him stay home from school today and participate in the police interviews.

"Maybe next time I'm ambushed by a gun-wielding murderer, you'll be there." Not if I could help it. Marcus being safely out of the way had been the one good thing about last night. Besides, I'd had my fill of being a hostage.

"They got the drop on you twice?" As he shook his head, sunlight reflected off his cap of black shiny hair. Disappointment rang in his tone. "You'd never last on the streets or in combat."

My son cast a significant look at Rabi, sitting in the shade of an awning. The man gave him a slow wink in response.

I sat back and sighed. With Gracie and Archie behind bars, nothing could bring me down. "Since I have my team as backup, I don't need to survive the streets, mean or otherwise."

Marcus rested his chin in both hands. "Kevin, you should have called me."

"Things happened pretty quick." Kevin grabbed a sliver of bacon off my plate. "She didn't invite me to her kidnappings either. We'll keep a closer watch next time."

Marcus's face brightened.

My mother, sitting next to my son, caught him in a tight hug. "I'm glad you were with me and Grandad. I'd have worried myself silly with all of you gone."

Marcus endured her concern and embrace with a barely concealed grimace. "I told you they'd be okay. We're professionals."

Remembering several heart-stopping moments of sheer panic, I blew a long breath across my steaming coffee. Last night hadn't qualified as a professional finale in my book. Only a lot of help and an amazing amount of luck had brought the case to a successful conclusion.

I took a drink, enjoying the hot brew as it burned my throat and warmed my veins. Then, I lifted the mug in salute. "To teamwork, family, and luck."

I whispered the final word under my breath.

Kevin shot a grin my way.

My dad clapped his calloused palms together, rubbing them with a sense of anticipation. "Marcus, be sure to e-mail us the articles. I can't wait to tell everyone back home how the Belden Detective Agency solved another case."

My son's grin widened. "I'll send you all the links. I have the cases cataloged."

Mom frowned. "I want a paper copy if possible."

"You're more than welcome to my paper." Mrs. C shuddered. A haunting sorrow lurked in her eyes. "I want to forget the entire affair."

I covered her hand with mine. Yesterday's revelations had been a hard blow for the woman. "If you hadn't left England, we'd never have met you."

"That's a silver lining for many a dark day, luv." Her expression lightened. She twitched her napkin onto her lap and reached for the hot sauce. "This is my home now, and here I'll be staying, eh?"

"I don't see why Gracie was so angry." Marcus's voice rang with outrage. "You should be mad at her. Why did she frame you after all this time?"

"Her vanity was her downfall, then and now." I answered when Mrs. C remained silent. Though my sympathy was in short supply for the self-centered Gracie, my mind could bend enough to understand her. "I think she had a need for public recognition for her art that was never fulfilled. Also, the buried guilt of lying to Mrs. C must have driven Gracie a bit crazy."

My mother sipped her coffee, hot and black, just the way she liked it. "Mrs. Colchester thought she'd killed that man all these years, yet she overcame the guilt."

"Mrs. C hit Gracie's lover in self-protection," Kevin said. "Gracie murdered him in a rage. She compounded her guilt by letting Mrs. C take the blame and encouraging her to run away, so Gracie could escape as well."

"That was for self-preservation. I see that now." The lady in question stirred her tea. She cocked her head to one side. A smugness colored her gaze. "Gracie wouldn't have made it out of London without me. Getting to France and the States? Never."

Marcus pointed to the older woman, then slid a telling look at me. "She knows how to survive the streets."

I drew a breath for a comeback but Mrs. C cut me off.

"Gracie never had a knack for undercover life." Mrs. C spoke as if she hadn't heard Marcus. She had a far-away look in her eyes. "She came close to being unmasked more than once. All she had to do was follow the rules."

I almost choked on my coffee at her words. The woman was a master at following her own path. Admittedly, most of the Belden Company fit that bill, but the older woman took first place. "Mrs. C, rule follower is not what I'd choose as *your* epitaph."

Mrs. C drew herself up in her chair. "I'm excellent at obeying my own dictates."

"Well aren't we all?" My murmur drew a chuckle from Kevin.

"Have you heard any official updates on the case?" Despite my mother's casual posture, her shining eyes had followed every word of the discussion.

My boyfriend had a knack for worming details out of the police. "The authorities believe Gracie and Archie are tied to the supposed discovery of several other lost masterpieces of surreal art. They're reviewing all his finds over the last two decades."

"The Infantino sketch has been withdrawn from tonight's auction." Mom swore her morning walk had been for exercise, but gossip had been the real draw. "Its authenticity will be re-verified by experts. Then, the Ponzers will have to decide what they want to do. Rumors are circulating about Jerrone's culpability regarding the old forgeries."

Pop waved a meaty, muffin filled hand at Mom's statement. "They'll ride out the storm. They bought those first forgeries back, didn't they?"

"That may be what saves them." Not that I cared very much. I sipped my coffee "The official story is that Neville was murdered because Gracie wanted the documentary to die with him."

"The Weatherington family will survive." A knowing tone underlay Kevin's words. "Notoriety will make the earlier pieces coveted items. Crime memorabilia has its own market."

"Speaking of criminals." Marcus's eyes sparkled with glee. He leaned toward me, jostling his plate in the process. "Are the police going to arrest you for hiding Jamie when she was a witness?"

"Those two hid her." I threw Kevin and Rabi under the proverbial bus without hesitation. Forget love or friendship, I'd been through enough. They could save themselves. "Besides, she didn't witness a crime and the police had already interviewed her. They're going to drop the matter. As long as we agree not to do it again."

My dad did a double take. "They believed you?"

I was searching for a retort to his incredulous tone when a knock sounded on the door. "That must be Holly. Right on schedule."

Last night's events hadn't dimmed the woman's perkiness one iota. Her blond curls were perfectly coiffed and her blue eyes were shining. No one would have guessed that, like several of us, she'd been up for hours with the police.

She stood just outside the French doors and surveyed our group with a smiling face. "The reservations are set for your activities today and this evening."

That's PR speak for "You've been banned from tonight's art auction". The resort wanted us kept away from the reporters who had suddenly invaded the place.

Keeping out of the limelight was fine with me. This high-brow art business had become a violent affair. Besides, when the resort and Weatherington had offered to pay to keep us busy, Marcus had been more than happy to provide a list of activities.

The day would begin with go-carts at the miniature speedway outside of town, followed by lunch and a tour of a local winery. Then a shopping spree at the Mineral Market, an abandoned mining headquarters that now housed an artist colony. Dinner was set for the most expensive restaurant in town - the Trail Blazer - located on the slowly revolving top floor of the tallest hotel.

Marcus, who had millionaire tastes on a pauper's budget, jumped to his feet. "Did you get the stretch limo?"

Holly nodded. "There's plenty of room for all of us."

"All of us?" I eyed her with a sinking feeling.

Amidst the bustle of everyone walking into the suite in preparation for leaving, I waited, with a growing sense of trepidation, for the PR rep to respond.

"My manager believes my presence will distract from the auction." Holly barely managed to keep a straight face. "I'll be accompanying your party today."

Her announcement ended on an unprofessional squeal usually reserved for a prize winner on a game show. "I can't believe my good fortune."

"Neither can I." My smile froze on my face. I was pretty sure a full twelve hours of this much perkiness would melt my mental gears.

"That's great news." Kevin put a hand on my back. A mischievous gleam twinkled in his eyes.

I glared at him and his enjoyment. I was ready to put the case behind me. Marcus and Holly were blatant enthusiasts for all things related to my cases. Being together would only inflame their nonstop chatter.

My mother touched Holly's arm. "How's Jamie?"

Holly's smile brightened by a few watts. "Thanks to Belden and Company, she's fine. She asked me to thank you all for helping her escape from Archie at the hospital and for hiding her. After she gave her statement to the police, she insisted on helping with tonight's auction."

I was relieved to hear the young assistant was doing well. "Her statement was key to clearing Mrs. C. Jamie saw Gracie's face at Rowdy Reptiles. She also remembered Mrs. C from the night of the murder. That was huge."

"You were the one who realized Gracie snuck into Rycliffe early Friday afternoon." Marcus, who'd been herding everyone toward the door, pointed a finger at me. "She picked the lock to the back door and planned to surprise Neville, but he was waiting for her in the library."

My parents exchanged knowing glances. It was my mother who eyed me with a half-smile. "Amazing how you figured that out. Almost as if you had experience sneaking in and out of places."

I flashed my best, angelic expression. Never confess. No matter what evidence is against you. "I must've read that twist in a mystery novel."

"Sure you did," Kevin muttered.

Mrs. C nodded encouragement. "Tracy has a very inventive mind."

"Thank you," I said in a self-righteous tone. Time to turn everyone's attention back to the murder.

"Neville being in the library was one of many things that went wrong for Gracie." The woman had spent years wanting to return home. To close the books on the first murder, she planned to kill two more people. "The only way to keep Mrs. C from realizing Gracie was guilty of the first murder was to kill Mrs. C as well."

With my crossword puzzle complete, I was ready to be done with the whole affair. My voice drifted to a stop.

Kevin shot me a supportive look and took up the story. "Gracie intended to shoot Neville using a silencer. Then, she'd turn on the fire and wait for Mrs. C, killing her by a blow to the head. When the bodies were found, Mrs. C would be identified as having killed both Daniel and Neville. Both cases would be closed. Gracie would be free to go home."

"Instead," Marcus whirled, stopping everyone in their tracks. "Neville confronted Gracie. He was fifteen when his father died. He'd seen her and he must have recognized her. They fought and she smacked him with the paperweight. When that happened, there was no way she could kill Mrs. Colchester and make it look like a double murder."

"Especially since I was late, wasn't I?" Mrs. C had recovered some of her usual zest. "I was supposed to be in the library at five-thirty, but with the broken stairs, I didn't go in until nearly seven."

"Thank goodness for that." Someone must have been watching out for Mrs. C. "Gracie couldn't risk hiding that long. She mixed with the attendees. When she saw you leave the library, she left the note, and snuck out of the building."

"The way you laid out the details was sheer genius." Holly gushed. "Gracie never signed in as an attendee that night so the police couldn't account for her."

Marcus interjected. "T.R.'s good at piecing clues together. It runs in the family."

Dad opened the main door, then turned to face the group straggling toward the exit. "Don't forget the video on Neville's phone. My little girl was on the money there."

"That was pretty obvious," I said in all sincerity. "Once I got over the shock, I knew the video had to be fake. Gracie could have made the recording any time. Neville wasn't in the video, only the muumuu and slippers to match Mrs. C."

The older woman smiled up at me. "My innocence wasn't obvious to the police. Without you and the others, I'd be living in the big house by now."

"The courts aren't that quick." Marcus told her with a knowing air. "You'd still be in the county jail."

"Exit to the left." Holly instructed. "The limo's waiting on the south drive so we can avoid the lobby."

As we filed out the door, Marcus looked over his shoulder. "Are you still going to be Mrs. Colchester? Or are you going to change your name again?"

"The past is dead." Mrs. C's smile was carefree for the first time in days. "This is the life I chose. I fought for it and I'm keeping it."

My dad turned and wagged a finger at me. "This talk of names reminds me... Who is this Trixie Belden that Marcus says we're related to? Is she the person in those books you used to read? I don't remember seeing her at any of the family reunions."

All eyes turned to me, even Rabi glanced over his shoulder with a smile on his usually serene expression.

"She's a distant relative." I gave my dad a sunny smile. No way was I about to confess to making up our relationship to the woman. "I'll tell you all about her after I win the go-cart race."

To see Tracy and the others solve their next case in FIVE CLUES TO A KILLER go to: https://www.amazon.com/Five-Clues-Killer-Crossword-Mystery-ebook/dp/B0B195QQ7S/ref.

DEAR READERS

Dear Readers,

Welcome to the adventures of Tracy Belden and her son, Marcus, along with their adopted family: Kevin Tanner, Mrs. Colchester, and Jack Rabi as they help solve Tracy's P.I. cases. While Tracy would prefer to drink flavored coffee and create crossword puzzles, she has to pay the bills. So, she puts her puzzle solving talents to good use as she dives into her cases.

While most of her cases are non-violent, the murder cases are often so complicated she despairs of solving them. However, Marcus, with the confidence of youth and his pride in the detecting heritage of the Belden family, never wavers in his belief that the Belden Agency can solve any case as long as they work together.

Among the many books I read while growing up was the YA mystery series involving Trixie Belden and her group of young friends. While no part of this book is based on those stories, Tracy did tell Marcus she was a distant cousin of Trixie's. Her good intentions were based on her efforts to get him off the streets, but her alleged relationship with Trixie is a claim Tracy is never allowed to forget.

I hope you enjoy your time in Langsdale, Nevada, and the stories of Tracy and her adopted family. If you like the story, please leave a review at your favorite bookseller or at Goodreads.

If you'd like to learn more about the other books in the Crossword Puzzle Cozy Mystery series, please visit my website or my author page on Facebook

Thank you for buying this book and giving me your time. I don't take either for granted.

Louise Foster

MEET THE AUTHOR

I didn't pursue a writing career until I was well out of college. However, a lifelong love of reading and solving puzzles proved to be good training when the writing bug bit. While I enjoy reading many different types of books, from thrillers to fantasy to science fiction, mysteries have always intrigued me.

Working on jigsaw puzzles as well as crossword puzzles with my family has also been a constant part of my life. A habit that carries through to today.

In the Crossword Puzzle Mystery Series, my love of writing and solving puzzles came together. I hope you love the quirky characters and their high-spirited adventures as much I enjoy writing them.

To learn more about the Crossword Puzzle Cozy Mystery series, visit my website www.louisefoster.com and sign up for my newsletter. You'll receive a free download of "One Across is Murder", the story of how Kevin and Tracy first met.

Find me on Facebook: Louise Foster, Author

https://www.facebook.com/Louise-Foster-Author-10751771750 8196/?modal=admin_todo_tour

I love to hear from readers: Louise.louisefoster@gmail.com

Thank you for giving me your time to read this book and your support by buying it. I don't take either for granted.

Louise Foster

Acknowledgements

I'd like to acknowledge a few of the many people who helped make this book a reality:

My editor, Mary-Theresa Hussey, for her awesome input.

Lee Hyat, who created my beautiful book covers.

Debbie Manber Kupfer, who used her skill and talent to create the crossword puzzles in this book and on my website.

Keith Jones for setting up my wonderful web-site.

CROSSWORD PUZZLE COZY MYSTERY SERIES

One Across is Death (Short Story Prequel) – *Tracy and Kevin meet for the first time when she finds him standing over her dead co-worker with the murder weapon at his feet. Tracy isn't sure the handsome stranger is guilty, but how can she solve this puzzle?*

A Clue to Murder (Novella Prequel) – Two years after Tracy and Kevin meet, his landlords ask her to find their missing nephews. When her investigation leads to a dead body, she fears the worst for the two teens, but she must find the boys and finish her puzzle. (Both prequels are available on my website: www.louisefoster.com)

An Ex in the Puzzle

Two Down in Tahoe

Adventures in Vegas

A Question of Murder

Five Clues to a Killer

Seven Furlongs to a Felony

Eight Letters in Betrayal

Glue Guns for Christmas (Novella)

Made in the USA
Monee, IL
10 June 2026

53029987R00181